DEATH'S PRELUDE

Praise for David S. Pederson

Death Overdue

"Deftly drawn characters, brisk pacing, and an easy charm distinguish Pederson's winning follow-up to 2019's *Death Takes a Bow*. Pederson successfully evokes and shrewdly capitalizes upon the time in which his mystery takes place, using the era's prejudices and politics to heighten the story's stakes and more thoroughly invest readers in its outcome. Plausible suspects, persuasive red herrings, and cleverly placed clues keep the pages frantically flipping until the book's gratifying close."—*Mystery Scene*

"David S. Pederson never disappoints when it comes to twisted and suspenseful mysteries...I highly recommend the Detective Heath Barrington mystery series, and *Death Overdue* in particular is suspenseful and an absolute page-turner."—*QueeRomance Ink*

Lambda Literary Award Finalist *Death Takes a Bow*

"[T]here's also a lovely scene near the end of the book that puts into words the feelings that Alan and Heath share for one another, but can't openly share because of the time they live in and their jobs in law enforcement. All in all, an interesting murder/mystery and an apt depiction of the times."—*Gay Book Reviews*

"This is a mystery in its purest form...If you like murder mysteries and are particularly interested in the old-school type, you'll love this book!"—*Kinzie Things*

Lambda Literary Award Finalist *Death Checks In*

"David Pederson does a great job with this classic murder mystery set in 1947 and the attention to its details..."—*The Novel Approach*

"This noir whodunit is a worthwhile getaway with that old-black-and-white-movie feel that you know you love, and it's sweetly chaste, in a late-1940s way..."—*Outsmart Magazine*

"This is a classic murder mystery; an old-fashioned style mystery à la Agatha Christie..."—*Reviews by Amos Lassen*

Death Goes Overboard

"[A]uthor David S. Pederson has packed a lot in this novel. You don't normally find a soft-sided, poetry-writing mobster in a noir mystery, for instance, but he's here…this novel is both predictable and not, making it a nice diversion for a weekend or vacation."
—*Washington Blade*

"Pederson takes a lot of the tropes of mysteries and utilizes them to the fullest, giving the story a knowable form. However, the unique characters and accurate portrayal of the struggles of gay relationships in 1940s America make this an enjoyable, thought-provoking read."—*Gay, Lesbian, Bisexual, and Transgender Round Table of the American Library Association*

"You've got mobsters, a fedora-wearing detective in a pinstriped suit, seemingly prim matrons, and man-hungry blondes eager for marriage. It's like an old black-and-white movie in book form…"
—*Windy City Times*

Death Comes Darkly

"Agatha Christie…if Miss Marple were a gay police detective in post–WWII Milwaukee."—*PrideSource: Between the Lines*

"The mystery is one that isn't easily solved. It's a cozy mystery unraveled in the drawing room type of story, but well worked out."—*Bookwinked*

"If you LOVE Agatha Christie, you shouldn't miss this one. The writing is very pleasant, the mystery is old-fashioned, but in a good meaning, intriguing plot, well developed characters. I'd like to read more of Heath Barrington and Alan Keyes in the future. This couple has a big potential."—*Gay Book Reviews*

"[A] thoroughly entertaining read from beginning to end. A detective story in the best Agatha Christie tradition with all the trimmings."
—*Sinfully Gay Romance Book Review*

By the Author

Death Comes Darkly

Death Goes Overboard

Death Checks In

Death Takes A Bow

Death Overdue

Death's Prelude

Visit us at www.boldstrokesbooks.com

DEATH'S PRELUDE

by

David S. Pederson

2021

DEATH'S PRELUDE

ISBN 13: 978-1-63555-786-2

This Trade Paperback Original Is Published By
Bold Strokes Books, Inc.
P.O. Box 249
Valley Falls, NY 12185

First Edition: February 2021

Credits
Editors: Jerry L. Wheeler and Stacia Seaman
Production Design: Stacia Seaman
Cover Design by Sheri (hindsightgraphics@gmail.com)

Acknowledgments

Thanks to my friend Eric Fahner for his infinite knowledge and invaluable research assistance on the *Queen Mary* and the boat train, and to my friends Ed Baskiewicz and Michael Vaughn for research assistance with New York and the New York streets. Thanks also to all my Facebook fans for voting on the name of the Quimby estate, and to the members of Fans of Ocean Liners on Facebook for their assistance with some research questions. Thanks to Liz and Mike for the suggestion of the name Wigglesworth for the butler, and special thanks to Delbert Slowik, who provided Heath's middle name, Alexander, in my "Give Heath Barrington a Middle Name" contest!

Special thanks to all my family, and my friends, who are my chosen family, and all my readers. Thank you!!!

And as always, thanks and all my love to my husband, Alan, the key to my lock.

Finally, thanks also to Jerry Wheeler, my editor with the most-est, and everyone at Bold Strokes Books who have helped me so much, especially Radclyffe, Carsen, Sandy, Cindy, and Ruth, Stacia, and Sheri.

This book is dedicated to my mom and dad,
who were always there for me growing up.
My mom is a wonder, and not at all like Heath's mother,
and my dad was gentle, funny, and loving.
He taught me to be true to my word, to be honest, and to be kind.

CHAPTER ONE

Friday Morning, September 10, 1937
New York City

The heavy brass elevator doors slid open, then the metal grate. The operator, a gray-haired, older man in a navy blue coat and cap, stuck out his head and looked at us with a bored expression. "Going down, folks?"

"Yes, lobby please," Verbina said, brushing past him as she stepped into the elevator cab. I followed, along with two bellboys pushing and pulling a luggage cart loaded to the top and then some.

"Yes, ma'am," the operator said as he glanced around the crowded car. "No room for anyone else, so I'll take you express." He whisked us six floors straight down to the plush lobby of the Plaza Hotel, where he opened the doors and grate once more and tipped his hat, still looking bored. Aunt Verbina and I stepped out hurriedly, followed by the two bellboys and the luggage cart, which was leaning rather precariously.

"I'll settle the bill, Heath. You get two cabs, the doorman will help you. Tell him we need to go to the Cunard Pier, and we're in a hurry." She glanced at her watch. "Goodness, it's ten thirty already, and the ship leaves at noon. Hurry now!"

"All right, Auntie."

I put on my fedora and walked quickly toward the 59th Street exit and out onto the street, the harried bellboys following, struggling to keep the luggage from toppling off the cart as it careened from side to side. Besides my garment bag, two large cases, and one small one that held my toiletries, Verbina had a steamer trunk, four matching oversized bags, three large hatboxes, one small one, a makeup case, a jewelry case, a garment bag, and a valise.

"Taxi, sir?" the doorman said, resplendent in a double-breasted navy coat with brass buttons and a matching brimmed cap.

"Yes, two actually. One for us, and one for all this luggage. Cunard Pier, number 90, 711 Twelfth Avenue, and we're in a hurry."

"Yes, sir." He blew his silver whistle and held up two fingers in a spotless white glove.

As the two Yellow Cabs pulled up and the bellmen began loading the bags, trunks, and cases, Verbina appeared on the sidewalk. She looked stunning, as always, in a turquoise dress, belted at the waist, and a matching bow hat. Over her arm was draped a red fox stole, and under her other arm was a simple red clutch purse that matched her belt and shoes. People nearby took notice, and I was proud to be her nephew. I walked up beside her.

"Did you get everything settled?" I said.

"Yes, I've paid the bill, including your one dollar and thirty-three cent room service charge for a bottle of Coca-Cola, crab salad, and a piece of blueberry pie."

"I'm sorry, I'll pay you back."

"It's all right, though you could have walked to the corner drugstore and gotten the same thing for less than half the price."

"It was the middle of the night, the drugstore was closed, and I was hungry."

She looked me up and down. "Goodness, you're twenty-two years old. Aren't you through growing yet? The way you eat, honestly, where do you put it? The country is in a depression, dear. We mustn't waste."

"I didn't waste any, I ate it all."

"Still, it wouldn't hurt for you to skip a snack once in a while, even though you're as thin as a rail."

"Yes, ma'am."

She glanced at the cabs. "Good. Are we all set, then?" she asked, ever so slightly out of breath.

"As soon as they finish loading," I said.

"Well, let's get in the first taxicab while they finish. No sense standing about in this heat. My, it's warm for September. Give the doorman and those bellboys something for their efforts, dear."

"All right." I tipped the bellboys and thanked them, and then gave the doorman a quarter as he opened the cab door and helped Verbina in. I slid in beside her as he closed the door once more with a satisfying thunk.

"Sailing today, lady?" the driver said as he turned to look at us, in an accent Verbina told me later was decidedly Brooklyn.

"Yes, on the *Queen Mary*, Pier 90, at noon. Make a right on Fifth to Fifty-seventh, then take Fifty-seventh Street to Eleventh Avenue, and take that to Fifty-fifth. Take Fifty-fifth to the river and the Cunard dock."

"From here I usually swing back along Central Park through Columbus Circle and then left on Columbus Avenue. I take that to Fifty-fifth and then down to the river, lady. It's more direct."

"*You're* more direct. If you wish to address me, you may call me ma'am or Mrs. Partridge. Take the route I stated. You'll avoid traffic and get there faster."

He shrugged and rolled his eyes. "Yes, ma'am, you're the boss lady." He faced front and started his meter as the bellboys finished piling the luggage and bags in and slammed the trunk lids down. And then we were off, zigging and zagging through the busy Manhattan morning traffic, the other cab following closely behind.

As we rounded a corner, I looked over at Verbina. "You look terrific, as always, Auntie. That color really suits you."

"Thank you, dear. It's something new I picked up for the crossing. You look handsome as ever, but I do wish you hadn't spilled coffee on your tan suit jacket at breakfast."

"Me too. Clumsy of me. I had to pack it still damp in my luggage. And since it was a suit, I had to change completely." I glanced down at my current outfit, which was a green single-breasted jacket with striped trousers, a yellow tie, and a matching pocket square. "But I guess this will do. Hopefully I can get the suit coat cleaned on the ship."

"Just give it to your room steward and they'll take care of it. That green jacket you're wearing now clashes with my dress, though, dear."

"Sorry, I didn't know we were supposed to match."

"Not match, but complement. A lady's escort's clothing should never clash with hers. Well, never mind, you can put something else on once we're aboard."

"Yes, Auntie," I said with a sigh. "Gee, I wish we could have had more time in New York besides just a day and half. There's so much to see and do here. It's an amazing city."

"It is indeed. You'll have to come back another time. But New York was just a stopping-off point between home and London this trip. We'll have two glorious weeks to explore the capital of England, its largest city, then back here for one night before heading home again."

"I'm looking forward to it all very much." I watched the sights of New York whizzing by out the cab window, craning my neck this way and that at the tall buildings and the masses of people. I didn't see any breadlines that day, but we did pass two soup kitchens with lines already forming on the sidewalk, and several men panhandling or selling apples for a nickel apiece on the street corners. It made me feel tremendously guilty, not just for ordering that room service, but for all Verbina had paid for this trip so far: the train ride from Milwaukee, the two-night stay in New York City—at the Plaza Hotel no less—and now a holiday in Europe, sailing first class on the *Queen Mary*. I considered myself fortunate indeed.

The cabs stopped at the pier, and a haggard longshoreman hurried over to gather up our luggage as Verbina paid the two drivers. Then she adjusted her hat and addressed the longshoreman as he began loading our bags and trunks on his large, flat cart, his muscles bulging beneath a sweaty work shirt. I tried not to stare.

"We're on the *Queen Mary* to Southampton, first class, or cabin class, as they're calling it nowadays," Verbina said to him. "The steamer trunk won't be needed on the voyage, but the rest should go in our cabins. Those two large brown ones, the black garment bag, and that small black one with the tan stripe are my nephew's.

The rest are mine." She handed him our tickets, and he marked each of the bags and trunks as another longshoreman with a bushy red mustache arrived to give him a hand. Auntie tipped each of them generously.

When the first man had handed Auntie back her tickets and she returned them to her handbag, she straightened up, gazed out at the small patch of brown water that was visible from where we stood, took in a deep breath, and said, "There it is, Heath, the Hudson River that will take us out to the Atlantic and over to England. And look! There she is, the majestic *Queen Mary*. Isn't she something? Almost brand new, you know, not even two years old. What a sight to see."

I sucked in my breath at the sight of the mammoth three stacker, its knife-edge prow almost touching the shore. "She's huge."

"One of the largest, in fact *the* largest, according to Cunard's brochures, *and* the fastest. Larger and faster than the *Aquitania*, and she'll beat *Normandie*'s speed record any day now, I'm sure of it."

"Yes, so you've mentioned. Definitely impressive, a killer diller for sure."

"A what?" she said, pulling on her gloves.

"Sorry, killer diller. You know, the best, the ultimate, like the bee's knees."

Verbina gave me a scornful look. "You're not in college anymore, you must learn to speak like a gentleman."

I sighed. "Yes, ma'am. Anyway, isn't her sister ship almost ready to sail?"

"The *Queen Elizabeth*, you mean? Construction began last December, but she won't be ready for a few years. Building a ship of that size takes time, you know. She's supposed to be even larger than the *Queen Mary*, if you can imagine."

I took another look at the mammoth beauty before us. "Hard to believe. I can't wait to get aboard."

"Nor I. As many times as I've sailed, this is always a thrill for me." Verbina consulted her watch. "We'll have to hurry. Oh, I do wish I hadn't worn these heels. The first class gangway is this way. We're on the main deck, adjoining cabins on the starboard side." We started walking briskly toward the terminal, each of us staring up at the looming hulk floating effortlessly and almost magically in the muddy brown water that lapped gently at her sides. A few gulls floated about, with more of them soaring above, squawking and chirping. The longshoremen, I noticed, had finished loading our luggage and had disappeared.

The boarding line was short, as it was close to departure time, and once we reached the front, a uniformed man with a white cap scanned our tickets and passports, then handed them back to Auntie and wished us bon voyage. I removed my hat and we climbed up the canvas-sided gangway into an opening on the side of the ship. We found ourselves on A deck, amidships, in a moderately sized foyer. The purser's office stood between two elevators, with long lines of people at the windows. Opposite that were three sets of doors leading to the main staircase. Masses of people scurried about like well-dressed squirrels up and down the stairs and the elevators, aided by a small army of uniformed pursers, stewards, and bellboys, all eager to assist.

Visitors mixed in with the passengers, all chitchatting loudly, gaping about, snapping photographs, and holding blowers, bouquets of flowers, and bon voyage baskets affixed with gay ribbons. It was loud, crowded, and stuffy, but the air almost crackled with excitement. No signs of the Depression resided here. This was the upper class, and though they may have lost some money in the great crash of '29, they didn't lose it all, and felt little guilt about displaying their wealth.

As I gaped at all the people I suddenly felt awkward and overwhelmed, and a bit unsure of myself. I was the son of a postal clerk and a housewife, put through college by a meager scholarship, my folks, a part-time job at Schuster's Department Store, and the grace of my Aunt Verbina. I felt out of place, unlike her, who was standing poised and confident by my side. She was an experienced traveler, but this was all new to me. "How many times have you crossed, Auntie?"

"Goodness, I don't keep track. Dozens of times, I imagine. This is my second sailing on the *Mary*. The first time on her was with David this past spring, of course. He had business in London."

She had taken out a gold compact from her purse and was studying her face in the small round mirror encased in its cover.

"Gosh, you've traveled so much. I remember Mom saying she's never been farther west than Minnesota and never farther east than the shores of Lake Michigan. And she's never been out of the country, not even to Canada."

"Ramona is a good woman, and a good mother to you, Heath. She sacrificed a lot when she married your father," she said, extracting a lipstick now and applying it with a steady hand.

"What do you mean? Pop's a great guy."

"I didn't say he wasn't. But he was, and still is, a working-class man. Not that there's anything wrong with being working class, but the finer things are generally out of reach for them, and Ramona knew that when she married him."

"He's done plenty well providing for us, I'd say, what with the Depression and all."

"Yes, he was lucky to get that job with the post office after they married. And then shortly after that they had you. Don't get me wrong, I'm glad they did, for as you know I don't have any children of my own, and I've loved spoiling you as much as your parents will let me."

"Why didn't you ever have children of your own?"

She put the top back on her lipstick, snapped the compact shut, and dropped them both back into her purse. "That's a rather personal question, but I'll allow it because it's you. To be honest, I'm not suited to being a mother. I'm better at being an aunt. I'm too selfish to raise a child. Unlike your mother, I married for social status, for money, and for the kind of life I always wanted, and I got it both times. I'm not saying I didn't love my first husband, and of course I love David, but it wasn't the primary motive to marry, nor do I think should it be. Good marriages are a business, a partnering of two people, of what each can bring to the table. David brought wealth and position, I brought refinement and respectability. A wealthy man should be married. It grounds him. In fact, every man should be married, eventually, in my opinion."

"Every man?"

"Well, not every man, obviously. Not priests, of course, and there are a few other notable exceptions."

"I don't think I ever want to get married."

She glanced up and flitted her gloved hand at me dismissively. "You say that now, but you're young, inexperienced, and naïve."

"I'm not naïve."

Verbina smiled and touched my cheek with that same gloved hand. "Oh, my dear boy, enjoy your youth. Cherish it. The world is your oyster. Live your dash to the fullest while you can."

"My dash?"

"It's the time between our birth year and our death year, the dash on our tombstones. To live your dash means to live your life as completely and fully as you can. Don't put things off, because we never know."

"Ah, I see. That makes sense. And I intend to."

"Good. It's fine to have your dalliances in your youth, but a time will come in the not-too-distant future you'll find you need a good woman to ground you."

"Being grounded doesn't sound like much fun."

"Marriage isn't supposed to be fun. It's a business, a partnership, like I said before."

"But are you happy? You seem to be."

"Oh my goodness, child, yes, I'm happy, for the most part. My marriages have allowed me to have those finer things in life—nice clothes, jewelry, a lovely home, and the opportunity to travel, though I admit I sometimes feel guilty about it all, with so many people out of work these days."

"I feel guilty about it, too, but none of these people seem to."

She glanced about at the crowd and shook her head. "The privileged class enjoying the finer things in life. I wasn't born into it like so many, and only came to it later when I married my first husband, so perhaps I value it more, and I understand what's it like not to have it. I give as much as I can to charity, and I volunteer in the soup kitchens back home when I'm able to."

"Yes, I know. You've got a good heart."

She laughed. "That's kind of you, Heath. These past years have not been easy for anyone, regardless of their social status or class. My friends the Connellys lost almost everything in the crash—their house, their yacht, nearly all their money, and he took his own life, leaving her alone and destitute. Fortunately, they didn't have children."

"What happened to her?"

"Sylvia moved back to Boston to live with her parents. So many lives have been ruined by all this. Still, President Roosevelt seems to be turning things around, what with his Works Progress Administration program and the new Social Security Act and all."

"He's done some good things, I think," I said. "But there's a long way to go yet."

"It's true, and I do worry about all that, my darling. But let's not think of those things now. This is your first trip to New York, your first transatlantic crossing, and your first trip to Europe. It's my gift to you, Heath. Your graduation present, as you know, but only the beginning of a world of travel for you, I hope."

"I hope so, too. It's awfully nice of you, Auntie. Extremely generous."

"Oh, you're worth it, even if you do fritter my money away on frivolous things like room service. You're the first on either side of the family to graduate from college."

"Yes, but I wasn't exactly in the top of my class, as you know. And I majored in literature with a minor in French."

"It doesn't matter. What does matter is that you graduated, and I'm proud of you, and so are your parents, of course. With a literature major, you may become an excellent teacher. I think you'd be quite good at that, and you'd have your summers off to travel. Yes, you should get a teaching job, I think. Most definitely."

"Jobs, any jobs, are hard to come by right now, Auntie, if not impossible."

"Not impossible for someone with a college education. But for now, let's get settled. My feet are killing me." She raised her gloved hand just high enough, and soon a bellboy in a short red jacket, white gloves, high black trousers, and a red brimless cap with gold braiding rushed to our side, beaming a toothy smile from ear to ear.

He couldn't have been much more than eighteen, if that. "Welcome aboard. My name is Albert, and I would be happy to assist you, Mrs.…?"

"Partridge. This is my nephew, Heath Barrington." She opened her handbag and handed him our tickets, which he glanced at with a practiced eye.

"Very good, Mrs. Partridge, Mr. Barrington. Please allow me to show you to your cabins. You're both on M deck, just one deck above where we are now. I'm afraid there's a bit of a wait for the lifts."

"Lifts?" I said.

"Elevators, Heath. This is a British ship, after all." She turned back to the bellboy. "I need to have the purser put my pearls in the safe, but that will just take a moment. I'll be right back." Fortunately, the line for the pursers office had mostly dispersed, and she was back shortly. "Now then, Alfred, the stairs are fine, thank you. Lead on."

"Albert, ma'am, and thank you, just this way," the bellboy said.

We climbed the stairs from A deck up to Main Deck and then followed Albert down a narrow corridor to Verbina's cabin. The keys to the staterooms were in the locks, removed as people checked in. Albert removed the key to M009, handed it to Verbina, and ushered us in. It was light and airy, paneled in a lustrous wood that positively gleamed. There were two beds, separated with built-in nightstands and a dressing table, the latter complete with a large round mirror attached securely to the wall. A metal fan was mounted to the ceiling and angled down.

"Your bathroom is just here, ma'am, and your cupboards are there. Your bags should be along shortly. If you require assistance unpacking, just press the call button for your stewardess. No need to dress for dinner this evening, first night out, you know." He turned to me. "Mr. Barrington, your cabin is just next door, and there is a connecting door between the two staterooms, should you wish to use it. If you'll follow me…"

He walked back out into the corridor, pausing briefly to let an old woman and another bellboy go by, and then stopped at M007, stepping aside as he handed me the key. It was a decent size, pretty much the mirror opposite of M009. The walls, as the bellboy proudly described them, were paneled in light Honduras mahogany, while the curtains, bedspreads, and such were in ivory satin with pink and green accents. The floor was covered wall to wall in a plush mint green carpet thick enough to sink my feet into. Both rooms, I noticed, had Bakelite punkah louvre ventilators.

"Your bags will be along soon, too, sir. Should you require assistance in unpacking, just ring for your steward. There's a call button by the door, or if you prefer you can use the telephone on the desk."

"Thanks. My tuxedo will need to be pressed," I said, putting my hat on the desk. "I can manage the rest."

"Of course, sir. Just ask your steward once your suitcases arrive. The first night out no one dresses, so we'll have it back to you first thing in the morning. Is there anything else you or your aunt require right now?"

"No, that will be fine, thank you." I gave him a fifty-cent piece and sent him happily on his way, in search of more passengers and more tips. That done, I used the bathroom, noting I had a full-sized tub with hot and cold water as well as salt water on tap. After washing my hands, I rapped on the connecting door.

Verbina opened it a moment later, looking shorter than usual because she had removed her hat and high-heeled shoes. I wasn't used to seeing her like that.

"My feet were killing me," she said. "Look what a bellboy just brought, a lovely bon voyage basket from your parents for both of us. Isn't that sweet?"

I glanced at the basket of fruit on the table and smiled. "Indeed, though they shouldn't have spent the money," I said, knowing they could ill afford it. "We shall have to write them a thank-you note."

"Oh, of course, we should each write a note. I rather thought my husband David would have sent flowers or something, but oh well, he's a busy man."

"Yes, he certainly is. By the way, I gave the bellboy who showed us to our cabins a fifty-cent piece. Do you think that was enough?"

"Of course. But don't overdo it. Generally speaking, tips are given at the end of the crossing. Five dollars to your cabin steward, five dollars to the dining room waiter, two dollars to the deck steward, and one or two dollars each for the bar, smoking room, gym, and pool stewards."

"Golly, that adds up to a fair amount."

"For services rendered. It's not required, but not tipping or tipping poorly is just as gauche as overtipping, and frequent travelers are known for how they tip or don't tip."

"I have a lot to learn, it seems."

"It will be second nature to you in no time. Now the bellboys you can tip as you go, as you just did. They generally get tips from the waiters, bar stewards, and cabin stewards, though, so no need to tip too much."

I felt like I should be taking notes. Just then we heard a gong in the hall and a bellboy shouting, "All ashore that's going ashore!" followed by the ship's whistle, loud and clear.

"Goodness, already?" Verbina said. "We've only just boarded, but then we were quite late. You shouldn't have dawdled over breakfast at the hotel like that, Heath."

"I'm sorry," I said for the fourth time. I didn't tell her, but the waiter in the hotel restaurant was fetching and attentive, and I really hated to leave, and then I had to go back upstairs to change my coat after spilling coffee on it while I was gaping at the waiter's attractive behind.

"Well, we made it, so all's well that ends well. Let me get my hat, shoes, and gloves back on, and we'll go up to the sundeck."

"What for?"

"For the send-off, of course. It's quite gay. Everyone throws streamers and blows blowers and waves at those on the pier."

"But we don't know anyone on the pier, Auntie."

"It doesn't make any difference. We wave, and they wave back, you see?"

I didn't really, but I was feeling rather agreeable, so after she'd dressed and I'd gathered up my hat, we joined the throngs crowding the rails on the sun deck, cheering, yelling, blowing, and waving as the old girl backed out into the Hudson, assisted by multiple tugs, and then swung around and headed slowly down the river toward the sea. "Well, we're off, and right on time. Twelve noon exactly," I said as I returned my pocket watch, which had belonged to my grandfather, to my pocket.

"I'd expect nothing less, and I'm sure the captain will be trying for another record-breaking crossing, and he'll do it if weather permits, I should think. We should pass the Lightship Ambrose by one o'clock, right on schedule. Let's have a light lunch while we wait for our luggage, shall we?"

I wasn't all that hungry and would have preferred to explore the ship, but seeing as how I was her guest on this trip and she was paying the lion's share of the expenses, I accompanied her toward the dining room on C deck, my hat in my hand. On our way down the stairs, we ran almost literally into a woman about my aunt's age, who was coming up the stairs. She was swathed in purple, with a deep purple hat that sported a white plume. She was wearing short white gloves, a fox stole much like Verbina's draped about her shoulders, and an alligator clutch tucked under her left arm that matched her shoes.

"Why, Verbina!" the woman said as we all stopped on the landing and stared at each other.

"Myrtle Obermeyer, what a surprise. I don't think I've seen you since you moved to Chicago."

"Goodness, has it been that long? I've been in Chicago almost two years," Mrs. Obermeyer said. "What are you doing on this ship? My gracious. Oh, and is this your new husband? I'd heard you remarried. My, he's quite handsome. Tall and young, too."

I blushed crimson and Verbina looked aghast. "Myrtle, for heaven's sake. This is my nephew, Heath. My sister's only child. My new husband is much older, and he couldn't come with us because of some silly work situation. I'm treating Heath to this trip. He's just graduated from college, you know."

She looked me up and down from head to toe. "Oh, how nice, congratulations. Aren't you going to introduce us, Verbina?"

"Of course, forgive me. Myrtle Obermeyer, I'd like you to meet my nephew, Heath Barrington. Heath, this is an old, old friend of mine, Myrtle Obermeyer, Mrs. Maxwell Obermeyer."

"Careful on the olds, dear, I'm younger than you are, remember."

"As you always remind me, Myrtle, but only by five months."

"Five months and six days."

"Yes. That means your birthday is this month."

"That's right, September the thirtieth. I'm a Libra, you know. Librans are known for being charming, graceful, and good humorists."

"But not modest, obviously."

"Oh, so witty. You're a Taurus, of course. Known for their stubbornness, hedonism, and a love of luxury and comfort. Quite spot on, I'd say."

"I had no idea you were such an astrology expert, Myrtle."

"I had a few encounters with a handsome medium named Omar last year. I treated myself for my thirty-ninth birthday."

"You treated yourself to Omar?"

"Certainly, darling. He also reads palms, you know. He told me I have one of the most fascinating love lines he's ever seen, very long."

"Of that I have no doubt. Sounds like it was a birthday gift that kept on giving. And now you turn forty on the thirtieth."

"I'm still thirty-nine, dear."

"For three more weeks, Myrtle, just three more weeks."

"Yes, but *you've* been forty for nearly five months. How has it been being in your forties, Verbina?"

"You'll find out soon enough."

"I do hope you'll get me a birthday present. Something tall, well-built, and handsome, just like this fellow here. How do you do, Mr. Barrington?" She held out her gloved right hand, palm down, and I wasn't exactly sure if I should kiss it like I'd seen in the movies, or just take it in mine and gently shake it. I decided on the latter.

"How do you do, Mrs. Obermeyer?"

"Oh, quite well, quite well," she said, withdrawing her hand.

"I'm a widow traveling alone, dear man. I didn't even bring my maid. Poor Maxwell has been gone several years now, I forget how many exactly." She looked me up and down again. "Are you single?"

"Myrtle! He's twenty-two years old."

She smiled. "That's old enough, and then some."

"In your mind, perhaps. What are you doing here, anyway?"

"Me? I was on my way up to the sun deck to see us off, but I'm afraid I'm too late. I waited forever for one of the lifts, then finally decided to take the stairs."

"Yes, we're well under way now, though not in open water yet," I said.

She shook her head, the white plume in her hat waving back and forth. "Such is life. My fault entirely. I took too long with a bottle of bubbly Frederick brought me as a bon voyage gift. Actually, I took too long with Frederick, too." She giggled at that, covering her mouth with her hand. "He was the last visitor off, I believe. Had we dillied and dallied any longer, he would have wound up sailing with us."

"Frederick?" Verbina said.

"Frederick Henry Hamilton, a dear pet. I met him at the Stork Club last week when I got to New York. He's simply charming and a divine dancer, among other things. He hated to see me sail, he was beside himself and he begged me to stay."

"Why didn't you?"

"Because when we first met he told me he was in banking. Turns out he's just a teller, and rather witless. Still, we had fun, and he saw me off with a bottle of Veuve, which probably cost him a week's salary. I promised him I'd write."

"Which you won't," Verbina said.

"I may, but then again you're right. I may not. Why keep his hopes alive?"

"You haven't changed, Myrtle. So, where are you headed, besides Hades eventually?"

She gave a false laugh. "Verbina, you haven't changed a bit, either, I see, except older. Still so, so witty. I'm on my way to Cherbourg to see my cousin Helen, Mrs. Arthur VanAllen."

"I wasn't aware you had a cousin in Cherbourg."

"They're from New York, originally. She and her husband live in Marseille, but they're meeting me in Cherbourg. I'll be stopping in Paris for a week on my way. So many French men there, you know."

"*Le ciel aide les hommes francais*," Verbina said.

"Don't speak French, Verbina. I can't understand a word of it," Mrs. Obermeyer said.

"It means, 'Heaven help the French men,'" I said, suppressing a smile.

"And if you can't speak French, how are you going to manage in Paris and Marseille?" Verbina said. "That is the native language, you know."

"My dear, I *always* manage, don't you worry. There are other ways to communicate."

"Yes, and you're fluent in all of them," Verbina said.

Mrs. Obermeyer shot her a look. "Practice makes perfect, I always say. And where are you two off to?"

"London," I said. "This is my first crossing."

"How charming. I know London well. Perhaps I should delay France and go on to London with the two of you," Mrs. Obermeyer said, touching my arm. "I'd be happy to keep you company, Mr. Barrington, and show you around. I know all the best night spots, and Verbina's never been one for nightlife. She gets tired quickly at her age, you know. You and I could have a very good time."

"Um, well, uh, your cousin is expecting you, though," I said.

"Exactly," Verbina said. "And besides, those French men…"

Myrtle pouted her lips briefly, glanced at Verbina, and then back up at me. "True, true. Well, I can certainly keep you company on the crossing while Verbina naps. Ocean voyages can be rather dull, you know. The Verandah Grill becomes the Starlight Club after dark, and it's *the* place to see and be seen. I'd be delighted to entertain you, so to speak. We could dance and drink the nights away, and toast the dawns." She squeezed my arm now as she moved closer to me. "Do you tango? Or do you prefer to rumba? The rumba is the dance of love, flirtatious and sensual."

"You're too kind, Myrtle," Verbina said. "But Heath's engaged to a lovely young woman back home, aren't you dear?"

I was taken aback by this unexpected lie, but picked up on it in a heartbeat. "Yes, that's right. Olive Grant. I miss her already."

Myrtle pouted again and released my arm. "Oh, dear, that's too bad, all the way around, I should say. But of course, shipboard dalliances are left at the pier, and I'm the picture of discretion. Where are your cabins?"

"M deck. I'm in 009," Verbina said.

"And you, Mr. Barrington?"

"Uh, 007."

"They connect," Verbina said flatly.

"How convenient. Are you *sure* he's your nephew? You sound awfully protective."

"Myrtle, don't be insulting. Heath is my sister Ramona's boy. You remember Ramona."

She tittered again, covering her mouth once more with a gloved hand that had large, garish rings on nearly every finger. I'd never seen anyone wear rings over a glove before. "Oh yes, of course. Don't mind me, I've had a touch too much champagne already, as I said."

"With Frederick," Verbina said.

"Yes. He was quite dashing, and he seemed so fond of me, poor man. I fear I broke his heart into little pieces." She looked me up and down again. "Perhaps I should find a nephew of my own to be my traveling companion. We could each have our nephews, wouldn't that be sweet? You know I can keep secrets."

"So you've said, the picture of discretion. But there are no secrets to keep," Verbina said. "Heath *is* my nephew, and he's engaged."

Mrs. Obermeyer smiled slyly. "Not much family resemblance, and you without your husband. Besides, as far as the fiancée goes, out of sight, out of mind, they say."

"As I said before, Myrtle, you haven't changed. I'd love to stay and chat, but we're just heading down to lunch," Verbina said, her voice rising in an annoyed tone.

"I'd join you but I'm not in the least bit hungry right now. I eat like a bird, everyone says so, like a little bird. It's how I keep my figure, you know. But we simply *must* catch up, it's been too long. I'll stop by your stateroom after lunch and we can order a bottle of bubbly. I'm on B deck. B17 in case either of you are ever in the neighborhood." She beamed at me and batted her eyelashes.

"We can meet in my cabin at two o'clock, M009. And if you want more champagne, we'll charge it to B17," Verbina said.

"Oh my dear, you're such a kidder. Perhaps I'll take a stroll about the Promenade deck until we reach the Lightship Ambrose and see whom I might run into. I'll see you both at two. Ta!" She turned and continued her climb up the stairs, clutching the railing for balance and support.

"Ta ta," Verbina said, calling after her.

"Nice to have met you," I said.

Mrs. Obermeyer stopped and looked back, exposing a good deal of her legs, as she had hiked up her dress for the stairs. "I have a feeling we may get to know each other quite well, my boy. The voyage is just beginning. Bye for now." She straightened her skirt and continued her climb up the stairs as we proceeded down the stairs.

"My goodness, Auntie, she certainly was something."

"Yes, she's something, all right. I met her years ago when we were young girls in finishing school. She can be a bit much."

"I noticed."

"And she noticed you. She likes younger men. All men, actually. I hope you don't mind my inventing a fiancée for you."

"No, not at all, I appreciate it. I have a feeling if it wasn't for Olive I never would have gotten rid of her."

"You still may have a fight on your hands, but at least you have a weapon at your disposal now. Myrtle doesn't take no for an answer very easily."

"Me and Olive against Myrtle, oh my."

"Stay strong, Heath, stay strong," she said as we reached the dining room.

CHAPTER TWO

Friday Afternoon, September 10, 1937
At Sea

The first-class dining room of the ship was magnificent, unlike anything I had ever seen, posher, even, than the dining room of the Plaza Hotel in New York, and far larger. The ceiling soared two decks high in the center, and on one end was a stunning map of the Atlantic, with a tiny crystal *Queen Mary* that apparently moved along two tracks, back and forth from Europe to America, on her summer and winter routes. The floor was covered in Korkoid, a type of linoleum, beautiful yet practical and new, and various types of gleaming wood were everywhere. The overall effect of the room was of spacious grandeur, and I took it all in like a hungry seagull.

After a few moments of my gaping, Verbina touched my arm and indicated a maître d' who was waiting patiently to show us to a table, set exquisitely with silver, crystal, and china, all laid out just as I had seen it in the movies. The menu was equally impressive, listing such delicacies as Potage Ecossaise, broiled fillets of haddock, Brussels sprouts, mashed carrots, baked jacket and pureed potatoes, rice custard pudding, biscuits, cheeses, and coffee, all included in the price of our tickets, and we could order as much as we wanted. I admit to being a bit enthusiastic, and I overate, so I was glad Auntie suggested we retire to our cabins for a brief rest after we had finished.

Back on M deck, my luggage had arrived, stacked neatly on

one of the beds in my cabin. I set my hat down on the desk, used the bathroom, and unbuttoned my trousers, giving myself a bit of breathing room. Then I put away the rest of my things with room to spare and rang for the steward to have my tuxedo pressed and my tan suit coat cleaned. He showed me how to stow my empty cases beneath the beds, took my tuxedo and suit coat, and left, letting me know he'd return later to turn down my bed. I slipped out of my green jacket and put on a dark brown one that still went with my striped trousers, and then, at just a few minutes to two, I rebuttoned my trousers, somewhat unwillingly, and knocked on the adjoining door.

"Oh good, your luggage came so you could change your coat," she said, looking at me approvingly. "Of course I'll be wearing my red dress tonight, so perhaps you could put on your black double-breasted before we go down to dinner."

"Can't I just wear what I have on?" I said, stepping into her cabin and closing the connecting door behind me. "Brown goes okay with red. Besides, the steward said no one dresses for dinner the first night out."

Verbina shook her head. "We're not in Milwaukee anymore, Heath. He meant formalwear, but one still must look one's best, and a sport coat is much too casual for dinner on board."

I shrugged. "If you say so." I glanced about, noticing her luggage had also arrived. The room was decidedly less tidy than it had been before, with hats, scarves, stockings, shoes, dresses, blouses, and whatnot strewn about and overflowing from her suitcases. A stewardess, I noticed, was busy trying to cram some of Verbina's unmentionables into a drawer in a bureau near one of the portholes.

Verbina declared, "Honestly, there just isn't enough room. I might have to store some of my hats and things in your cabin."

"That's fine, I have more than enough space."

She gave me a disgusted look. "Of course you do. Men."

"Can't help it," I said with a grin.

"In my next life, I hope to come back as a wealthy gentleman. Life is so much easier. A dark suit, some sport coats, a tuxedo and evening coat, a couple pairs of trousers, and a few ties, and you're all set, not to mention your underthings are so much simpler." She looked over at the stewardess. "That's enough for now, Marie, thank you."

"Yes, ma'am. And it's Louise, ma'am."

"What? Yes, Louise, that's what I said. Come back while we're at dinner and finish up what I don't get done."

"Yes, ma'am," the stewardess said as she left, probably glad to escape.

Verbina looked about once more. "I knew I should have brought my own maid. It's simply hopeless."

"You'll get it straightened out."

She sighed. "Yes, in time to repack everything for the boat train. It's the same every crossing. You'd think I'd learn."

A knock came from the door to the corridor.

"Oh, for heaven's sake, now what? Oh, it's probably Myrtle," she said, glancing at her watch. "I forgot about her. Answer that, will you, dear?"

"Yes, ma'am." I moved a few feet and opened it to find Mrs. Obermeyer swaying slightly from side to side, from either the motion of the ship, the champagne she'd had earlier with Frederick, or both.

"Oh, Mr. Barrington, did I knock on the wrong door? I was looking for Verbina. You know, your, uh, aunt." She had removed her rings and gloves, along with her plumed hat.

"This is her cabin, Mrs. Obermeyer. I'm just visiting."

"Just visiting? Of course you are. You should visit me some time, on B deck. B17, in case you've forgotten. I can be very friendly. Have you ordered the champagne? It is two o'clock, you know, and I believe I'm right on time."

"Please come in, Mrs. Obermeyer, yes you are, and no, I don't believe we have ordered the champagne," I said.

She stepped in, brushing a little closer to me than was necessary, as I closed the door behind her.

"My goodness, Verbina, did your trunks explode?"

"Very funny, Myrtle. I'm just having trouble fitting everything in, that's all. Heath, ring for a bottle of champagne and three glasses, please. Use the phone on the desk, ask the switchboard for room service."

"Yes, ma'am," I said. The white telephone was inset with a notice that read *You can telephone to any part of the world whilst at sea.*

When I finished, Myrtle looked over at me and smiled. "You know, Heath, your Aunt Verbina and I went to finishing school together."

"Yes, she mentioned that."

"Except you never finished finishing school, Myrtle."

"Neither did your sister."

"My mother?" I said.

Myrtle looked at me. "Is she really your mother? I mean, Verbina's really your aunt?"

"Yes, and yes," I said, annoyed.

"Well, isn't that interesting?"

"I *told* you he was my nephew, Myrtle."

"Of course, but there isn't much of a family resemblance. I didn't really believe it. I just thought—"

"I *know* what you thought," Verbina said crossly.

"Well, no harm done, and now you really *must* visit me in my cabin, Mr. Barrington. It's a long crossing, and we can play a game of mah-jongg. I brought a brand-new set along that I purchased in New York."

"I'm afraid I don't play mah-jongg, Mrs. Obermeyer."

"Even better," she said, touching my arm once more. "I can teach you. I can teach you lots of things."

"There are plenty of other things to do on board, Myrtle," Verbina said. "There's quoits, shuffleboard, ping-pong, deck tennis, the masquerade ball, a funny hat contest, exercises in the gymnasium, and motion pictures. None of which take place in your cabin."

Myrtle waved her hand dismissively at Verbina. "I can't play tennis, and funny hat contests bore me. But I can be quite entertaining in private." She looked at me and smiled, squeezing my arm again, and I felt myself blush as I returned her gaze. Mrs. Obermeyer was attractive for an older woman. Her hair was a brilliant shade of chestnut and stylishly done, and she had an hourglass figure, curved in all the right places, but I certainly had no interest in getting to know her better. At least not the way *she* wanted.

"Remember Heath has a fiancée," Verbina said.

"Oh fiddlesticks, I'm just being friendly. My goodness, it's warm in here, isn't it?" Mrs. Obermeyer said as she tugged at her dress and shifted about, fidgeting with her waistline.

"Myrtle," Verbina said. "Surely you remember from Miss Albright's Finishing School for All Bright Young Ladies that one does not tug at one's undergarments in mixed company."

"Gracious, I can't help it, Verbina. My girdle is killing me, and it's hot in here."

"You were talking about my mother before," I said, trying to get her back on track.

"Hmm, what? Was I? Oh, yes, your mother went to Miss Albright's with us for a time, then she met and married your father, poor dear."

"Why do you say that?"

"Well, because your father *was* a poor dear, my dear. We all enrolled in finishing school way back in 1913, to help us find rich husbands, of course. Me, your mother, and Verbina here."

"Myrtle, really."

"It's true, no use denying it. We were sweet sixteen, your mother was seventeen. None of us were born to the privileged class, unfortunately, so we were bound and determined to marry into it. Your aunt and I succeeded, eventually. Your mother, on the other hand, well, she ended up marrying for love, as she put it. She left the school in June of 1914 to get married."

"And I was born in January of 1915," I said. "But that means—"

"That you were premature," Verbina said quickly, and then looked at Mrs. Obermeyer. "Ramona's husband is a good man."

Myrtle looked over at her. "Oh, I'm sure he is. Quite handsome, too, as I recall." She looked back at me then. "How is your mother, by the way? I haven't seen her in years."

"She's just fine. She and my father are quite happy."

"And live in a nice little working-class house in a nice little working-class neighborhood in Milwaukee, I suppose," Mrs. Obermeyer said.

"That's right, what's wrong with that?"

"Oh, nothing, nothing, my dear. Has the Depression been horrible to your family?"

"No, my father works for the post office and provides for us amply, thank you very much."

"Oh, I'm so glad. No offense meant, Mr. Barrington. So many people are out of work these days. It's just been dreadful."

"It doesn't seem to have affected you."

"Heath, don't be rude," Verbina said.

"It's all right, Verbina. Maxwell left me quite well off when he died, and I invested in real estate, gold, and the railroads rather than the stock market. And I spend my money so that it trickles down to the masses, you see? What good would it do anyone, including me, gathering dust in a bank vault? Spread the wealth, I always say. Roll it around."

"I see," I said. "How generous and philanthropic of you."

"Fill in what now?" she said, tugging at her girdle once more with one hand and fanning herself with the other.

"Nothing, Mrs. Obermeyer."

"Hmm, yes, well now, about this young woman you're engaged to, this Olive...?"

"Uh, Olive Smith," I said.

"I thought it was Grant?" Mrs. Obermeyer said.

"Right, right, Olive Grant Smith," I said.

Mrs. Obermeyer raised her painted on eyebrows. "I see. Well, I hope she comes from a good family, at least. I'm not familiar with any Grant Smiths."

"She's just a nice girl from a nice family," I said.

"Hmm. What does her father do? Hopefully, he's employed."

"Her father? Yes, he's a, he's a dentist," I said, at the same time Verbina said, "He's a lawyer."

"A lawyer dentist," I said.

"A lawyer dentist? How queer. You don't seem quite sure, neither of you."

"It's a new profession, Myrtle," Verbina said.

"Indeed. Hmm. Do you have a photograph of this Olive? I bet she's a lovely girl."

"A photograph?" I looked panic stricken at Aunt Verbina and then back at Mrs. Obermeyer. "Uh, no, I left it at home."

"No photograph of your fiancée on such a long trip? No remembrance of your betrothed?"

"I, uh, just, didn't bring one along," I said.

"How about a locket of her hair? Or a letter, perhaps, with a lipstick print?"

I shook my head. "Um, no, afraid not."

Mrs. Obermeyer looked triumphant. "Hmph. I thought as much. Olive Grant Smith. You two aren't fooling me in the least. There is no Olive Grant Smith, is there? And you're not engaged, Mr. Barrington, to her or anyone else, are you?"

"Well, uh, I, uh," I stammered, feeling myself blush again.

"Oh, all right," Verbina said. "So he's not engaged, but he's not interested in you in the least, so retract your claws."

"Really, Verbina. I'm insulted. I was just being friendly. Can't a woman be cordial to a handsome young man? I don't see why you both had to lie to me. Why you felt the need to deceive me," Mrs. Obermeyer said, still swaying from side to side and front to back.

"Of course you don't. You never do. Now move that hatbox on the sofa aside and have a seat, Myrtle, before you topple over," Auntie said as she settled into the upholstered chair.

A rap on the door was a welcome interruption, and I opened it, allowing a handsome white-jacketed steward to enter, carrying a silver tray with an ice bucket, a bottle of Veuve Clicquot champagne, and three coupe glasses, which he set up on the small rimmed table that held the fruit basket from my parents, next to the easy chair Verbina had chosen.

"Shall I open it, sir?"

"Yes, please," Verbina said, answering for me.

We all watched and waited expectantly for the pop, and we weren't disappointed. He poured the three glasses expertly, returned the bottle to the ice bucket, and then removed two items from under his arm. "This is the daily ship's bulletin, madam, for the remainder of today. Tomorrow's will be under your door in the morning. I've also brought the first-class passenger list for your perusal," he said, handing both items to Verbina. "May I be of further assistance?"

"No, thank you, that will do. Sign for that, Heath, will you, dear?"

"Yes, ma'am." I scrawled my name as directed, he thanked me and then left, closing the door behind him. I handed the coupe glasses out and then stood back, looking from Mrs. Obermeyer on the sofa to Verbina in the chair.

"Well, what shall we drink to?" Myrtle said, raising her glass.

"To a life of travel and adventure," Verbina said.

"Hear, hear," I said, because I remembered someone saying that in a movie once. We drank, and I found the bubbles delightful.

"Now then, come sit by me on the sofa, Heath. You don't mind if I call you Heath, do you? No use standing about. Make yourself comfortable," Mrs. Obermeyer said, patting the seat cushion next to her and smiling demurely. She was not one to give up easily.

"*I'll* sit by you, Myrtle, and we can look over the passenger list and ship's bulletin together. Heath, you take my chair," Verbina said.

"If you insist," Myrtle said, looking annoyed. I sat in the upholstered chair vacated by Verbina, careful not to spill any of my champagne. Once settled in, I crossed my legs, noticed a hole in one of my socks, and quickly crossed my legs the other way, hoping neither of them had seen. By then, they both seemed intent on reviewing the passenger list. Auntie scanned it with an expert eye while holding her champagne glass in her other hand.

"What or who are you looking for?" I asked.

Verbina glanced in my direction. "Oh, I'm just curious, that's all. Maybe there's a wealthy, single young gentleman on board for Myrtle, here."

"Wouldn't that be nice? Perhaps a Vanderbilt or a Rockefeller. If they're wealthy enough, they don't have to be that young."

"Naturally," Verbina said, looking at the list once more. "And perhaps there are some lovely single young ladies aboard, from the best families, of course, that you may be interested in, Heath, now that the cat's out of the bag about your nonexistent fiancée."

I resisted the urge to roll my eyes. "If there were, why would they be interested in me? I am not from one of the best families. I'm working class, as Mrs. Obermeyer pointed out."

"That may be so, but you're an American traveling first class, and you're young, quite attractive, if I do say so myself, and you have a college degree. All that in itself will do, as Myrtle will agree, I'm sure."

"Marry well and marry often, I always say," Mrs. Obermeyer said. "But in the meantime it never hurts to have a little fun. Forget the young ones. An older, shall we say, experienced woman may be just what you need before you go settling down with some silly young girl."

"Quiet, Myrtle," Verbina said as she turned her attention once more to the list in her hand and took another sip of champagne. "Oh my, as I live and breathe. William Haines is on board."

"Really? *The* William Haines?" Myrtle said.

"I can't imagine there's more than one," Verbina said. "At least not in first class."

My ears perked up. "The actor?" I recalled his amazingly handsome face from the movies, including his first talkie, *Navy Blues* in 1929, the year I turned fourteen. I think I went to see that film ten times and had all the dialogue memorized. And who could forget him in *Just a Gigolo* in 1931? I certainly couldn't, nor did I want to. I still had a copy of *Motion Picture* magazine that had a spread of him in it along with a shirtless picture of Buster Crabbe. Carole Lombard was on the cover. I told my mother Miss Lombard was the reason I was keeping the magazine in my bedroom, tucked safely in my nightstand.

"*Former* actor," Mrs. Obermeyer said. "He hasn't made a

picture in two years. I heard he started his own decorating firm. Does it say who he's traveling with?"

"It lists a J. Shields," Verbina said.

"That figures. That would be Jimmie Shields, his partner, shall we say, in the decorating business, among other things we won't discuss."

"What do you mean?" I said. "What other things?"

"Nothing, dear. Nothing. His personal affairs are not for your ears," Verbina said, "and none of our business."

"He's a public figure, or was. I think that makes his life everyone's business." Mrs. Obermeyer clucked. "Rumor has it he and your first husband Michael would have gotten along famously."

"Uncle Michael? What about him?" I said.

"Never mind, dear. Michael and I divorced amicably and he left me quite well off and happy," Verbina said.

"And he moved to San Francisco, way out in California," Myrtle added.

Verbina looked at Mrs. Obermeyer. "And I married the distinguished and wealthy David Partridge, a partner in a law firm, and one of *the* Partridges. So we're both better off," Verbina said. "Leave Michael alone and be quiet."

"Gladly," Mrs. Obermeyer said. "I only meant that William Haines is rumored to be a homosexual."

"You shouldn't speak of such things in front of Heath, Myrtle."

This time I did roll my eyes. "I'm twenty-two, Auntie, not twelve. I've heard rumors that William Haines was a homosexual. That he *is* a homosexual, and I know what that means."

"Where on earth did you hear that?" Verbina said, looking surprised.

I shrugged. "I don't know, around. I think it's terrible Metro-Goldwyn-Mayer fired him and basically forced him to retire from acting. I read all about it in *Photoplay* magazine."

"Why is a young man like you reading *Photoplay* magazine? You're not exactly the clientele they cater to," Mrs. Obermeyer said.

"I like movies, that's all."

"I see. Well, I'm sure no one forced Mr. Haines to do anything.

I hear he's doing quite well as a decorator, him and that Mr. Shields. I heard he even did Joan Crawford's place," Mrs. Obermeyer said.

"Golly. Maybe he could do my place when I finally move out of Mom and Dad's someday."

"I doubt you could afford him, dear," Verbina said. "Besides, gentlemen don't hire decorators."

"Or read *Photoplay* magazine, apparently," I said. "And yet I do. Maybe he could decorate your apartment, Auntie."

"I wouldn't object, but I don't need a decorator no matter how handsome he is, and David wouldn't allow it."

"Nor would I. I wouldn't have a man like that in my house, decorator or not. Some people say it's contagious, you know," Mrs. Obermeyer said, shaking her head. "It's an illness."

"*If* it is an illness, and I don't think it is, you certainly don't have to worry, Mrs. Obermeyer," I said. "You are one hundred percent heterosexual, and then some."

"Why, Heath, apologize at once," Verbina scolded.

I hung my head. "I'm sorry," I said, though I really wasn't.

"You certainly should be," Verbina said.

"Oh, it's fine, Verbina, and quite true," Mrs. Obermeyer said, chuckling. "He was just being a little cheeky, that's all, and I probably deserved it. Who else is on the passenger list? Anyone of note? Anyone single and *not* a homosexual?"

Verbina went back to the passenger list.

"Well, let me see. Upton Sinclair, he's certainly interesting, and oh, this is a surprise, Lord Quimby is on board."

"I thought he was dead," Mrs. Obermeyer said, a faint look of surprise on her face.

"Not Lionel Quimby, Simon, his son," Verbina said. "The new Lord Quimby."

"Oh, of course. How silly of me," Mrs. Obermeyer said.

"Who or what is a Lord Quimby?"

Verbina looked over at me. "A man from a very good family in England. He's a baron now that his father has passed on. It's an inherited title. Doesn't list a valet, but not surprising, I suppose."

"What exactly is a valet?" I said.

"A gentleman's gentleman. A good valet maintains his employer's clothes, polishes his shoes, runs his bath, sometimes even assists with shaving and dressing. They're getting a bit out of favor now these days, but it's an important position," Verbina said.

"I think Simon considers himself a modern, so he probably doesn't employ one. I don't believe his father did, either," Mrs. Obermeyer said.

"I've never had one, and I don't think I'd want one," I said.

"You're not of a certain lineage or income, my dear. But of course you're still a gentleman, though clearly in need of some tutelage," Mrs. Obermeyer said.

"Yes, so it's been pointed out," I said, looking at Verbina.

"Lord Simon Quimby," Verbina said again. "It's been quite some time. My first husband, Michael, and Simon's father, Sir Lionel, had business together once or twice, and we all met in London a few years ago. Michael and I, Lionel, Simon, and Charlotte Quimby, Simon's younger sister. We dined at Wiltons, such a lovely restaurant."

"And I was there with Maxwell, don't forget," Mrs. Obermeyer said. "That was the last trip he took. He died right after we got home. Oh, it must have been at least seven or eight years ago now. Letitia Birdwell was there too, I remember."

Auntie nodded. "That's right. She and Lionel Quimby were courting at that time. I wonder whatever happened between them. They seemed so well suited to each other."

"Yes, dear Letitia," Mrs. Obermeyer said. "I see her regularly these days. We both belong to the Woodlawn Women's Club. I sponsored her, as a matter of fact. Did you know she'd moved to Chicago, too?"

"Yes, I remember the Endicotts discussing that last season."

"You must be careful what you say around her, though, she's such a gossip," Mrs. Obermeyer said.

"So, you make sure you sit right next to her, of course," Verbina said.

"Be nice or I won't tell you what happened between her and Lionel Quimby."

"Oh. all right, Myrtle, I'm sorry," Verbina said. "Do tell."

"Well, Sir Henry Longfellow had set Letitia up with Lionel Quimby, as Lionel's wife had died many years prior. Letitia, a distant cousin of Sir Henry's, was living in London at the time, and apparently Lionel and Letitia hit it off."

"That's old news. I just said Letitia and Lionel were courting for a time."

"Of course, but nothing of note ever happened. It ended abruptly."

"You mean they never married," I said.

"Correct. The official reason given was that Letitia was homesick for America, but personally I think she was afraid of the Quimby curse," Mrs. Obermeyer said, lowering her voice. "I ran into Simon, you know, Lord Quimby I guess I should call him now, on the *Aquitania* last spring. It was all rather peculiar," Mrs. Obermeyer said. She finished her glass and held it up for a refill. I obliged and helped myself to a banana from the fruit basket while I was at it.

"Thank you. Now then, where was I?"

"You were saying you ran into Lord Quimby on the *Aquitania*," I said.

"Oh, yes, most peculiar. He had made fast friends with a young man from Philadelphia—I forget his name, Sturgis or something. Anyway, just before we docked in New York, this young man was found dead in his first-class cabin." She paused and looked at each of us in turn, waiting for a reaction.

"Dead? From what?" Verbina said at last.

"The final verdict was natural causes, a heart condition or something. But he was only in his twenties. There was a rumor he had been poisoned. It was most peculiar, if you ask me."

"So what does that have to do with this Lord Quimby fellow?" I said.

"They had just met on board and had become friends. Don't you find that odd? So many peculiar deaths around him in such a short span of time. Simon's mother died shortly after Charlotte was born, and Simon was just six years old. Then, two years ago, their father, Lionel, was killed during a burglary at their estate," Mrs. Obermeyer said.

"My goodness," I said. "That's awful."

"Yes, but the burglar was never caught. I hate to say it, but some suspected Simon, including Letitia."

"As she won't hesitate to tell you, I'm sure," Verbina said.

"Well, she *does* know the family. Letitia kept in touch with the Quimbys after moving back to the States, and she's visited a few times. She's kept me apprised of the goings-on. She even attended Sir Lionel's funeral, and she told me the circumstances surrounding his death were, shall we say, unusual?"

"How so?" I said.

Mrs. Obermeyer looked at me, her cheeks glowing, relishing being in the spotlight. "He was murdered in his bedroom on the second floor with a house full of people. Simon and Charlotte were there, of course, and Simon's cousin, Walter Wittenham, and Mr. Wittenham's wife and child. It happened near bedtime, but not in the dead of night, if you'll excuse the expression. Why would a burglar climb up to a second-story window, crawl in, stab Sir Lionel in his bed, and then flee?"

"Of course he'd flee," Verbina said. "He wouldn't exactly stay for tea."

"No, but why choose a second-story window? Why not break into a first-floor room? And why not wait until everyone had gone to bed and all the lights were out? Sir Lionel's bedroom light was on when he was found. What burglar in their right mind would climb into an open window where a light was on and someone was inside?"

"It does seem unusual, I must admit," I said.

"It most certainly does. That's why some people think it was an inside job, made to look like a burglary. And just one year ago, Simon's sister, Lady Charlotte, died. Such a tragedy."

"I remember hearing about that," Verbina said. "Tragic. It was even covered in the *New York Times*. She was only twenty-three years old, I believe."

"Goodness, that's about the same age as I am now," I said. "What happened to her?"

"The papers said it was an accident, but Letitia thinks she may have been murdered," Mrs. Obermeyer said. "Just like her father."

"Accidental poisoning is what the *New York Times* reported," Verbina said.

"Well, yes, I know, but honestly, how does an adult *accidentally* drink poison? Simon was twenty-nine at the time, so he's thirty now. He's never married, either. I believe Letitia said he was engaged last year, but it ended abruptly, probably because of the curse," Mrs. Obermeyer said. "It's all been because of the curse."

"What is this curse you keep talking about?" I said.

"Utter nonsense is what it is," Verbina said. "Lionel Quimby himself told me about it. Pure rubbish, voodoo, and witchcraft."

"I wouldn't be so sure," Mrs. Obermeyer said. "The curse is stronger than ever. You see, Simon's father, Lionel, did something to upset a Gypsy woman when Simon was just a young boy. She put a curse on the whole family."

"Honestly, Myrtle, how can you believe in such things?" Verbina said, finishing her champagne as I poured her another.

"Because it's true. Sir Lionel's wife died shortly after childbirth, Charlotte was born simple, Lionel was murdered, Charlotte was poisoned, either by accident, or—"

"And what of Simon? Nothing bad has befallen him," Verbina said.

"Not that we *know* of. But his engagement ended abruptly. And what if he *did* kill his father? I would certainly say that was bad. And then the mysterious death of his sister, and that fellow on the *Aquitania* last year…"

"Why would some people think he killed his own father?" I said, peeling the banana and taking a bite. "Or have anything to do with his sister's death?"

"Jealousy, plain and simple. I think there's some truth to it, too. Charlotte adored her father, and Simon felt left out," Mrs. Obermeyer said. "Besides, Letitia told me Lionel could be controlling, and he kept Simon under his thumb, unwilling to let him do as he wanted or be who he wanted."

"You don't know that to be a fact, Myrtle," Verbina said.

"But it makes sense," Mrs. Obermeyer said.

"Even if it were true, to murder someone over it? His own father? His sister?" I said.

"Oh, *I* don't think he did it, of course," Mrs. Obermeyer said, placing her hand on her bosom, "but people *do* like to talk."

"Namely you and Letitia Birdwell," Verbina said.

"Well, in her defense, the murderer of Sir Lionel was never found, you know," Mrs. Obermeyer added. "And an accidental poisoning is unusual in an adult."

"Hmm, well, since accidental poisoning is unlikely, has anyone considered Charlotte Quimby's death may have been a suicide?" I said.

Mrs. Obermeyer shook her head and held up her empty glass, which I refilled once more. "No, because there was no note. Simon is the one that found her, still alive, supposedly, and he claimed her last words to him were something about a letter she'd left somewhere in the house, but one never turned up. Then he changed his tune to say it was an accident. Quite odd, if I do say so myself. That's why the rumor mill has it that Simon killed her, too, slipping her the poison. Of course, I don't believe it, never have," Mrs. Obermeyer said. "Still, if it *was* suicide, the question is why? And why wouldn't she leave a note or a letter in plain sight, if in fact she *did* leave a note or a letter?"

"Poor Charlotte," Verbina said. "I remember her as not quite right, if you know what I mean, but a pretty girl. Sweet and shy."

"Yes, a lovely girl. Innocent. I certainly don't believe it was an accident."

"Myrtle, please."

"Just putting in my two cents' worth, Verbina."

"That's about all it's worth."

"Sounds pretty awful all the way around," I said. "I imagine it all went to court."

"Of course, they investigated both times and got lots of testimony from the servants, the doctor, the inspector constable, the family, and Simon. In the end, they determined an unknown intruder bent on burglary killed Lionel Quimby, and then a year later that Charlotte died from an accidental poisoning."

"Enough of all this morbid talk," Verbina said. "What is the name of the Quimby estate? I can't seem to recall it. Michael and I went there for dinner one evening while we were in London. We motored down in a rented automobile. Oh, the evening was just lovely. Heather Wood? No, Heather something, though. Heather*wick*, that's it. The dinner ran quite late—at least seven courses—and then cigars and brandy for the gentlemen in the library, while the ladies retired to the drawing room for sherry. Lord Quimby offered to have us spend the night, and I wanted to, as I was so tired, but your Uncle Michael would have none of it. He said he'd paid for a London hotel, and by God he was going to use it."

"I seem to recall you telling me he wanted to get back to London in time to see a nightclub singer he liked," Myrtle said, raising a painted-on brow. "Some late-night cabaret singer. I think *that's* the reason he didn't want to spend the night at Heatherwick."

"Michael liked the London shows, of course," Verbina said, shooting Mrs. Obermeyer a look.

"And he certainly liked that one," Mrs. Obermeyer said with a smirk. "What was the name of the singer he admired so much? Maurice? He was fetching, I seem to remember you saying. You both made it back to London in time for Michael to catch Maurice's last show while you went to bed. Michael didn't get back to the hotel until the wee hours of the morning. As I recall, you were upset by it all."

Verbina glared at her. "Maurice had a nice voice."

"And he was quite a performer, I'm sure," Mrs. Obermeyer said. "A man of many talents, on- and offstage."

"Finish your champagne, Myrtle. Oh, I'd love to manage an invitation to Heatherwick."

"And how, pray tell, would you manage that? You can't just invite yourself to someone's home," I said, finishing my banana and dropping the peel in the waste basket.

"Goodness no, that would be gauche. One merely makes the

subtle suggestion, that's all, as in, 'How are things at Heatherwick? I remember the dinner we had there, so lovely. I hope someday to get the opportunity to return.'"

"And then he says, 'Why don't you come down then for a few days while you're in London?'" Myrtle said.

"Well, yes, that's the idea. Hopefully, anyway," Verbina said.

Hopefully not, I thought. The idea of spending a weekend at some musty old cursed estate with people I didn't know, including one who might be a murderer, held not even the slightest appeal to me. Not when we could be in London attending late-night cabaret shows with handsome singers by the name of Maurice. "But wouldn't you rather stay in London, Auntie? There's so much to do there."

"Oh, we'll have plenty of time to do and see all you want, don't you worry. Besides, Lord Quimby may not even invite us. And we have to arrange to run into him first."

I didn't say much after that, and I was glad when Mrs. Obermeyer finally excused herself. I went back to my cabin to change for dinner, taking an apple along for good measure. I put on my black suit with a red tie that complemented Verbina's red dress, and I pulled on a new pair of socks, setting aside the ones with the hole in them for my mother to darn when we got home.

At precisely eight o'clock, Verbina and I entered the dining room on C deck, her on my arm, and we were shown to our table for the crossing, a six-top near the center of the room but off to the side. We were the last to arrive, so we introduced ourselves to our dining companions and then took our places. I had been hoping for an attractive young man or two at our table, but unfortunately such was not the case.

To my left was a dull minister from Indiana and his shrewish wife, and across from me was an opinionated octogenarian from Wales who needed to weigh in on every subject. Next to her was Verbina, and to her right, a boorish American psychologist by the name of Dr. Uriah Feldmeyer, who informed us he was traveling alone on his way to a conference. Still, the food was excellent, and the waiter handsome and attentive. We dined on grilled fillets of whitefish, boiled potatoes, Clover Club salads, and vanilla ice cream with pears, along with plenty of wine and champagne. When the meal was over, Verbina and I excused ourselves and retired to the lounge, where we listened to a capable jazz singer before retiring early to our cabins, both full and contented.

CHAPTER THREE

Saturday Morning, September 11, 1937
The North Atlantic

I slept well Friday night, lulled to sleep by the motion of the ship slipping through the ocean, and I awoke refreshed. After a shave, I dressed in my new gray windowpane suit with a light blue tie I'd bought just for the trip, and knocked on the connecting door just after nine.

"Good morning," I said as Verbina opened the door. "Ready for breakfast? Some goo and the moo?"

"I beg your pardon?"

"Pancakes, syrup, and milk, of course," I replied with a smile.

She frowned. "College slang again. I've told you, Heath, a gentleman must speak properly."

I sighed. "Sorry, I know. Old habits. I'll try to keep it to a minimum."

"Better to stop it altogether. You're a college graduate now, and an adult."

"Yes, ma'am."

"Don't forget. You're judged by how you speak, how you dress, the company you keep, and how you behave."

"I'll try to do better. I *will* do better."

"Good. You slept in this morning. I've been up since seven."

"You have?"

"I had things to do. I've just been to see the deck steward, the chief steward, and the purser and found out Simon Quimby is staying on A deck and usually promenades on the sun deck just after breakfast, counterclockwise. He has breakfast delivered to his cabin at eight o'clock, and almost always has the same thing, fried eggs, sausages, tomatoes, mushrooms, bread, and a slice of black pudding, with tea and buttered toast. He's a frequent passenger, and his routine is well known, a creature of habit, as they say."

"He sounds dull. But honestly, Auntie, you do amaze me sometimes. How did you find all that out?"

"I have my ways, Heath. Charm and a little money usually does the trick. Now, we've already missed this morning, so tomorrow we will need to be out on deck looking our best right after breakfast. That means we must be in the dining room no later than seven thirty."

"Goodness, that's early for me. You go ahead. I'll order breakfast in and do some reading, and maybe write some postcards to Mom and Dad and Cousin Liz and her folks."

"No, no, no. You must come with me. A united front, you see. Besides, you can be charming when you want to be."

"Gee, thanks, but I certainly don't feel like being charming to someone I've never met just to get him to invite us to his house for the weekend, when I'd rather stay in London anyway."

"Tut, tut, my boy. You'll smile and be polite and attentive, and that's that. It wouldn't hurt you to learn a few things about manners from a proper English gentleman. You've gotten a bit cheeky lately, and as I said before, you could clearly use some tutelage."

"I thought this was supposed to be a vacation," I said, rolling my eyes toward the ceiling and then back down again.

"It is, my dear. A holiday, as they say on the Continent, but one must never stop learning and expanding oneself, either. Tomorrow morning, knock on my door at seven fifteen sharp, dressed and ready, understand?"

"Yes, ma'am," I said, knowing it would do no good to argue.

"Good, now let me get my handbag and we can go down to breakfast. Did you look over today's daily bulletin?"

"Uh, no, I didn't see it."

"The steward should have slid it under your door. You probably just didn't notice. Regardless, there's shuffleboard and ping-pong this morning followed by hot bouillon and crackers at eleven. That should take us to lunch, then perhaps we can find Myrtle and a fourth for bridge, or maybe the two of us can play backgammon until it's time for tea. And if you like, we can sit on deck for a bit, reading, and watching the people stroll by. I took the opportunity earlier to reserve two deck chairs for us, on the port side."

"You have to reserve them?"

"Of course. If you don't, who knows whom you may end up sitting next to, or where. As it is, all the decent ones on the promenade were spoken for already, so we're on the sundeck. The stewards put your name on a card and slide it into a plate affixed to each chair to mark its exclusivity."

"I never would have thought of reserving a deck chair. I thought you just took any old one."

"That's why you still have a great deal to learn, my boy. Now then, once settled into our chairs, the deck steward will provide us with steamer rugs, hand warmers, and hot bouillon and tea, if we so desire."

"Hand warmers and steamer rugs?"

"Oh, yes. Very necessary this time of year. This is the north Atlantic in September, and it gets quite chilly on deck, even on the covered promenade, and there's always a stiff breeze on the sun deck. The steward will also provide reading materials if requested, but I've brought my book."

"I have my book, too. I'm reading one of Oscar Wilde's novels."

"Interesting choice."

"I find his life fascinating."

"He was an interesting man, I must admit. By the way, I also brought along Mothersill's seasick pills, should you need them."

"I've been fine so far."

"Yes, you seem to be a good sailor, but the sea has been relatively calm up until now. It will get rougher, trust me."

"Okay, I'll let you know if I get queasy."

"Please do. Anyway, as I was saying, all that will take us to teatime. Perhaps after that, we will have an opportunity for a nap before we must dress for dinner."

"That sounds, uh, nice and relaxing," I said, though I wanted to say boring.

"Of course it does. We must also find time to visit the library to write some postcards and letters."

"Yes, I do need to write that thank-you to Mom and Dad for the bon voyage basket, and tell them how things have been going so far."

"Certainly, and I shall do the same, from my perspective, naturally. Oh, I almost forgot. There's an afternoon movie in the lounge—*Jezebel* with Bette Davis, I know how much you like her."

"I do. She's aces for sure, snazzy. The snake's hips."

Verbina scowled at me.

"Very good, I mean. A fine actress. I was only teasing, truly."

"Teasing, indeed. Dinner tonight is formal, don't forget."

"I won't. The steward returned my tuxedo freshly pressed this morning, and they got the coffee stain out of my suit coat, too."

"Good, and make sure to have your shoes shined. Dinner's at eight, as usual, followed by some dancing, or cutting a rug, as I believe I've heard you call it."

I laughed. "That's perfect, Auntie."

She smiled then. "Well, they do have the most wonderful orchestra on board, for dancing or rug cutting."

Her turn of a phrase made me grin. "I'll do my best not to step on your toes."

"Please do. I told your mother you'd benefit by some extra dancing lessons, but we'll make the best of it."

And that we did. By the time we finally returned to our cabins close to midnight, having danced waltzes, two-steps, and even a foxtrot, we were both exhausted but content, and we both slept well once again, the day not having been quite so dull as I'd imagined it might have been.

CHAPTER FOUR

Sunday Morning, September 12, 1937
The Mid-Atlantic

I had requested a wake-up call for six, and unfortunately, the telephone rang promptly. I answered it groggily, thanked the operator, and hung up. I was tempted to go back to sleep but forced myself out of bed and into the bathroom, though I would have preferred at least another hour or two under the covers.

Dressed in my freshly pressed and cleaned tan suit, with the turquoise tie Verbina had given me for my last birthday, I knocked on the connecting door at seven fifteen sharp, my hat in my hand. She looked a little tired herself but was dressed in a lovely pink dress with a black hat, upon which was fastened a pink rose made of silk. A black cardigan sweater was draped loosely about her shoulders.

"Good morning. You look lovely as always," I said after she'd opened the door and stepped aside, allowing me to enter.

"Good morning, Heath, and thank you. I always find pink to be complementary to my complexion. I'm glad you're on time, and I think I'm ready. Nice tie, by the way."

"Thanks, a special lady bought it for me."

"She has excellent taste. Shall we go?"

"We shall," I said. I opened the door from her cabin to the passage and closed it behind us as we went to the dining room. We arrived at exactly seven thirty and were seated shortly after. I'd never seen Aunt Verbina rush through a breakfast before, but that morning she did. I had ordered grapefruit, Bonny Boy Toasted Oats, griddle cakes, and coffee, but I'd barely started on the griddle cakes when she was telling me we had to go. At precisely eight-twenty, we were up on the sun deck, my hat pulled low to keep it from blowing off in the wind and my tweed coat drawn tightly about me. Auntie, for her part, was holding her dress down with one hand while periodically checking her hat with the other, hoping her hatpins held. She had wisely opted to put her sweater on and button it up.

"Now what?" I said, looking from right to left.

"Now, my dear, we stroll clockwise, slowly, until we run into him."

"Why doesn't he promenade on the promenade deck, where it's enclosed and far less windy?"

"Too many people down there, I suspect. The promenade deck is the equivalent of the Champs Elysée in Paris, the place to rub shoulders with the well-to-do. I imagine Lord Quimby wishes to avoid all that. Besides, the sun deck offers more fresh air and, well, sun. The promenade deck can be rather gloomy."

"I've never known you to be a fresh air aficionado, Auntie, especially on a day like this."

"Well, it is a bit cool and breezy up here, and I should have brought my coat, but we must do what we must do. Shall we?"

"I guess we shall," I said. We walked arm in arm slowly down the deck, alternately into the wind and then with the wind at our backs as we reached the other side of the ship and began again. We passed the gymnasium and the Verandah Grill and strolled beneath the lifeboats hanging from the sports deck above. As we strolled, I gazed into the face of each dull-looking older man who went by, wondering if that could be him, but Verbina just nodded at each in turn, occasionally murmuring a "good morning" as we passed. The men and women nodded and murmured their replies. One fellow who approached I thought looked promising. He had a small black mustache atop thin white lips, and he appeared sinister, with a beak nose and small, dark, close-set eyes that peered at us as we passed, but that apparently wasn't him, either. Verbina just smiled and kept walking.

"Why don't we just ask one of these people if they've seen Lord Quimby or know him?" I said after a while, getting cold and weary as we made our second lap around the deck. I gazed longingly at the folks huddled beneath their steamer rugs, holding cups of hot coffee, tea, or bullion.

"Honestly, Heath. It's not proper to initiate a conversation with a stranger unless you've been formerly introduced. You should know that by now."

"Well, it all seems rather silly, I think."

"Silly or not, those are the rules in polite society, and rules must be obeyed. Therefore, when passing a stranger one gives a perfunctory good morning and a nod, nothing more."

"But maybe this Quimby chap decided not to walk this morning, or maybe he slept in. Couldn't we just sit in our deck chairs under a cozy rug and have some tea or coffee and wait for him to go by?"

"No, I think it best that we come across him as we stroll. Besides, it's hard to see people clearly from a deck chair, they're all so bundled up with their hats pulled low and their coats closed tight."

"All right, but once more around and then I'm sitting down," I said. "It's cold."

"And leave me to promenade by myself?"

"I could go and get your coat for you from your cabin if you like."

"Thank you, but I'm fine. Besides, I think I see him just ahead, coming this way now."

Auntie tugged on my arm and nodded ever so slightly at a well-built, rugged-looking, handsome man striding toward us, his hat pulled low, as everyone's seemed to be, to keep it from blowing off in the wind.

"How can you tell? I can't see his face very well."

"I can't be certain, but he has that look about him." Auntie guided us into his path, causing him to stop short.

"I beg your pardon," he said, lifting his face into the wind to look at us, his cheeks ruddy and rosy. His eyes looked far away, as if he had been asleep and suddenly jolted awake. There was a sadness about him.

"Why, Lord Quimby, is that you? What a delightful surprise," she said.

The man stared at the two of us, removing his hat as he did so, a crease across his forehead from where it had been. His eyes cleared a bit and his expression softened.

"Pardon? Do I know you?" He looked from me to Verbina, and then back to me.

"Oh, you probably don't remember, you meet so many people, and it's been a few years," Verbina said.

He studied her for a moment, and then turned his attentions back to me, and I felt my heart flutter. He was surprisingly dreamy. "I'm sorry, I don't—"

"We had dinner at Wiltons in London with your father and sister once several years ago, along with Miss Birdwell and Mr. and Mrs. Obermeyer, and then shortly after that my husband and I dined at your home," Verbina continued. "We had motored down from London in a rented automobile. The evening ran late, and your father wanted us to stay over, but my husband insisted on returning to the city that night, much to my chagrin."

Suddenly he smiled brilliantly in recognition. "Oh, yes, of course, Mrs., don't tell me, Mrs. Weatherall, isn't it? Of Milwaukee?"

Verbina beamed. "Yes, that's right, only it's Mrs. Partridge now. How nice of you to remember."

"Of course I remember. You and your husband were charming."

"You are too kind, my lord. Mr. Weatherall and I divorced, however, and I've since remarried."

"Oh, I see."

"I know some people find divorce scandalous, but I assure you it was quite mutual and we're both the better for it. I'm married to David Partridge now, an attorney and a senior partner at Cross and Young in Milwaukee. And he's one of *the* Partridges of the pharmaceuticals company, you know."

"How nice, I didn't know that. Is Mr. Partridge with you?"

"No, David doesn't like to travel for pleasure much, as he does it often enough for work. And besides that he gets quite afflicted with *mal de mer*, poor dear. So, I'm traveling with my nephew here. Heath and I do love a good morning constitutional, don't we, dear?" she said, looking my way.

"Hmm? Oh yes, nothing like a brisk morning walk, I always say," I said, realizing I couldn't feel my fingers and toes any longer, but I suddenly didn't care.

"Heath, I'd like you to meet Lord Simon Quimby, and Lord Quimby, this is my nephew, Heath Barrington."

"A pleasure to meet you, Mr. Barrington," he said, pulling off one of his brown leather gloves and extending his right hand as he held his hat in his left.

"Oh, it's my pleasure entirely, Lord Quimby," I said, taking his hand in mine. His skin was cool but soft, and I felt electric charges surge through my body as we touched, sensation returning to my ice-cold fingers.

"Heath. Is that short for Heathcliff?" he said.

"Yes. My mother read *Wuthering Heights* while she was expecting me. I was either going to be Heathcliff or Catherine."

"You make a better Heathcliff, I think," he said, his eyes now bright. He seemed a tad cheerier, too.

I chuckled. "Yes, I think so, too."

"Heath prefers to be called Heath rather than Heathcliff," Verbina said. "Though personally I think Heathcliff sounds more dignified."

"Heath's a fine name. Rugged and masculine. And I'm sure your life will have a happier ending than your namesake in the book," he said.

"I certainly hope so!" To my young eyes, Simon Quimby was about the prettiest thing I'd ever seen on two legs, better even than the actor William Haines. His hair was the color of sunlight glinting off a wheat field, with just a touch of sandy brown, and he had blue-green eyes that looked like the color was lifted directly from the sea rushing by us. And that voice, deep, lyrical, and so, so English. It was impossible for me to conceive a man so handsome could be a murderer. He just couldn't. "Gee, I've never met a baron before."

He smiled again. "I hope I don't disappoint you. And how is Mrs. Obermeyer?" Lord Quimby said, turning to look at Verbina.

"Oh, she never changes," Verbina said, laughing. "I hadn't seen her myself in a couple of years, but actually we just ran into her on board yesterday."

"Really? Such a small world. Extraordinary."

"Indeed. She mentioned she saw you on the *Aquitania* last year."

I watched as his expression changed just ever so. "Yes, I did see her then, though we didn't have much of a chance to visit. It was a rough crossing, in many ways."

"I'm sorry to hear it. Hopefully, this trip will be better for you. Mrs. Obermeyer is getting off at Cherbourg, traveling to Marseilles via Paris to visit her cousin, while Heath and I are continuing on to Southampton and then London."

"Well, we must all get together for a drink before Cherbourg. What is taking you to England, Mrs. Weatherall? I mean, Mrs. Partridge?" he said, pulling his glove back on.

"Heath has never seen London."

He glanced at me again. "Ahh, well, you'll love it, I'm sure, Mr. Barrington. Where are you staying while you're there?"

"The Grosvenor, near Victoria Station," I said.

"We're taking the train from Southampton to London, arriving at Victoria," Verbina added.

"A splendid hotel, Mrs. Partridge, and an excellent location. A wise choice."

"Yes, I've stayed there before. I hadn't originally planned on a return trip to England so soon, but I wanted Heath to experience it before, well, before things get any worse over there."

He furrowed his brow. "It's already gotten pretty bad, I'm afraid. Tensions are high. Prime Minister Chamberlain is cautiously optimistic about keeping us out of any conflicts, but I think it's inevitable. Hitler and Germany are threatening the world. The Depression has hit Germany particularly hard, and the people look to Hitler to help them. They're following him like sheep. Rumor has it he wants to annex Austria and possibly Czechoslovakia."

"Horrible. I'm glad the United States isn't involved," Verbina said.

"If things get worse, I hope we can count on your government's support. We'll need it, I'm afraid."

"Oh, pish posh. It won't get that bad, mark my words. But if they did, President Roosevelt would of course give full support to England and all of Great Britain. How are things at Heatherwick, by the way?"

He raised his eyebrows in surprise. "You remember the name of my home?"

"Oh my, yes. And I remember it as being so elegant, so lovely."

"I bet it's beautiful," I chimed in unexpectedly, even to myself. "I've never been to an English country estate before." Suddenly the idea of spending a weekend at this handsome and charming man's home seemed delightfully appealing.

Simon smiled then, and I noticed he had dimples and a cleft chin. I felt a sudden urge to place my index finger in that cleft and just hold it there.

"Oh, it's not all that much. Just a big old house in the country, really. Drafty in the winter, stuffy in the summer, and frightfully expensive to maintain. It can't compare to the wonders and excitement of London. You're sure to have a grand time, Mr. Barrington."

"I'm looking forward to London, and please call me Heath. I'd like it ever so if you did. But we'll have plenty of time to see the sights. We don't sail home for two weeks, and a weekend in the country sounds so peaceful and relaxing. Are you heading back to your house now?"

"That's right, after six weeks in America, and I don't travel again for almost three long months. Perhaps the two of you could visit me while you're in England."

"Oh, we'd like that very much, wouldn't we, Auntie?"

"Heath, honestly!" Aunt Verbina admonished, but Simon only laughed.

"All right, Heath, why don't the two of you come down on the Friday train and stay at Heatherwick through breakfast on Sunday? Would you like that?"

I couldn't help but grin like an idiot. "Gee, that would be swell, Lord Quimby."

"Please forgive my nephew, Baron, he's not typically so forward."

He smiled warmly. "It's all right, Mrs. Partridge. I'd be chuffed to bits if you'd both come, truly. I'd very much like the company. Please say yes."

"Well, we've so many things on our itinerary that we want to see and do, and we were planning on going to the theater Friday night, but I suppose we could go Sunday evening instead."

"A capital idea. You'll get better seats for the theater and better pricing on Sunday, too. If you take the eleven thirty train to London, you'll be back at your hotel by one at the latest, in plenty of time for a Sunday matinee or early evening show. Leave your trunks and things in London, no need for formalwear at Heatherwick. I don't stand on tradition like my father did."

"Well, if you're absolutely certain, Lord Quimby. We don't wish to intrude."

"It would truly be my pleasure, and please call me Simon, each of you."

"In that case, we'd be delighted to accept," Verbina said.

"Splendid. Take the ten thirty out of Waterloo Station to Brockenhurst. I'll meet you at noon at the station there."

"You're very kind, Baron."

"Simon, please," he said. "So, what do you two have planned for the rest of your day?"

"Well, of course we'll be attending Sunday services in the main lounge at ten. The captain himself presides over that."

"Yes, I've heard. Nondenominational. Splendid, but not really my cup of tea," Simon said.

"I dare say Captain Townley is rather fetching and a good speaker, so I'm rather looking forward to it," Verbina said. "After that we'll lunch, and then I'm attending a lecture in the hall on

Renaissance philosophy. Should be quite interesting, I think, though Heath doesn't agree, so I'm going by myself, unless *you'd* care to join me."

"I imagine Renaissance philosophy would indeed be interesting, but I agree with Heath that a lecture can be a bit dry at times. I had enough of those in school."

"*C'est la vie*. Naturally Heath and I will be taking tea at four in the lounge. You're more than welcome to join us for that."

"You're most gracious, Mrs. Partridge, but I promised a friend of the family I'd have tea with them this afternoon."

"Another time, then."

"I certainly hope so, and I shall look forward to it." He looked at me. "So, what will *you* be doing then, young man, after lunch, while your aunt is at the lecture?"

"Me? Oh, gee, I don't know. Maybe go to the library and read, or write some letters or something like that, or I heard there's a movie, or maybe cards, or a walk, or the gymnasium, or something..." My voice trailed off as I realized I was babbling.

He smiled that smile again. "Well, since you've no definite plans, and you've never been to London before, would you care to join me for a cocktail in the bar on the promenade deck? I can give you suggestions on things to see and do in that fair city. I know it quite well."

"Gee, that would be wonderful. I'd like that a lot!" I tried to keep the excitement out of my voice, but I feared I had little success.

He looked into my eyes, and I in his, and I felt my frozen feet melt into the decking. "Splendid. Let's meet in the cocktail lounge on the promenade deck at one thirty. Will that work for you?"

"Oh yes, absolutely," I said, trying not to gush.

"Good, then that's settled. So glad to have run into you again, Mrs. Partridge, and to have met you, Heathcliff," he said, putting his hat back on. "Heath, I mean to say."

"Likewise, Simon," Verbina said.

"Cheerio, then," he said, and he continued on his way.

"Cheerio!" I echoed enthusiastically, calling out after him with a wave.

CHAPTER FIVE

Sunday Afternoon, September 12, 1937
The Mid-Atlantic

The first-class lounge and cocktail bar was located at the forward part of the promenade deck, just one deck up from the main deck, where my cabin was. I entered from the port side and was immediately taken by the beauty of the room, including the joyful painting, *Royal Jubilee Week*, behind the semicircular bar. So taken was I by the décor, I almost didn't notice Simon Quimby entering on the starboard side. Almost, I say, because his style and grace could never be surpassed by mere manmade decorations.

I strode over to him, nervous and grinning, and he smiled, too, moving toward me with the elegant confidence and poise that came from good breeding, I supposed. He had changed his clothes and was now sporting a gray, vested suit with a blue polka-dot bow tie. Neither of us were wearing hats. I was still in my tan suit, and I wondered if perhaps I should have changed, also. Simon, however, didn't seem to notice or mind that I was wearing the same outfit, or if he did, he was too much of a gentleman to say anything.

"Hello, Heath. I'm so pleased you could join me for a drink."
He extended his right hand and we shook once more, and once more I felt that electric spark course through me. He didn't seem as sad as he had when we first met. In fact, he seemed rather cheerful.

"Thanks for asking me," I said, staring at him and trying to hide my excitement. "You look terrific. I love polka dots." I bit my lip, realizing that sounded peculiar, but he didn't seem to notice.

"Polka dots? Oh, my tie, yes. I like them, too. And thank you, you look nice, also." He held up two fingers, signaling the waiter, who led us to a small round table on the raised platform by the semicircle of windows across the front that gave a panoramic view of the rolling rough Atlantic and the endless horizon.

"What will you have, then?" Simon asked.

"Have?" Suddenly I felt foolish. I had no idea what to order. My parents mainly drank beer, and Verbina usually ordered Pink Ladies. The few times I'd gone out with the fellows in school we had beer or sometimes wine, but none of those options seemed appropriate right now. "Gee, I'm not sure. What are you going to have?"

"A dry vodka martini, with three olives, my usual."

"That sounds good, I'll have the same."

"Excellent." He gave the order to the waiter, along with a request for a relish tray to nosh on.

When the relish tray and the drinks came, we toasted to adventure and new friendships and I took a sip. Overall it was a pleasant sensation, but I didn't care for the olives much, which must have shown on my face.

"Not to your liking?"

"Hmm? Oh, I like the martini well enough, but I guess I'm not too keen on the olives."

He reached over and took them from my drink, sliding them rather seductively one by one into his mouth. "I love them, personally. But you need *some* kind of garnish. What will it be?" He perused the relish tray on the small table between us. "Radish? No. Carrot? Hardly. What about a pickle? Do you like pickles?"

"Yes, very much."

"Than a pickle it shall be." He used the olive toothpick to spear a small pickle out of the dish and then deposited it into my drink. "Give that a try."

I took another drink. "Different, but overall pleasant. I like it."

"Really?"

"Absolutely."

He grinned. "Than a vodka martini with a pickle shall be your drink from now on. Here's to it!"

We clinked our glasses once more, drank, and laughed. I was still nervous, and we lapsed into silence while I tried to think of something to say that wouldn't make me sound like a dolt or a child, but finally he started talking about London, and I relaxed a little bit, just listening to him. He gave me recommendations on things to see and do, though I knew I wouldn't remember even half of them, distracted as I was by his handsomeness. And now and then I asked a question I thought sounded at least halfway intelligent. But then, during another pause in the conversation I found myself suddenly blurting out, "I bet you have a gaggle of girls waiting for you at home." I instantly regretted it and felt foolish again.

Simon looked surprised. "What brought that on?"

"I don't know, just that you're so handsome, and an Englishman and all, a baron, no less, and you live in a big manor house in the country."

"Well, thank you, but I don't know about all that. As for girls, it's more like the mothers and fathers of a gaggle of girls wanting to marry off their daughters to a baron."

"Lucky you," I said, smiling and feeling a little less stupid.

"Eh, I suppose. My father instilled in me from early on that I should produce an heir because I was the last male Quimby. But now he's gone, and so much has happened. I'd like to just live my life, to be who I am, you know?"

"Yes, I think I do know. And I feel the same."

"But it's easier for you. I'm not sure it's possible for me."

"Why is that?" I said.

"It's hard to explain. Has anyone ever pressured *you* to produce an heir?"

"Well, not exactly. I know my parents would like a grandchild someday, but Mom's in no hurry to be a granny, and I'm only twenty-two and just out of college."

Simon smiled. "Congratulations on your graduation."

"Thanks, it was a long four years."

"I can imagine. So, what are your plans for yourself now that you're a college graduate, young man? How do you intend to live your life, to be who you are?"

"Oh, I've been clerking at Schuster's Department Store during school. Mr. Schuster himself said I could be promoted to head clerk soon, and then even a floor manager someday."

"And a fine floor manager you'll be, I'm sure."

"I guess so, but it's not really for me."

"No?"

"No. Aunt Verbina thinks I should be a teacher or a professor. I majored in literature in college, and I'm quite a fan of Oscar Wilde. In fact, I'm reading one of his books now."

"Ah, Mr. Wilde, quite the Irish gentleman. I've read many of his works myself, and I've seen a few of his plays. He was a talented, though tormented, man."

"Yes, I think so, too. Sad, really. He's one of the reasons I majored in literature."

"Well, I could certainly see you as a professor or teacher. You have a gentle demeanor, and you're obviously quite intelligent and well spoken."

I felt a little calmer. He was easier to talk to than I had imagined. "Thanks, but I'm not so sure I want to teach, either."

"Oh? What would you like to do, then?"

"I don't know for certain, but I've actually been thinking about joining the Milwaukee Police Department this fall, once we get back."

Simon raised his eyebrows in surprise. "Really? How interesting. We call policemen bobbies in England. You don't seem the type, frankly."

"What do you mean?"

"Oh, no offense meant. It's just that you appear kind, gentle, thoughtful, intelligent, and well-spoken."

"That seems offensive to policemen in general."

"Sorry, I'm not saying it well, I guess. I think of police as hard, rough, and tough, I suppose. Why do you want to go into that line of work, especially after four years of college?"

I didn't say anything for a bit, contemplating how much I

wanted to share. Talking with him seemed so natural, like we'd known each other for years. "Two things, really. One happened when I was just seventeen. I got jumped in a bad part of town by four thugs, and a police officer came to my rescue."

"I say, what were you doing in a bad part of town by yourself at seventeen?"

"Looking for trouble, I guess, only it found me. Then, in my second year of college, I did something else stupid. I was twenty, it was a beautiful fall day, and I went for a walk in a park down by the river."

"Yes? That doesn't sound stupid."

"It wasn't, yet it was. I'd heard rumors men had been known to congregate there, you see, and I was curious. But sometimes the police make arrests for loitering, and stuff."

"Loitering? Isn't that what parks are for?"

I felt myself blush. Was I saying too much? "Yes, but some men did stuff in the park with each other. I was in the wrong place at the wrong time. I'd never been there before, but I'd heard about it, like I said, and I was wondering if the rumors were true. A plainclothes Milwaukee Police detective approached me, and thankfully took pity on me. He did me a kindness."

"Oh, I see. I think."

"Because of his kindness, I wasn't arrested. My folks never knew, no one did. I don't like to talk about it, naturally, but I thought then and there that perhaps I should go into law enforcement, even become a detective maybe and help others like me, do them a kindness, if I could. And I'm pretty good at solving mysteries. I have been since early on."

"I bet you are, and I imagine you'll be a first-rate policeman and detective, if that's what you really want."

"Yes, I think that is what I want."

"Dangerous work, though. I hope you'll be careful."

"I will. I'll try to be, anyway. My folks don't like the idea, of course, and my Aunt Verbina will be livid when she finds out. I'm an only child, and I just have one first cousin. Her name's Liz, my dad's sister's kid. I have a second cousin by the name of Chuck.

He's Liz's dad's brother's son, but I don't know him all that well. So, we're a small family, you see, and they want to keep me close, keep me safe."

"That's understandable."

"Yes, I suppose. Mom and Dad want me to use my college education, maybe go into banking or something, or keep working my way up at Schuster's, and eventually get married, have those children—"

"I'm sure you'll make a fine husband to a nice young lady and have lots of beautiful children."

I scowled. "But I don't *want* to be somebody's husband, Simon, or have children, beautiful or otherwise. Like you said, I just want to live my life, to be who I am."

Simon looked thoughtful. "Do you really know who you are? Are you still that same young man that was in that bad part of town or in the park that day?"

I shrugged, finishing my drink. "I don't know, frankly. I guess not, in some ways. Heck, I don't think I'm even the same fellow I was yesterday."

"Wise words," Simon said as he signaled for the waiter and ordered two more martinis. "We all change a little, every day, but not all of us realize it."

When the drinks had been delivered, Simon took my olives and put another cocktail pickle in mine. I picked it up, took a drink, and looked at him. "Do you know who *you* are?"

He took a drink of his. "I've never known, but for me it's different, I think, like I alluded to before."

"Because you're a baron, and because you feel pressured to produce an heir?"

"Yes, to a degree. People expect lots of things from me."

"What people?"

"Family, society, the public."

"Doesn't sound much different. People expect things of me, too. Maybe we're more alike than we think."

"It might be fun to find out," he said, polishing off his martini and looking at me with a gleam in his eye.

My nervousness returned in waves, and my palms felt sweaty all of a sudden. It made it hard to hold on to my glass, so I finished it and set it down carefully on the small rimmed table. I was warm and excited, anxious and fidgety. "I think it might be, too," I said, my voice almost cracking as I nibbled on the vodka-soaked pickle.

"And I think we should have another drink."

"I think if I have another drink right now, I'll be under the table," I said, staring at him again.

"That would be amusing, but probably not socially acceptable. Well, then, if we're done drinking, why don't we go for a swim? You packed your bathing costume, I assume?"

"I did. My aunt told me about the pool on board."

"It's definitely something to experience. I'll settle up here. You go get your suit and meet me at the pool, deal?"

"Deal."

"Enter on C deck and then come down the stairs to the changing rooms."

"Got it, see you soon, and thanks for the drinks."

CHAPTER SIX

Sunday Afternoon, September 12, 1937
The Pool

I hurried to my cabin, grabbed my swimming suit from the drawer, and dashed off a note to Verbina, which I slipped under her door before racing to C deck, my heart pounding with nervous excitement. He was nowhere in sight as I gazed down from the balcony at the clear blue water moving up and down and side to side in the pool below. I went down the tiled double staircase and the attendant showed me to the men's dressing rooms as he handed me a fresh towel.

Even though it was quite warm and humid inside, I couldn't help but shiver as I alternately felt hot and sweaty and then cold and clammy. I changed into my suit and had a look at myself in the mirror. I was too skinny, too pale, too tall, and too gangly. What did Simon see in me if, in fact, he did see anything in me? Maybe he was just being polite. Maybe it was all my imagination. I looked at myself again and wished I'd splurged on a new bathing costume, but I'd already spent too much on clothes for this trip, and I hadn't planned on doing a lot of swimming. My swimsuit was a two-piece, with navy trunks and a blue and white horizontal stripe crab back top made of wool knit. The two pieces were held together with buttons at the waist, which I always had trouble buttoning, but today I managed.

I left the dressing area, set my towel on a lounger, and got cautiously into the water, which felt cool to my skin, but I quickly adjusted as I paddled into the center of the pool, continually scanning every face and body for him. I wondered if he'd changed his mind or caught sight of my gangly body and left. Then, suddenly, there he was. He strode out from the dressing rooms, clad in black trunks that somehow made him even more handsome, his torso bare and firm. Of course he would have the latest in bathing attire. I waved an arm, and he smiled and climbed in, effortlessly swimming over to me, despite the water continually sloshing side to side and back and forth with the movement of the ship.

"Hello, there, Heath."

"Hiya, Simon."

We splashed about, and he showed off swimming laps, floating on his back, and holding his breath underwater, and I nearly drowned staring at the sight of him in his bathing trunks and bare torso whenever he climbed out to retrieve a towel or a drink of water.

Too soon the bell rang, signaling the end of men's swimming, and I frowned, not eager to get out just yet.

"It's close to teatime," Simon said, looking just a tad melancholy again. "I suppose your aunt will be waiting."

"I left her a note that I was going swimming with you."

"But we've been in the pool almost two hours. It's close to four," he said, glancing at the clock on the stairway landing.

"Really? Boy, it seems as if we just got here."

Simon looked at me for a few seconds, his eyes merry. "I agree. I can't remember when I've had this much fun."

"Me, either. I guess I did promise Auntie I'd meet her for tea in the lounge, though, and then we'll have to get dressed for dinner, I suppose."

"Yes, I suppose. And that family friend is expecting me. I have an idea—"

"Yes?"

"We could meet for an after-dinner drink in the smoking room and then stop by the Verandah Grill, the Starlight Club it's called after dark, and listen to the music tonight, if you like."

I grinned. "I'd like that very much, Simon."

"Capital," he said, grinning back at me. "Let's meet in the smoking room at nine thirty then, sound good?"

"Sounds capital!"

We both laughed as we climbed out of the pool, showered, toweled off, and changed back into our street clothes. As we headed out, Simon tipped the attendant, which I had neglected to do.

CHAPTER SEVEN

Sunday Evening, September 12, 1937
The Mid-Atlantic

Dinner that evening seemed to be eternal, and eternally dull, sandwiched in as I was between the Indiana minister, Reverend Doddard, who picked his teeth nervously and quoted scripture, and the opinionated octogenarian on my right, Mrs. Byrne, who droned on about the escalating tensions in Europe and what should be done.

Aunt Verbina was seated across from me, next to the minister's shrewish wife, who complained to the waiter, and to all of us, about every item of food and drink she was served, and told her husband that next time they would be taking the French Line, and to hell with the price. Her husband, who was busy with his toothpick, simply nodded and said, "Yes, dear, but please remember Matthew 5:34, 'But I say to you, Do not take an oath at all, either by heaven, for it is the throne of God,' to which she replied, "I'll take any oath I please, Edgar, and I'll thank you to keep your scripture to yourself and be quiet. And stop picking your teeth. It's disgusting."

"Yes, dear," Reverend Doddard said quietly. He dropped his head and began moving his fork around his plate absently, pushing the food into little separate but equal piles. "I'm sorry."

Dr. Feldmeyer, a psychiatrist on his way to St. Albans, was seated on Mrs. Doddard's left. "Actually, Mrs. Doddard, you should honor your husband, not belittle him, especially in public."

Mrs. Doddard looked suddenly furious. "I beg your pardon. Are *you* married, Doctor?"

"Why no, I'm not, I just meant—"

"Then I'll thank you to keep your opinions to yourself."

"They're not just opinions, dear lady, they're facts. I may not be married, but I'm an expert on abuse, spousal and otherwise. I wrote a paper on it that was published in the *Annual Review of Clinical Psychology*."

"Bully for you," Mrs. Doddard replied, glaring at him.

"I'd say you're the bully," he said, not backing down. "Your husband has been displaying classic symptoms of someone abused."

"Rude. I've never laid a hand, not even so much as a finger, on him."

"I meant mentally abused, madam. People who have been abused, mentally, physically, or sexually, often exhibit traits of self-doubt, self-loathing, and anger. They often blame themselves for the abuse, sometimes to the point of hurting themselves, or in extreme cases even suicide."

Reverend Doddard blushed scarlet. "Oh, Dr. Feldmeyer, my wife doesn't abuse me. I just tend to talk too much sometimes. A bad habit of mine, I'm afraid, of quoting scripture. Hazard of the trade, I guess." The reverend dropped his fork and began picking his teeth again.

Dr. Feldmeyer looked triumphant. "My point exactly. You, the victim, Reverend, are deflecting blame from your abuser and putting it on you. And I think your constant teeth picking is a nervous habit brought on by her constantly ridiculing you."

"I don't constantly ridicule him, that's ridiculous. Tell him, Edgar, and stop picking your teeth! Honestly, the very idea that I'm a bully—"

"Hitler is the real bully. The bully of civilization," Mrs. Byrne the octogenarian, said, clucking her tongue.

"Are you comparing me to Hitler?" Mrs. Doddard said.

"What? No, of course not. Don't be ridiculous," Mrs. Byrne said, staring back at Mrs. Doddard. "But something must be done in Europe, and I'll tell you all just exactly what should be done and how." And she proceeded to do so for the next several minutes, much to our dismay, in between biting comments from Mrs. Doddard and Dr. Feldmeyer, who continued to scowl at each other.

When the main course was finally cleared just after nine and dessert was offered, both Auntie and I declined, even though a seven-layer chocolate cake, my favorite, was one of the options. I just couldn't listen to any more of it, and thankfully, neither could Verbina. We made our excuses, said our good nights, and left, Verbina taking my arm as I guided us out of the dining room and back to her cabin.

"That was excruciating," she said, as we strolled up the stairs. "I'll be damned if I know how we're going to survive another dinner tomorrow night with those people."

"If I may quote the good reverend, 'And he who swears by heaven swears by God's throne,' Auntie," I said jokingly, and we both laughed.

"Pardon my French," she said. "I do feel rather sorry for that man, though."

"So do I, Auntie, So do I."

"Perhaps we should dine in the à la carte restaurant tomorrow and avoid the whole lot of them."

"That, I think, is a terrific plan. I'll see to reservations in the morning."

"Thank you, dear. That woman, all of them actually, have given me a terrific headache. I think I shall lie down for a bit."

"That's a good idea," I said.

"What will you do?"

"Me? Oh, I promised Simon I'd meet him in the smoking room for an after-dinner drink."

Verbina looked up at me with a queer expression. "You're becoming fast friends."

"Yes, I suppose so. I must say I'm enjoying his company, that's all. He's an interesting man."

"He seems to be enjoying your company, too. Drinks in the bar together, swimming in the pool, now more drinks in the smoking room…"

"What's wrong with that?"

"Nothing, of course, not a thing. But there are so many lovely young ladies on board who I'm sure would enjoy your company, too, and Simon's. Here we are on our third night out and you've not mentioned a single girl you've seen or met."

"Oh, well, he, uh, did say something about going to the Starlight Club afterward. It's a pretty big deal in the wee small hours of the morning, and sure to be full of lovely young ladies."

"That sounds nice, then. Have a good time tonight, Heath, but don't overdo the alcohol. You're not used to cocktails, late hours, and such."

"I'll be fine, honestly. What are your plans after you lie down for a bit?"

"Don't worry about me. After I rest a while, Myrtle and I will go and listen to the orchestra. Some gentlemen are always available to dance with, and apparently Myrtle has her eye on some Frenchman she met this afternoon. I'll see you in the morning for breakfast."

"It's a date," I said. "Give my best to Mrs. Obermeyer." I gave her a peck on the cheek before dashing back down the corridor, my heart racing once more.

The smoking room was on the promenade deck just past the long gallery, with large windows on both sides. Multicolored leather furniture, carpets, and linoleum gave it a smart, sophisticated feel I admired. Simon, resplendent in his tuxedo and black tie, was waiting at a small table by the fireplace. As I approached, he stood and we shook hands before we both sat down again. He had taken the liberty of ordering me a vodka martini with a pickle, and we toasted to the English.

"You wear a tuxedo quite well, Heath," he said. "You clean up nicely."

I smiled, pleased at the compliment. "Thank you, and so do you. Tuxedos are so easy. I never have to consider what to wear. I think Verbina, on the other hand, tried on at least three different dresses tonight before deciding on a blue floor-length with a matching bolero jacket, the first one she'd tried on."

Simon laughed. "Typical. How was dinner?"

"The food was excellent. I had the sirloin of beef with horseradish cream. Our table mates, on the other hand, were a bit boorish, rude, and dull."

"Oh, I'm sorry to hear that. Dinner at sea is always a gamble, a roll of the dice. Fortunately, one meets interesting people more often than not. You could ask the maître d' if he could reseat you and your aunt, perhaps at a table for two."

"Gee, I'd hate for them to think us impolite. Instead, I thought perhaps I'd make reservations for Auntie and me in the Verandah Grill for tomorrow evening, and explain if anyone asks that we just wanted a change."

"Good thinking. If the hosts tell you they can't seat you, feel free to use my name to Oliver at the desk."

"Thanks, I will. It should be a nice change of pace, though as I say, the food in the dining room has been excellent and plentiful."

"Yes, it's easy to overeat onboard. Have you been enjoying the trip overall, then? Table mates notwithstanding?"

"More than I ever would have imagined."

Simon smiled. "Good, me too. Crossings are generally fairly routine, even boring, but this one has taken an unexpectedly pleasant turn."

"It's been anything but routine or boring for me, tablemates notwithstanding, but then this is my first time. I've never been abroad before."

"Ah, a virgin."

"Yes, sir." I blushed and laughed, and we drank some more, toasting the Americans this time, and we talked a great deal about everything and nothing until it was nearly midnight.

"I think they're getting ready to close up the smoking room, Heath," Simon said, glancing about. "If you're hungry, they serve a cold buffet supper at midnight in the dining room."

"Gosh, no, I'm not hungry in the least. Are you?"

"No, not really. Interested in the Starlight Club, then?"

Not wanting the night to end, I nodded. "Sure, it sounds like fun."

"It can be. It's one deck up, on the sun deck, almost directly above us. It can also be loud and crowded. The later it gets, the louder it gets, and it can go quite late, sometimes until three in the morning."

"I don't mind. I'm not tired at all."

"Me neither. Lots of single young ladies will be there, anxious to dance with us, I suppose."

"Oh," I said, not thrilled with that idea, and I think he could tell by my expression. "Yes, I mentioned that to my aunt. She seemed pleased."

"Your aunt has your best interests at heart, I'm sure, or what she thinks are your best interests anyway. But if you're not up for crowds or dancing, we could have champagne in my cabin instead, if you like."

I swallowed hard, my heart thumping. I wondered if it was visible to the naked eye. "Ah, gee, I'd like that, sure."

"Great. Let's go, then." He signaled for the waiter and paid our bill, and when he'd finished I stood up and nearly lost my balance.

"You all right?" he said, standing up and reaching out an arm to steady me.

"Yes, fine," I said. "Maybe I've had one too many martinis."

He smiled that smile again, his beautiful eyes sparkling in the light. "The sea's gotten rougher, and we're rolling and pitching a fair amount. Don't worry, I won't let you fall over."

"Thanks," I replied, thrilling at the touch of his hand on my arm. His cabin was on A deck, and we climbed down the two flights of stairs side by side, his hand still on my elbow, as we made idle chitchat until we reached his door. He unlocked it and then ushered me in, closing it behind him and turning on the dressing table lamp, which gave off a soft, pink glow.

"So, this is your cabin."

"Yes, do you like it?"

"Sure, it's charming. I thought you'd be in a suite, though, being a baron and all."

Simon shook his head. "Suites are a waste of money. I spend little time in my cabin on board and do little entertaining, present company notwithstanding."

"I suppose that makes sense. Amazing how every cabin on board has a different look, a different feel."

"But the beds are the same. Soft and comfy."

"Oh, yes. I suppose they are. The same, I mean," I said, glancing at the double bed and then back to him. "Mine's been very comfortable."

"You're nervous."

"Me? No, I'm not, not at all," I said, which wasn't entirely true.

"Good, you've no need to be. Would you like some champagne, then? Or a martini with a pickle?"

"No, I'm good, real good," I said, holding on to the back of a chair. I could feel the room rocking up and down and side to side, and I felt slightly nauseous.

"Yes, you are good."

"I am?"

"You are. Though you look a little pale, even in this light. Should I ring for some peppermint tea?"

"No, thanks, I'm a little queasy, but I'll be fine." I didn't want any interruptions just then. "You look really handsome tonight, Simon, if you don't mind my saying so. That's a really handsome tuxedo, I mean. It fits you well."

"I don't mind you saying so at all. I couldn't help but notice you constantly staring at me, Heath, from the time we met on deck. And I must say, I've found myself staring at you, too."

"At me? Why?" I said, genuinely surprised.

"Because you're a handsome man, though you don't seem to know it. Tall, dark hair, green eyes, nice build, broad shoulders. You filled out your bathing costume quite well, too."

I felt myself blush, my face on fire. "Oh, well, gee, uh, thanks. You looked awfully good in yours, too."

"Thanks." He moved closer to me and touched my left cheek with the back of his right hand. "You're blushing."

"It's just hot in here, that's all."

"You're hot in here."

"Yes, I am. I mean, maybe we should turn the fan on or open a porthole or something."

"Or lie down."

I backed away a bit, confused, excited, nervous, and scared. "What?"

He slid off his tuxedo jacket and undid his bow tie, tossing them both over the desk chair. "If you're still feeling queasy, I mean. You might feel better on the bed, horizontal."

"Oh, right. No. I'm fine being vertical." I couldn't take my eyes off him, standing there in his dress shirt and trousers, so attractive, so desirable. He undid his collar button and the first few button studs, along with his cufflinks, and set them on the dresser before he kicked off his shoes.

"I like you, Heath, and I think you like me, too, unless I'm painfully mistaken. Am I mistaken?"

I tried to speak, but no words came out, so instead I just slowly shook my head. I was trembling.

"Good, I'm glad. I didn't think I was wrong, but I can't be too careful. I trust you can be discreet?"

"Discreet? Me? Gosh, yes. I'd never say anything, ever. Would...would you?"

He looked deeply into my eyes and smiled mischievously. "About what? We're just two friends getting to know each other, that's all." He moved closer to me again, slipped my jacket off, and undid my tie, adding them on top of his. Then he undid the first few buttons and studs of my shirt while I stood there trembling. He took off my cufflinks next, setting them on the dresser next to his.

"Have you ever done this before, Heath?"

I swallowed. "Done what?"

"This, with a man. With anyone, really."

Once again I shook my head, my lips quivering. I didn't think kissing Doris Kincade and copping a feel in ninth grade counted, or that time my second cousin Chuck and I masturbated in front of each other in a tent while looking at a picture of Jean Harlow in a swimming suit when I was seventeen.

He took my head in his chin and held it gently. Then, almost as if in slow motion, his lips grazed mine. "Should I stop? Would you like to leave?"

This time I found my voice. "No, and no. I'm okay. I want to stay."

He hugged me then, wrapping his strong arms about my body and kissing my neck, which caused me to nearly faint. We pulled apart just enough for our lips to meet again, tenderly at first, then passionately, aggressively. He undid the rest of my shirt studs and buttons as I kicked off my shoes, and then I tripped and fell on the floor trying to get my socks off. He came down with me and we lay there laughing for a few moments before he rolled on top of me and kissed me again. Quickly his massive hands were at my belt buckle and I felt my trousers and then my undershorts being pulled down. I was naked on the floor of his cabin, raging with an excitement I'd never felt before. Soon he was naked, too, and then, almost too soon, definitely too soon, it was all over. We both lay there panting and sweating for a while, and then he got to his feet and padded to the bathroom. I heard water running, and then he returned holding a wet cloth.

"I warmed it for you. You'd better clean up."

I wiped myself as I sat up. "Thanks."

"Cigarette?"

"No, I don't smoke."

"Mind if I do?"

"Not at all."

I watched him standing naked as he lit up and inhaled, then exhaled a cloud of white gray smoke that curled up to the ceiling, the tip of the cigarette glowing amber in the dark. "I only smoke occasionally. Like after this."

"Has there been many times like this for you?" I said, not really sure I wanted to know.

He picked up his white boxer shorts and pulled them on, steadying himself against a chair as he did so. "Not many. A few. I have to be careful. Are you okay?"

"I couldn't be better. A little cold, though, all of a sudden."

"Right, me too. We'd better get dressed. Besides, it's after one in the morning. Your aunt may be wondering, if she's waiting up."

"Oh, let her wonder. I'm an adult."

"Yes, you are, very much so, and I'm glad of it," Simon said, pulling on his undershirt and then his dress shirt. "But your aunt is a nice lady, and we shouldn't worry her."

I sighed and stood up. "I suppose you're right." I picked up my clothes and dressed slowly, putting the soiled washcloth on the back of the chair. "Can we do this again?"

Simon smiled, and then walked over and kissed me gently. "I'd like that, Mr. Barrington, but I'm not so sure we should have even done it once."

"What? Why? It was wonderful. I mean, *I* thought it was wonderful. Didn't you? Did I not do it right?"

He laughed and hugged me. "You were perfect, and it *was* wonderful."

"*I* thought so. We're like Heathcliff and Catherine from *Wuthering Heights*. Passionate, all-consuming—"

"And look what happened to them."

"Well, it will be different for us."

"We don't know each other very well."

"I think we know each other pretty well after that."

He smiled indulgently. "Yes, but that's only a part of getting to know someone."

"What do you want to know? Ask away, my life is an open book."

He handed me my tie. "Here. Your life may be an open book, but mine's not."

I took the tie and draped it around my neck as I stared into his eyes. "What do you mean?"

"I mean I have a past, Heath. Secrets, things you wouldn't understand."

"Try me. I'm great at keeping secrets, and I'm an understanding fellow."

"My secrets are deep, wrapped in a mystery."

"I'm good at mysteries, too."

He continued to get dressed. "Yes, so you've said. You want to be a detective someday. But right now you're sweet, young, too trusting, and a bit naïve."

"I'm not naïve, and I'm twenty-two, not a kid anymore."

"I think we've established you're not a kid anymore. And I'm thirty, nearly thirty-one, with a lot of baggage."

"I can handle baggage with the best of 'em. You can trust me."

"Can anyone really trust anyone? Can we even trust ourselves?"

"I'm afraid I don't understand."

"Look, Heath, how deep is the ocean?"

"How deep is the ocean? What's that got to do with anything?"

"Just answer me."

I thought for a moment. "Well, gee, I don't know, exactly. Pretty deep. I know Lake Michigan has some deep parts, with lots of shipwrecks, but nothing compared to the Atlantic."

"Some scientists believe the ocean is over eight thousand meters deep. And some secrets are deeper than that, and should stay that way."

"I don't care about your secrets. I don't care about your father's death or your sister's, or the Quimby curse, or that young man on the *Aquitania* or anything!"

He looked taken aback. "Who told you about all of that?"

"Mrs. Obermeyer mentioned it."

Simon looked disgusted. "Goodness, that woman does like to talk. Such an old gossip. I wonder where she gets her information from? But I had nothing to do with that man's death on the *Aquitania*. I only just met him on board. He died from a heart condition. Still, rumors persist about that, my father, my sister—"

"I don't care. I know you're not a murderer, if that's what you're worried about."

"I'm glad you think I'm not a murderer, though some people do."

"What other people think doesn't matter to me. It's none of my business. I think you're swell."

"I think you're pretty swell, too, but there's also something else you should know, something I don't think even Mrs. Obermeyer is aware of."

"What?"

"I'm considering getting married."

"I don't…what? Married? To a woman?"

"Yes, that's generally how it works. I was engaged last year to someone else, but it didn't work out. This girl's name is Ruth. She's one of the St. Jameses of Philadelphia. I've just been to see them this trip."

"But how? Why?"

"It's what I am expected to do. Marry, produce an heir, grow old, and die."

"That sounds dreadful."

"I suppose it is in some ways, especially to people like you and me."

"But you told me earlier that wasn't important. You said you just want to live your life, to be who you are."

"That's still true, Heath. But I can't be selfish, either. And I can't just keep going from smoky encounter to smoky encounter the rest of my life. Maybe it would be best if I settled down."

"So, I'm just a smoky encounter?"

He sighed. "No, that's the hell of it for me. You have a name, a personality, and I'd like to consider you a friend."

"Do you have many friends, Simon? I don't mean like this, but friend friends."

He inhaled deeply and blew out a large cloud of smoke. "I still keep in touch with a few chaps from boarding school, but we're not close. I can't be honest with them. They wouldn't understand. And the old local constable and I go back a few years, but in general I'm out here in this world by myself now days. How about you?"

"A few fellows, I suppose, but like you, I can't be honest with them about myself. Besides, most of them are all interested in different things than I like. Football, basketball, girls—"

Simon chuckled. "Sounds very all American. In England it's cricket, rugby, and girls."

"Girls are universal, I guess."

"And it's a better world because of it. Sometimes I think they should be in charge. There would be less war and less anger. Girls are just as smart as men, and I think they are more compassionate and kinder."

"I suppose so. Is this Ruth St. James compassionate and kind? And is she pretty?"

"She's pretty enough. And she seems kind, I suppose, but I barely know her, to be honest. Her father, Wendall St. James, arranged it all. It's not official yet. Nothing's been announced, and I haven't even made up my mind for sure. But he's made it known he wants Ruth to be the next Lady Quimby."

"Do you have a photograph of her? A lock of her hair? A love letter with a lipstick print?"

Simon gave me an odd look. "Uh, no. Like I said, I don't really know her all that well at this point. Why?"

"Just something someone asked me once about a girl I'd invented. A fiancée."

"Oh, well, I can assure you Ruth St. James is very real and very much a woman."

"Why didn't you tell me all this before?"

"Because I like you. I didn't want to scare you off, and I didn't think it mattered."

"But you think it does now?"

He shrugged his shoulders and put out his cigarette. "I don't know, maybe."

"It matters to me. If nothing's been announced, you don't have to go through with it."

He went to one of the portholes and stared out at the darkness. "That's true. You've confused me."

I took a deep breath and let it out slowly. "And you've certainly confused me. I really like you, Simon," I said as I walked up behind him.

He turned and touched my cheek with the back of his hand again and smiled. "I know you do, more than I thought you would, and I like you, too, more than I thought I would, which is why I had to tell you, don't you see? Look, we arrive in Cherbourg on Tuesday. Let's enjoy our remaining time on board, and then you and your aunt can come see me at Heatherwick on Friday. We'll have a nice visit, and then you'll both go back to Milwaukee."

"I don't want to go back to Milwaukee."

Now he sighed. "But you have to, and I think I have to get married."

"Why?"

"Maybe it will help me move forward from the past. It's ironic, in a way. My getting married and having children is what my father always wanted. It's what we fought about most. He had fiery red hair and a temper to match. But now that he's gone, well, I see perhaps he may have been right."

I took a step back and looked at him in the dim light. "I don't know what your past is exactly, but I don't think burying it deeper will help you move forward. I think only uncovering it will do that, bringing it to light, sharing it."

He looked startled for the briefest of moments. "You may be wise beyond your years, Heath. But you have a whole life ahead of you, fresh and new."

"And I want to share it with you. I could stay on, be your manservant or something, your valet. Your wife wouldn't have to know."

"My God, you're a treasure. But that wouldn't be fair to you, and it would be torment for me. Maybe if I marry, the Quimby curse will be broken."

"You don't really believe in curses, do you?"

"I don't know. I never used to, but you've no idea what my life has been like, what all has happened, what's really happened. When I finally came to terms with my feelings, I felt ashamed and frightened. Blaming it on the curse made it easier to accept."

"I can understand that. We all believe and do things that make our lives easier. But it's not real, Simon. I'm real, you're real. Together we could be very real, flesh-and-blood real."

"Maybe you're right. Maybe I have been hiding behind that curse, I don't know. But I do know that right now you should go back to your cabin and get some sleep. I'll see you after breakfast, okay?"

I had a lump in my throat, and I felt tears in my eyes that I didn't want him to see. "Okay, I'd better go." I started to leave.

"Heath?"

I stopped but didn't turn. "Yes?"

"We still have all day tomorrow and tomorrow night. Plus the weekend at Heatherwick. And you can write me, if you want. When you get back to Milwaukee, I mean, but you'll have to be discreet."

"I'd like that. Will you write back?"

"I will."

"And promise me something?" I said, my voice quavering.

"What?"

"That you'll think seriously about not getting married."

"I'll think about it, Heath, but someday you'll meet someone else and forget all about me. Hurry up now, get going."

I nodded but I'm not sure if he noticed, and then I proceeded to the door and down the passageway to the stairs, holding onto the walls to steady myself against the roll and pitch of the ship crashing through the waves.

CHAPTER EIGHT

Monday Morning, September 13, 1937
The Mid-Atlantic

The ship's horns, melancholy, deep, and resonate, woke me from a fitful, dreamless sleep. I opened my eyes slowly, unwillingly, and looked about my cabin. Nothing had really changed, yet so much had changed. I got up feeling anxious, sad, and tired, the horns continually and regularly sounding their mournful cry. The seas had calmed, and the ship wasn't rolling and pitching nearly as much as it had the night before. A glance out the porthole told me we were now in fog, which was the reason for the horns, of course.

Being in fog would force the captain to slow down, which meant we wouldn't be breaking any speed records this crossing, but I didn't mind. I was in no hurry to reach Southampton and say goodbye to Simon, even if I would be seeing him again at his home a few days later. The thought of that both excited and saddened me. I brushed my teeth and put on my black suit with a dark green tie, for it seemed fitting to my mood, and knocked on the connecting door at fifteen minutes to eight.

"Good morning, Heath," she said. She was still in her dressing gown and slippers.

"Good morning."

"I'm afraid I'm running a tad late, but I'm almost ready. I've done my hair, makeup and nails, so I just have to get dressed. Did you sleep well? I think you were out rather late also."

"I got in a little after one, I believe. We had a nice time."

"Oh good, I'm so glad. I wish I could say the same. Myrtle finally landed that Frenchman she was interested in, and the two of them danced all evening. I felt like the proverbial third wheel. I left them clutched in a tango about midnight and came to bed. I tossed and turned all night."

"I'm sorry to hear it, Auntie, truly."

"It's fine, I still had a nice enough time. Watching the two of them try to dance while the floor was heaving up and down and from side to side was quite comical. Most couples gave up, but they soldiered on, oblivious to everyone else, it seemed."

"Mrs. Obermeyer is nothing if not persistent," I said.

"She certainly is that. How about you? Meet any lovely young girls in the Starlight Club?"

"Hmm? Oh yes, sure," I lied. "But as you said, dancing was challenging, so we mostly just sat and chatted."

"Nothing wrong with that, my dear. I bet you were the handsomest man there."

"You flatter me, Auntie, but you forget Simon Quimby was also present."

"Simon is nice looking, isn't he?" She gave me a look, one eyebrow raised.

I felt my face redden. "He's okay, I guess. I just meant the girls seem to like him more than me."

"I see. Well, don't sell yourself short, Heath. You're handsome, smart, and charming, and any girl would be lucky to have you. It pays the devil to be jealous of Simon."

"Thanks," I said, "but I'm not jealous of him, just making an observation." I wished right then and there that I could tell her what had really happened last night. How I had lost my virginity to him, how I felt like I was falling for him. How we made love, and when it was all over how he practically pushed me away, telling me he was thinking of getting married. But instead I had to dance around the truth, tell lies, and make excuses. Such was my life. "He's very popular with the ladies."

"I'm sure he is, and I'm sure he's well known in the Starlight Club. Oh, by the way, speaking of the Starlight Club, don't forget to make reservations for us in the Verandah Grill for dinner this evening."

"Right, thanks for the reminder. Shall I say eight o'clock?"

"That will do, but if they don't have anything open at eight, I can do seven or whatever they have. Even dining at nine would be preferable to sitting through another meal with those people."

I smiled in spite of my mood. "Okay. Why don't I take care of that now, and you can get dressed and go on to breakfast. I'm not all that hungry, but I'll meet you in the dining room shortly."

"Not hungry? I never thought I'd hear you say those words." She looked me up and down. "And you're not as chipper as you usually are. Are you feeling well?" Her hand went to my forehead.

"Sure, I'm fine. Just a little tired is all. Maybe a little queasy from last night, too. All that motion."

"You don't feel warm. Probably all those cocktails, no doubt. Some good black coffee and a hearty breakfast will do you good. Go make the reservations, and I'll see you in the dining room. I'll wait at the entrance for you. Oh, and why don't you ask Simon if he'd like to join us for dinner later?"

"Gee, I could, I suppose."

"Certainly you could, and you should. Ring him up before you go, dear, and tell him I said hello, too."

"Yes, ma'am."

"Oh, I almost forgot. Myrtle and her French friend want you and me to play bridge with them after breakfast. I told them I'd ask you."

I made a face. "Bridge? With those two? I was hoping to do something with Simon today, maybe go swimming again."

"We won't be playing cards all day, only for a few hours. There will be plenty of time for swimming later if that's what you want, but we mustn't be rude to Mrs. Obermeyer and her friend."

I heaved my shoulders. "All right. I'll give Simon a call and then see about the reservations. I'll meet you in the dining room."

"Don't forget to say hello for me, and don't dawdle."

"Right," I said. "I won't." I returned to my cabin, made sure the connecting door was securely shut, and then picked up the phone on the desk, asking to be connected to Lord Quimby's stateroom. After a moment, I heard a click, and then his unmistakable voice, deep and resonant.

"Hello?"

"Oh, hello, good morning. I hope I didn't wake you. This is Heath."

"Yes, good morning. No, I've been up for some time. My breakfast was just delivered. Fried eggs, sausages, tomatoes, mushrooms, bread, and a slice of black pudding, with tea and buttered toast."

"Sounds delicious."

"I like it. Did you sleep well?"

"Not really. It was rather fitful. And then when the fog horns started—"

"Yes, that is rather annoying, even worse on deck, so I think I'll skip my morning constitutional today and stay indoors instead."

"Would you like some company? I promised Verbina I'd play bridge with her and Mrs. Obermeyer and a friend after breakfast, but I could make an excuse of some sort. She says hello, by the way."

"Tell her hello back."

"I will. So, are you up for a visit?"

"I'd hate for you to disappoint your aunt, Heath. Besides, I need to catch up on my reading and some of my correspondence."

"What about later, then? We could go swimming or something."

"I've already packed my bathing suit, and I don't wish to get it wet again. I'm afraid I really do have a lot of paperwork and whatnot to muddle through. Sorry, old boy."

I felt like I was being put off, but Mrs. Obermeyer wasn't the only persistent one. "Well, you have to eat dinner. Verbina wanted to know if you'd like to join us in the Verandah Grill. I'm going to make a reservation."

"I remember. Don't forget to use my name with Oliver if he

tries to tell you he's full up for tonight. I would enjoy dining with you and your aunt, and I very much appreciate the invitation, but I'm afraid I have other plans."

I swallowed, envisioning all kinds of things. "That family friend you had tea with yesterday?"

"Yes, as a matter of fact. Mrs. Wessel. She knew my mother, and she's traveling alone, so I offered to dine with her, and she was gracious enough to accept."

I breathed a sigh of relief. "I'm glad it's not a male friend."

"Heath, these phone lines aren't private, and my breakfast is getting cold, so I really must go."

"But I want to see you before we get off tomorrow."

"All right, why don't we meet in the smoking room again then, after dinner? Once you've made your reservation, let me know what time it is for, and we can arrange to meet roughly an hour or so after that. Sound good?"

"Okay, I'd like that. I'll see you tonight, then."

"Yes, goodbye."

I heard him disconnect and my heart sank a bit more. He had been friendly but not too friendly. Almost like we were just chums. Was that what he felt, or was he just being cautious? I hung up the phone, left my cabin, and went to the Verandah Grill, which was bustling with passengers who preferred the less formal atmosphere for their morning coffee. I made arrangements for a table for two for dinner that evening, at eight forty-five, the best they could do, and I didn't even have to use Simon's name. That done, I wrote down the information on a piece of paper, folded it, and gave it to a bellboy to deliver to Simon's cabin. It was coming ten before I finally made it to the dining room. I found Verbina waiting for me at the entrance as promised, somewhat impatiently. She was dressed in a tailored light green skirt with a matching jacket, red blouse, and a small white hat with a red band.

"What took you so long?" she said, looking briefly at her watch.

"Sorry, I phoned Simon first but he has other plans for this evening. He said to say hello back, by the way. Then I had to wait in the Grill until they could attend to me, but I was able to get us a table at a quarter to nine this evening."

"Goodness, I shall be famished by then, but at least we have a reservation. Speaking of being famished, let's eat, it's quite late in the day already." We found a smallish table for two off to the side, and I waited as the maître d' sat Verbina, and then I took my place across from her. I ordered the oatmeal with a side of toast and eggs, black coffee, and orange juice, and found I was hungrier than I thought I was, as I ate it all. Verbina had coffee, toast, blackberry jam, and two eggs over medium.

"Feel better?" she said, as the waiter cleared our plates.

"Yes, somewhat. What are the plans for today? Are we still playing bridge?"

"Yes, most definitely. Myrtle and her French friend discussed it with me last night. She wants us to get to know him."

"Why?"

"That's just Myrtle. She seems rather smitten. I thought we'd play in the Long Gallery. it's rather quiet there most of the time."

"All right. I'm not very good at bridge, but I guess I could give it a whirl, if you like."

"I do like. Bridge is a good game to know in the social circles, and just what you need to take your mind off whatever or whoever it is you're dwelling on."

"What makes you think I'm dwelling on anything?"

"Or anyone," she said. "Call it my intuition."

"Fair enough, but you're wrong, I'm just tired. When do we play?"

"I told them we'd meet them at eleven, so we have just enough time to use the ladies' and gentlemen's lounges, then stroll the promenade deck to the Long Gallery and find a table. You and I will be partners against the two of them."

The Long Gallery was located on the port side of the ship, with lots of windows overlooking the sheltered promenade and the sea beyond, which was still covered mostly in just gray, dull fog drifting by. The inside of the gallery, however, was warm and cozy, with charming area rugs covering the Korkoid floor, small tables and chairs in groups by the window, and columned torchiers giving off a soft amber glow.

Mrs. Obermeyer and her newfound friend were already there, and she introduced him to us as Monsieur Antoine Chevrolet. He spoke with a decidedly French accent and kissed the back of Auntie's hand the way they do in the movies. We took our seats, and then we cut for deal. Monsieur Chevrolet had high card, so he dealt. As he did so, I studied him. He seemed not young but not old, not attractive but not ugly, and he could possibly have been wealthy, but I wasn't sure and frankly didn't care. He had a thin, dark mustache curled at the ends and wore spectacles perched on his long, narrow nose that gave him an almost comical look.

We played the first hand well enough, Verbina keeping score. We were ahead, though Myrtle and Antoine didn't seem to mind or even barely notice. In fact, they were paying little attention to the game at all, so it was fairly easy for Verbina and I to keep our lead. Still, I was envious of Mrs. Obermeyer and Antoine, as they flirted with each other openly across the bridge table and called each other sickening pet names like *mon tresor* and *mon chou*, along with Cuddles and Sugar Lips. Frankly it turned my stomach more than the rolling and pitching of the ship had the night before. *They* didn't have to hide their feelings, their emotions, or their true selves. They didn't have to pretend and lie. It was therefore with some satisfaction that Verbina and I won both of the two games we played.

"Well, Myrtle, that makes sixty-three cents you two owe us. Fancy another game?" Verbina said, shuffling the cards expertly.

"Dear me, no, you two are much too good. We'll just settle up, shall we?"

"No checks, please," Auntie said, setting the deck aside.

"Oh, Verbina, you're such a kidder." Mrs. Obermeyer put her hand on Antoine's across the table. "Cuddles, do you have sixty-three cents for my dear old friend here?"

"Of course." He looked at Auntie. "A Frenchman who does not pay his debts is a man without honor, madame." He extracted a franc from a leather purse and handed it to Verbina. "And a man without honor is not a man. You may keep the change."

"*Merci,*" Auntie said.

"Goodness, I can't believe we lost both games. I'm afraid I lost in the ship's pool last night, too," Mrs. Obermeyer said.

"The ship's pool?" I said. "I was swimming there yesterday. It's lovely."

She tittered and giggled like a schoolgirl. "Oh, dear, not *that* pool, the ship's pool."

"What do you mean?" I said.

"Honestly, Myrtle," Verbina said. "Don't confuse the boy." She turned to me. "She means people wager money on how many miles the ship will go in one twenty-four-hour period. The smoking room steward announces the winner each day during cocktail hour. The currency is always pounds eastbound, dollars westbound. They call it the ship's pool. People have been known to win several hundred dollars, but personally I don't partake in it."

"Well, I do," Mrs. Obermeyer said. "But I'm afraid this crossing just hasn't been lucky for me, at least not monetarily speaking." She smiled at Antoine and giggled again.

"What do you Americans say? Unlucky at cards, lucky at love?" Antoine said, smiling back at Mrs. Obermeyer, his thin mustache twitching.

"Yes, that's how the saying goes," Verbina said. "Would you two like to join us for lunch?"

"You are *très* kind, Mrs. Partridge, but I have made reservations for Myrtle and me in the à la carte restaurant for both lunch and dinner this evening, followed by a night of dancing under the stars."

"There won't be any stars tonight. The fog is supposed to last until morning," I said happily.

"Then we shall make our own stars and our own moonlight, right, *mon chou?*" Antoine said, gazing at Mrs. Obermeyer like a love-starved puppy with worms.

Myrtle giggled and snorted. "That's right. Tomorrow we both get off in Cherbourg, and then we're going on together to Paris."

"What about your cousin in Marseille?" Verbina said.

"I'll take the train down to see her and her husband for a couple of days, but then Antoine has invited me to his villa in Nice. That's near Cannes, you know."

"That seems rather sudden," Verbina said.

"*Oui*, perhaps, but again as you Americans say, one must make hay while the sun is up, yes?"

"While the sun shines, my love bug, and yes, I agree. Now that I'm over thirty, there's no time to waste on silly formalities," Mrs. Obermeyer said.

"Now that you're over *thirty*?" Verbina said, raising her brows.

"That's right," Mrs. Obermeyer said, giving Verbina a scathing look.

"Well, technically that's true, I suppose," Verbina said, turning to Antoine. "You live in a villa?"

"Just my family home, madame. A small villa on the coast, quite empty since my wife died three years ago," Antoine said, and then he gazed at Mrs. Obermeyer. "It is very beautiful there, but it will still be outshone by you, *mon tresor*."

I made a small gagging sound and stuck out my tongue almost unconsciously, but instantly regretted it as all three of them looked at me in surprise.

"Heath," Verbina said, "where are your manners?"

"I apologize. I swallowed wrong."

"Indeed. Well, perhaps we should get you some water. Heath and I will be heading to the dining room, then. Thank you for playing," Auntie said.

"My pleasure, our pleasure, *madame, monsieur.* I hope to see you before Cherbourg, but if not, I'm sure we shall meet again at some point. It's a small world."

"Very true, Monsieur Chevrolet. By the way, your surname is so interesting. Are you at all involved in the motor cars?"

His laugh was annoying. "I am asked that frequently. But no, the name actually means goat farmer in French."

"Goat farmer?" Myrtle looked aghast. "I thought you said you own a winery."

"*Oui*, my dear, that's true. My family owns a vineyard, several actually, not goats. I'm afraid I know little of automobiles, or goats for that matter, but a great deal about grapes."

"Thank heavens," Myrtle said, looking relieved. "Grapes make wine, you know."

"Yes, they do, and wine makes money, I imagine," Verbina said.

"*Oui*, Mrs. Partridge, our vineyards have been doing well in spite of the Depression, or perhaps because of it. People still drink. Your silly Prohibition a few years ago put a dent in the export market, but the American tourists traveling overseas more than made up for it."

"How interesting," Verbina said.

"Isn't it, though? He's such a treasure," Mrs. Obermeyer said with a dreamy sigh.

"Treasure is just the right word," Verbina said. "Myrtle, dear, we'll see you off tomorrow and wave to you on the tender. You must promise to write and tell us all about your experiences in France."

"I most certainly will, when I have time. I suspect we'll be very busy, though, won't we, sugar lips?" she said, reaching across the table again for his hand and giggling all over again.

"*Oui, mon chou.* Feeding each other very tender, sweet, plump grapes."

I resisted the urge to gag again or roll my eyes. I think I would have preferred it if he *was* a goat farmer. Auntie and I both stood, followed by Antoine and Myrtle, who moved next to each other, gazing longingly into each other's eyes and holding hands.

I don't think they even noticed when we had walked away.

"I suppose that was rather rude," Verbina said, as we descended the stairs to C deck. "We didn't even say a formal goodbye."

"I don't think they cared. At least Antoine has taken Mrs. Obermeyer's attention off me."

"That is something to be thankful for, I suppose. But honestly, feeding each other grapes."

"I know, tender, sweet, plump grapes. I almost lost my appetite for lunch."

"And you sticking out your tongue and making that gagging sound. It was most embarrassing."

"I'm sorry, Auntie. It was a foolish impulse."

She stopped and looked at me, a twinkle in her eyes. "But a funny one. Let's eat."

Chapter Nine

Monday Afternoon, September 13, 1937
Nearing Cherbourg

After lunch, we had our tea in the lounge, accompanied by a harpist. "Remember what I told you yesterday, dear," Verbina said, looking at me as I stirred my Earl Grey with my spoon. "Never clink your spoon against the cup. Simply hold it vertically and move it back and forth like a paddle."

"Oh, yes, right. Sorry," I said.

"Take small sips, don't slurp, and put the cup on the saucer between each sip. Never cradle the cup in your hand, hold it by the handle only."

"Yes, ma'am. Coffee seems so much simpler."

"Once you get the hang of it, you'll find it most pleasurable," Verbina said as she set her cup and saucer back down on the table and sighed contentedly. "High tea at sea is one of my favorite things about the English ships. Splendid tea with clotted cream, scones with jam, cucumber sandwiches, chocolates, and pastries."

"It is rather pleasant, rules notwithstanding."

"You know, Heath, the Pfister Hotel in Milwaukee does high tea. We should do that sometime, just the two of us."

I smiled at her. She was so different than my mother, but Mother would have been more like her if she hadn't married for love and had a child, so I guess I was content to have Mother as she was, and have Verbina for my aunt. "I would like that very much. It could be our monthly date. And I promise to remember my tea etiquette."

"Splendid. I always enjoy spending time with you." She glanced at her watch, which was suspended from her neck like a pendant. "Oh my, it's after five. I suppose we should go back to our cabins, gather up our things, and pack our bags once more in preparation for disembarking."

"Yes, I suppose so. And then it will be just about time for dinner. The reservation is for eight forty-five, don't forget."

"I remember, dear. On the last night out, no one dresses for dinner, just like on the first night, so you can pack your tuxedo."

"All right. I'll keep out my windowpane suit for the evening, and I can wear it again tomorrow with a different tie."

Verbina looked at me. "Men. You know quite well I can't be seen wearing the same thing, but you can."

I grinned. "Sorry, Auntie. I didn't make the rules, silly as they may be. Shall we?"

"We shall."

It only took me about forty-five minutes to finish packing, but Verbina, on the other hand, struggled mightily getting everything repacked, swearing that either a case had gone missing or her wardrobe had increased along with her waistline while on board. With the assistance of her cabin stewardess, she finished, and we set everything out in the passageway to be collected, except for the things we'd need the next day, which would go in the cases we planned to carry ourselves.

Finally, at twenty-five minutes after eight, we went up to the Verandah Grill on the Promenade Deck, where, after just a brief wait, we were seated at a table for two by a window on the starboard side. The fog had lifted a bit, but the horns still droned on. There was nothing to see outside, so we turned our attention to the lovely room as we listened to some light jazz played on the white piano above the dance floor. It was filled with tables at the moment, but it would be cleared later when the café converted to the Starlight Club.

We both dined on the swordfish with crispy rock shrimp,

scampi with garlic butter, and bistro fries. It was just as delicious as the food in the main dining room, and the company at the table was far more pleasant. We shared a bottle of wine and lingered over dessert and coffee, enjoying ourselves despite the fact that I was anxious to see Simon.

"So, what shall we do after dinner?" Verbina asked in between bites of her chocolate torte with fresh whipped cream and raspberries.

"After dinner? Oh, well, um, Simon asked me to join him in the smoking room for a drink."

"That sounds nice. I could use a sherry, and I enjoy Simon's company. Let me just pay the bill here, and we'll be off to see him."

"Oh, uh, fine, fine. I thought maybe you'd want to go to the lounge for dancing, though," I said.

"No, I don't think so. I'm a wee bit tired, and my feet could use a rest. Besides, Myrtle will be there with her Frenchman, and I really don't want to play the third wheel again tonight."

I smiled to myself at the irony of that statement, and I was more than a little disappointed she wanted to tag along.

Verbina gazed at the check the waiter had discreetly deposited on a silver tray. "My, it does seem decadent to pay for our meal here when we could have eaten for free in the main dining room, but this was certainly more pleasant."

"Yes, I agree. Thank you for dinner, and for everything."

"You're most welcome, my dear, and thank you for the company."

After the bill had been paid, we strolled to the smoking room, Verbina on my arm. As usual, Simon was there before us, occupying a table for two by the fireplace. Ever the gentleman, he stood when he saw us and signaled a waiter for another chair before we even reached him. If he was disappointed Verbina had joined us, he never let on. He was polite and charming as we all chatted about the crossing, Mrs. Obermeyer and Antoine Chevrolet, and our plans for London. I enjoyed being in his company, even if it wasn't just the two of us. And then, just like that, it was eleven thirty, and I noticed Auntie stifling a yawn behind her handkerchief as she looked at her watch.

"Oh my, excuse me, gentlemen," she said.

"Of course, Mrs. Partridge," Simon said. "Would you like another drink?"

"Goodness, no thank you. It's been a long day, and I'm afraid we have an even longer one tomorrow. I think we should be getting to bed, Heath, and let Simon get some rest, too."

I glanced at Simon, who didn't look at all tired, and then back at Verbina. "Please go on ahead, Auntie, I'm not the least bit sleepy," I said, though truthfully I was a bit.

"Perhaps you're not, but maybe Mr. Quimby is."

I looked at Simon again, but he just smiled and held up his hand. "My day tomorrow will not be as long as yours, Mrs. Partridge, and I had a nice lie down this afternoon, so I'm not ready for bed just yet."

Verbina looked doubtful. "You bachelors. So carefree, it seems."

"I suppose Heath hasn't mentioned it, but I may not be a bachelor much longer," Simon said, almost too casually. "I have to enjoy myself while I can."

"You're to be married?" Verbina looked almost shocked. "I had heard you were engaged last year, but that it was called off."

Simon looked uncomfortable. "Well, yes, that was to Lydia Fortner."

"Lydia Fortner. Why do I know that name?" Verbina said.

"Her father is Peyton Fortner," Simon said, "of the Chicago Fortners."

"Oh, yes! The Fortners. They lost almost everything in the crash of '29 and are just barely scraping by...oh dear, I shouldn't have said that."

"It's all right, Mrs. Partridge. It's true. Mr. Fortner had been hoping for a large inheritance to turn things around for them, but it didn't happen. Regardless, it just didn't work out with Lydia and myself. I'm thinking now of proposing to Ruth St. James, of the Philadelphia St. Jameses, but it's not official, nothing's decided yet."

"How wonderful, congratulations."

"Thank you, Mrs. Partridge, but it's not definite yet, as I said."

"I've heard of them. Quite a well-to-do family. Not affected at all by the crash. Old money, and lots of it."

"Yes, well, as Simon said, Auntie, nothing is definite yet."

"Still, it sounds promising." She looked at me with a queer look once more. "Well, I must be off. Don't be too late, Heath."

"I won't, I promise," I said as we all stood up. I gave her a peck on the cheek, and she squeezed my arm.

"Good night, Mrs. Partridge," Simon said.

"Good night, gentlemen. Sleep well, and thank you for the drinks, Simon. We shall see you tomorrow, I'm sure." She gathered up her fox stole and her handbag and tottered off as Simon and I sank back down into our club chairs, our glasses empty, the drinks gone.

"Why did you have to mention Ruth what's her name to my aunt?"

"St. James. And why not? It's the truth. Besides, I got the impression she was beginning to suspect something. Good to keep them guessing."

I frowned. "I suppose. But why bring that up? You said yourself it's not definite."

"Is anything in life definite, Heath?"

"Don't go getting philosophical on me."

Simon laughed. "All right. Another refill?" he said.

I set my empty glass on the table and tried to hide a yawn behind my hand. "No, thank you. I think I've had enough alcohol for one night."

"And you're not tired, eh?" Simon said, looking at me, a twinkle in his eye.

"Maybe a little," I said, half smiling.

"It's okay. Me, too, to be honest. I suppose I should be getting to bed before too long."

"Oh. I guess I should too, I suppose. By the way, how was your visit with that family friend, what was her name, Mrs. Vessel?"

"Wessel, and it was nice. It was good to hear her talk about my mother, about the old days before the curse, before everything, really."

"I'm sure," I said.

"I was only six when my mother died, just after Charlotte was born. Still, I remember her. She had beautiful, kind, loving eyes."

"Like yours."

He laughed lightly. "Maybe. I don't think of my eyes as beautiful, but I'm glad you do. I miss her, and I think of her sometimes, wondering if she was happy, if she felt loved."

"She loved you," I said, "and that must have made her happy."

"I suppose so. I wish I would have known her more." He glanced at his watch. "My, it is getting late. I suppose they'll be wanting to close up here soon."

There were only a few people left in the smoking room. "I could walk you to your cabin, if you wish."

Simon set his empty glass on the table next to mine. "I would like that. You know I would, and I know you would too, but nothing has changed from what I said last night."

"I see," I said, though I wasn't sure I really did. Everything was so confusing. Since I met Simon, I had alternating feelings of joyous rapture and deep despair, sometimes simultaneously.

"I've given it a lot of thought, Heath. I don't want to lead you on more than I already have. My life is complicated."

"I think maybe I do understand, Simon, and you're not leading me on, honest. I know what I'm getting myself into. I just want to spend another night with you before we disembark. Is that okay?"

He looked at me thoughtfully. "All right, I suppose that might be a lark. But I don't think anything can happen between us when we're at Heatherwick. Too many eyes, too many ears. We must keep our distance."

"Do you not want Verbina and me to visit anymore? I don't want you to be uncomfortable with us there after what's happened between us," I said, almost holding my breath waiting for him to answer.

"Your aunt is looking forward to it," he said at last.

"She is. But she'd understand. I don't want to come if you don't want us to be there."

"Heath, it's not that I don't want you there. I very much do, that's the bloody problem."

"I'm confused," I said, feeling frustrated again.

He took out a cigarette but didn't light it, turning it over and over between his fingers. "What do you want from all of this? From me?"

Now it was my turn to pause. I couldn't just blurt out that I was falling in love with him, and that I wanted to be with him now and always, though that was how I felt. Finally, I looked into his beautiful eyes and said, "I like you, and I like spending time with you. And I think you could use a friend. You don't seem to have many of those. Just some chaps from boarding school, I believe you said, and the local constable…"

Simon smiled, and I felt a tug at my heart. "You're right about that."

"Then let's be friends, once and for all, considered and done. We can be ourselves with each other. We understand each other at least."

"I'd drink to that, but our glasses are empty."

"Let's go to your cabin, then, shall we, and have a nightcap there?" I said hopefully.

"I thought you've had enough alcohol for one night."

"I guess there's always room for one more. By the time we get to your cabin, I'll be ready."

"You're sure then? Just a lark, nothing more? No strings attached, as they say?" He lit the cigarette and put his lighter back in his pocket.

"No strings, no ropes, no chains, I promise. Friends come and go like the waves on the ocean, but true friends share a bed, I always say."

"You're a crazy American, you know," Simon said, laughing. "But right now I think I could use a true friend, and another drink." We both stood, he left some money on the table to cover the bill, and together we went to his cabin for one last night. It was considerably cleaner and tidier than the previous evening, with most of his belongings already packed for disembarkation the following day, but he did have a bottle of whiskey and two glasses on the table.

"Make yourself comfortable," he said. "I'll pour. I don't have any ice, but I could ring for some if you like."

"No, straight up is fine. How did you manage to get a whole bottle of whiskey?"

"A little money to the right person can manage all sorts of things. You'd be surprised."

"And two glasses?"

He grinned. "I thought maybe you'd come back. Good to be prepared, regardless."

I didn't reply, but I took off my shoes, jacket, and tie, along with my cufflinks, and had a seat in one of the chairs as he poured the drinks, his back to me. I couldn't help but admire the view, as he was pretty from all sides.

He handed me one of the tumblers and we toasted to last nights, which made me feel rather melancholy.

"You all right, then?" Simon asked.

"Hmm? Oh, yes, fine. Just not used to straight whiskey, I think. It burns a little going down."

"It takes some getting used to." He slipped off his shoes, jacket, and tie, and had a seat next to me.

"You know, Simon, I feel like I've known you a lifetime."

He gazed at me over the top of his glass. The lights were low, soft, and fuzzy. "But you don't really know me at all, Heath."

"I think I do. More than you think I do, perhaps."

"You definitely *think* you do," he said. "But we've only just met. I'm practically a stranger."

I took a larger drink this time and coughed. "I'd like to get to know you more, then."

"There are parts of me even I don't understand. And I'm not sure I want to."

"You're deeper than the ocean, I believe you said." I finished my whiskey.

He laughed lightly. "Something like that."

"But it doesn't matter to me. If it mattered, I wouldn't be here."

"Maybe you *shouldn't* be here."

"No, I should be. I'm exactly where I want to be, where I need to be. Where I belong."

"Innocence," Simon said. "Such a fleeting thing. It's something to hold on to as long as you can. But at the same time you have to be careful. You're too trusting, Heath."

"I trust *you*," I said.

He stared at me for what seemed an eternity before speaking again. "Why? You've no reason to. As I said, you don't really know me, nor I you."

I shrugged. "An instinct then, a feeling."

"Instincts and feelings can get you hurt, or worse. There are a lot of not nice people in the world more than eager to take advantage. Another drink?"

I shook my head. "I'd better not, I'm feeling a trifle woozy."

"Maybe it's because of what I put in your last one."

"What? What do you mean?"

"Just a simple sleeping potion, but effective. Phenobarbital."

"A sleeping potion? Why? Why would you do that?" I stared incredulously from the glass to him.

"Because you know too much about me now. You know some of my secrets."

"But, but I would never tell, I told you that, you know that."

"I can't take chances, I'm afraid. Once you're asleep I'll take you out on deck. If anyone sees us, I'll just say you've had too much to drink. But it's late, and the decks are deserted."

"And then you'll throw me overboard?"

"Perhaps. It's a good thing you were so trusting."

I stared at him hard. "You didn't slip me a Mickey, Simon."

He looked puzzled. "A what?"

"A Mickey. A Mickey Finn. It means to spike someone's drink."

"What a curious expression. But how do you know I didn't, uh, slip you a Mickey, as you say?"

"Because I know you more than you think I do, like I said before. And I really do trust you."

"If you do, you're one of a very few. But trust has to be earned,

Heath, not given. You'd do well in life to trust no one until they *prove* they can be trusted."

"That seems rather cynical," I said. "Shouldn't we trust people until they've proven they *can't* be trusted?"

"By that point you could be hurt or dead. You're right, I didn't put anything in your drink, but I *could* have."

"But you *wouldn't* have."

He sighed. "No, of course not. I was just trying to make a point that you shouldn't be so naïve, so trusting, so gullible."

"I'm not! It's not like I make a habit out of going back to strange men's rooms."

He reached over and touched my cheek. "I know, I'm sorry. Maybe that wasn't fair of me."

"Or nice."

"I just don't want you to get hurt, now or ever."

"Nor I you," I said.

"Too late for that, I'm afraid. But it's our last night on board, and here we are all doom and gloom."

"Yes, and I promised myself that wouldn't happen," I said.

"My fault entirely."

"I won't argue that!" We both laughed, and things seemed all right again.

"Why don't we get a little more comfortable and slip into bed for an hour or two?"

"I like the sound of that," I said, feeling better still.

"Good, and I like the sound, and the sight, of you."

We made love again, this time in the comfort of his bed, and it was even better than the night before. Tender, passionate, and romantic, and then we fell asleep, my back to his chest, the ship gently moving up and down and side to side.

"Hey, sleepyhead," I heard Simon say, rousing me from a lovely dream. "It's almost four in the morning. You'd better get back to your cabin."

I turned over and looked at him in the darkness, reaching out my hand to his face, feeling the stubble of his beard. I placed my left index finger in the cleft of his chin and felt my heart throb.

"I suppose," I said at last. "It was a wonderful night."

"I agree, but the sun will be up soon, and it won't do for you to be here much longer. Someone may see you leaving."

Unwillingly, I turned over again and got out of bed, padding to the bathroom in the darkness. When I returned, Simon had turned on the bedside lamp and was sitting up in bed, smoking a cigarette.

"Good morning," he said.

I smiled. "Good morning."

"What would your aunt say if she knew?"

"I think she'd be better about it than my folks. She's more worldly, you know. But I don't think it would be good for her to find out, so I guess I have secrets of my own."

"Indeed. Better get dressed."

"Right." I put on my clothes by the dim light, not bothering to tie my tie or put my cufflinks back in. I slipped them into my pocket. I saw Simon's boxer shorts lying on the chair, and on an impulse slipped them into my other pocket when he wasn't looking. Then I walked over to him, still in bed, and gently kissed him. "See you later," I said.

"Yes, later."

I stood there, staring down at him as he looked up at me.

"What is it?"

"I was just thinking about what you said last night and earlier to Verbina. About getting married."

He blew a cloud of smoke off to the side. "You'd like Ruth, Heath. She's a lovely girl. Maybe you'll find a girl someday."

I shook my head. "I don't want to find a girl someday. Or any day."

"You say that now, but you're young. People aren't yet asking you questions about when you'll settle down, get married, have children. Your parents, your friends, your relatives, and your aunt aren't pressuring you."

"I don't care."

He inhaled once more and then blew more smoke. "You will care someday, believe me. Hurry up now, get going. It's starting to get light out."

I had a tear in my eye again that I hoped he couldn't see. "All right, I'll go now, but I don't believe you." I turned and left, closing the door behind me. As I heard it latch and catch, I felt a lump in my throat I couldn't swallow.

CHAPTER TEN

Tuesday Morning, September 14, 1937
Cherbourg

I awoke to the sound of persistent knocking from the connecting door. Groggily I opened my eyes and glanced at the clock, noting it was a couple minutes past eight. "Just a minute," I shouted, hoping to quell the knocking. Unfortunately, it didn't. I crawled out of bed, pulled on the trousers I had been wearing the night before, and stumbled over barefoot to answer it.

"Oh good, you're up," Verbina said, stopping in mid-knock after I'd opened the door. She looked me up and down.

I rubbed my eyes and yawned. "I wasn't, until you knocked."

"Clearly. I must have knocked twelve times or more. You look terrible."

"How kind of you to say so," I said, still yawning. "Sorry, I didn't get much sleep."

"You and Simon dancing until dawn?"

"Hmm? What?" Images of Simon leading me in a foxtrot popped into my head, and I found the idea rather pleasant.

Verbina raised her voice. "I said, did you two go back to the Starlight Club after I left last night and dance with all the pretty girls again?"

"Oh, right. Yes, something like that," I said, relieved.

"Goodness. Youth, how does one ever survive it?" She stepped back and looked at me, shaking her head. "Do you always sleep in your trousers and undershirt?"

"Huh?" I looked down at myself and then back at her. "No, of course not. I put my trousers on to open the door."

"Where are your pajamas? I bought you that nice red silk pair just last Christmas with the idea that you'd have them for this trip."

"I know, I'm sorry, but I don't typically wear them. I find pajamas uncomfortable, much like this conversation, Auntie."

"Well, don't tell your mother, she'd have a stroke."

"The fact that I sleep in my boxers and undershirt is something I don't think she needs to know, and I really wish you didn't know, either. It's embarrassing."

"She won't hear it from me. You may not realize it, but I'm quite good at keeping secrets, all kinds of secrets. So if you ever have something you wish to tell me, anything at all—"

"I'll keep that in mind. Did you need something?"

"Oh, only breakfast. Shall I go on down by myself?"

"No, no, if you can give me ten minutes, I'll be right with you."

"Only ten minutes? Men. I swear in my next life—"

"I know, you want to be a man. Trust me, it's not all it's cracked up to be. I'll hurry."

"All right, dear, just knock when you're ready."

"I will." I closed the door and opened the drapes covering the portholes. The fog had lifted, and we were now in brilliant sunshine, which sparkled on the water rushing by. I stripped off my trousers once more, along with my boxers and undershirt, and draped them over the back of a chair, and then had a quick rinse and a shave, managing only one small nick on my left jawbone from my razor. I toweled off, dressed as quickly as I could, applied my aftershave and hair tonic, combed my hair, and then rapped on the door.

"Nine minutes, twenty-two seconds. I'm impressed," Verbina said, staring at her watch and then stepping aside to let me enter.

"Thanks. I would have been quicker if I hadn't cut myself shaving."

She squinted up at me, examining my face closely. "I see that.

You should put some mercurochrome on that, I have a bottle in my train case—"

"It's fine, Auntie, just a small nick, though the aftershave stung mightily. Let's go eat."

"All right, it's your face."

"I've learned to live with it. Shall we?"

"We shall." We exited her cabin and went down to the dining room, where we dined on porridge and eggs, lots of black coffee, slices of black pudding, and a couple of pastries we couldn't resist, though probably should have. When we were finished, we found our evening waiter, tipped him for his service throughout the crossing, and said goodbye.

"He was an excellent waiter, so attentive," Auntie said as we left the dining room.

"Yes, it's too bad he had to put up with the likes of Mrs. Byrne, Mrs. Doddard, and the rest of them for four nights," I said. "Bad enough we had to deal with them for three."

"He gets paid to deal with them, and hopefully, as obnoxious as our table mates were, they are at least good tippers," Verbina said.

"That, Auntie, I wouldn't count on, if I were him."

Arm in arm we went to the promenade deck, four decks up, which was bustling with morning pedestrian traffic strolling clockwise and counterclockwise, nodding and murmuring at each other as they went. Along the inside, in rows of adjustable folding wooden deck chairs, sat the rest of the lot, watching as the rest of the upper crust passed by. Verbina and I went to the windows, where we noted a small brass plate affixed to the deck.

"What's that?" I said.

"Hmm? Oh, that commemorates Lord Burghley, the Olympic athlete."

"What about him?"

"Last year, in 1936, he completed a full quarter-mile circuit of the ship in only fifty-eight seconds, can you imagine? And he did it in full evening dress. It was truly remarkable."

"I would imagine. Of course, he was a high hurdler in the Olympics, as I recall. I suspect he's in excellent shape," I said.

"Most definitely."

"And those legs of his. They're quite muscular. I remember seeing photos of him in his track shorts, impressive."

Verbina looked at me sharply, and I feared I might have overspoken.

"He's rather handsome, too, don't you think?"

"I hadn't noticed."

"Hmm," she said. "I wonder."

"What time do you have, Auntie?"

"Changing the subject?" she said, consulting her watch. "Well, it's just fifteen minutes after ten. We have a few hours before Cherbourg. Any thoughts on what you might like to do? The last day is always difficult."

"Why don't we just walk for a while? After a heavy breakfast like that, I could use the exercise, and here on the covered promenade deck it's considerably warmer than on the sun deck."

"All right, dear, clockwise we shall go. A nice walk will be good for me, too, and I don't have my heels on."

We strolled about the deck for almost an hour, discussing our plans for London and guessing at what a weekend at Lord Quimby's would be like, and then I challenged her to a game of Wahoo in the starboard gallery. She beat me two games to one, after which we had our final lunch in the dining room.

"I could get used to this," I said, as the waiter cleared my plate. "Wonderful food, excellent service."

"I *am* used to this," Verbina said. "It's the only way to travel." She consulted her watch once more. "It's nearly one in the afternoon, so we'll be in Cherbourg shortly. I suppose we should find Myrtle and say our goodbyes."

"Yes, I suppose so," I said. Verbina stood, as did I, and we left the dining room arm in arm. We arrived in Cherbourg at two minutes past one, exactly four days, one hour and two minutes after departing from the dock in New York. The *Queen Mary* didn't break any records this crossing, but she was still a swift and beautiful ship. We found Mrs. Obermeyer and Mr. Chevrolet on A deck, in the first-class entrance foyer, locked arm in arm, waiting for the doors to open so they could proceed to the tender that would take them to Cherbourg.

Mrs. Obermeyer was swathed in emerald green from head to foot, and positively glowing, her cheeks red and rosy.

"Oh, Verbina, Heath, how nice of you to go to all the trouble of seeing us off." I found her sentiment amusing, as we only had to climb two decks from the dining room to do so.

"Of course, Myrtle, it was so nice to catch up with you. You *must* keep in touch," Verbina said, clutching Mrs. Obermeyer's outstretched hand over the red dividing rope. They kissed each other quickly on the cheek.

"Oh, I will, darling, I will. Do have a nice time in London, and please give my regards to Lord Quimby. I'm so sorry we weren't able to visit with him this trip, but you know, things do come up." She glanced at Antoine, resplendent himself in a beige double-breasted suit with a red, orange, and brown striped tie and a bowler hat in his hand.

"Yes, dear, of course. I'm sure he's disappointed he didn't get to say hello, but there will be other times," Auntie said.

"*Mais oui, mais oui!*" Mrs. Obermeyer said. "That means *but yes*, you know. Antoine taught me that."

"You're an excellent pupil," I said.

Mrs. Obermeyer looked at me. "Thank you, but I'm also an excellent teacher. I'm sorry you and I didn't get to know each other better, too, but hopefully we'll have other opportunities."

"Um, yes, I'm sure."

The doors opened, and the bellboys began escorting passengers to the gangway.

"Well, this is it," Mrs. Obermeyer said.

"*Oui, au revoir, madame, monsieur,*" Mr. Chevrolet said.

"That means goodbye," Mrs. Obermeyer said.

"Yes, Myrtle, we know. Have a good time, and be sure and write," Verbina said.

"I will! Toodle-oo!" she called out, and they disappeared through the doorway and were gone.

"They make quite a pair," I said.

"They certainly do, but they're a good match, I should think. Quite symbiotic."

"Oh Auntie, is there no romance in you at all?"

"Romance? What is romance but a temporary feeling of excitement and mystery that will soon fade? Still, I wonder what will happen with them. Anyway, I suppose we should go up to the sundeck and wave goodbye. We did promise, after all."

"Yes," I said. "I suppose so." We climbed the stairs up and found a spot along the rail overlooking the tender bobbing up and down in the ocean below.

"Do you see them?" Auntie said, both of us peering over the railing.

"No, not yet."

"I suppose they're still getting settled. I think we have a few minutes before it leaves," Verbina said. "I'm just going to powder my nose. I shan't be but a minute. Hold my spot, will you?"

"Of course, Auntie," I said. I watched her walk away, then turned my attention again to the activity on the little ship below, side by side with the *Queen Mary*, both anchors dropped.

It seemed almost odd being on deck without the ever-present and constant wind we'd experienced the last several days, and I was enjoying the calm and fresh air, oblivious to my surroundings.

"Have a match?" a man said, coming up alongside me, his voice deep and familiar.

I turned to look at him, startled, and realized it was Simon, dressed in a tweed suit and green tie, with a rakish hat, looking for all the world like a movie star, only better.

My face was suddenly beaming. "Hey there. I was wondering where you were today, and what you were up to."

"My usual breakfast, my usual constitutional, then a brief go-round in the gymnasium. I'm a creature of habit. Sleep well?"

"Yes, I did, though not long enough. But it was worth it."

Simon glanced about, making sure no one was listening. "Good, I'm glad. No regrets, I think."

"None on my part."

"Glad to hear it. Now about my original question…"

I looked at him, puzzled. "Sorry?"

"Do you have a match?"

"Oh, yes. I always try to carry matches."

"Even though you don't smoke?"

"I have friends that do, and they always seem to be matchless."

He laughed an easy laugh. "And since I'm your friend now, I guess that fits."

I joined in his laugh. "I guess so," I said, striking a match and lighting his cigarette for him.

He took a few puffs and then blew the smoke out toward the ocean. "Thanks."

"Sure." I put the matchbox back in my pocket. "What happened to your lighter?"

"I forgot it in my cabin."

"Oh."

We stood side by side, almost touching but not quite. It was rather awkward for some reason.

"Where is your aunt?" Simon said at last.

"Powdering her nose. She'll be back soon."

"I see. It's been quite a crossing."

"Yes, it has. Far better than I ever would have imagined."

"Has it? Ah, here comes your aunt now. Hello, Mrs. Partridge," Simon said as Verbina approached.

"Oh, hello, Simon, how nice to see you again so soon. Is the tender still here?"

"Yes," he said, pointing at it over the rail. "They're taking on mail and the rest of the passengers now."

"Oh, good. I promised Mrs. Obermeyer we'd wave to her and Mr. Chevrolet."

The three of us glanced over the rail at the many passengers on the tender's small deck. "Do you see them?" Simon said.

"No, I still don't. Wait, that's her, in the green. Mr. Chevrolet is the one in the tan suit, glasses, and the bowler hat," Verbina said, pointing and waving.

We all waved then, and Mrs. Obermeyer and Antoine, catching sight of us, too, waved back, until at last, at a quarter after two, the tender departed, loaded down with passengers, luggage, and mail. When she had gone, the *Queen Mary* raised anchor and we were under way again at two thirty.

CHAPTER ELEVEN

Tuesday Afternoon, September 14, 1937
Approaching Southampton

"How long before we reach Southampton?" I said as the tender disappeared from view and we began picking up steam.

"About five hours, maybe less," Simon said.

"We should go back to our cabins to finish packing," Verbina said. "We also have to give our tips to our steward and stewardess and freshen up before tea at four."

"I suppose," I said, turning to look at her, her cheeks rosy from the wind that was now rather brisk again. "I feel rather melancholy about it all, though, I must say."

"That's natural. One almost always does at the end of a crossing. At the end of anything, actually. But remember, an end is also a beginning," Auntie said.

"To what?"

"That remains to be seen," Simon said, and I swear he had a twinkle in his eye that made my heart thump.

"That sounds promising," I said. "And hopeful."

"One must always have hope. Now, I should get my pearls from the purser's safe before the lines get too long," Auntie said. "And I want to exchange that franc Mr. Chevrolet gave me."

"Why don't you take care of that, then, and I'll meet you back in the cabins? I just want to get a little more fresh air."

"All right, dear, see you soon. Ta ta, Simon. Will we see you before we disembark?"

"Possibly, Mrs. Partridge, but if not, I'll see you on Friday at Heatherwick. I'll pick you up at the station in Brockenhurst."

"Yes, I'm looking forward to that, we both are. See you downstairs, Heath." Simon and I tipped our hats, and Verbina headed to the purser's office on A deck.

I checked my pocket watch, noting it was a quarter of three. "Just over an hour until teatime," I said. "Would you like to join us?"

Simon shook his head. "Thank you, that's very kind, but I'm having drinks with Billy Haines and his friend in their suite this afternoon, and then we're all having a light early dinner together."

"You know Mr. Haines? The movie actor?" I said.

"We're acquainted. He's a nice man, talented in many respects. They both are."

"And Mr. Haines is devilishly handsome," I said. "I've seen all his pictures."

"Well, yes," Simon said quietly, glancing about and nodding at an old biddy standing nearby, watching us. "You shouldn't say things like that out loud in public, Heath. You never know who's listening."

"Sorry," I said, as the old biddy turned and moved slowly on down the deck. "What's he like?"

"What's Billy like? Strong, brilliant, talented. I admire him. Did you know he thumbed his nose at Louis B. Mayer and up and quit when the old man wanted him to marry a starlet to quash rumors that were circulating about him?"

"Gosh, I heard he was fired."

"They didn't fire him, he quit. He has more guts than I'll ever have. And now he has reinvented himself as a decorator and is doing fabulously well for himself."

"I'm glad."

"Me too. He didn't let the bastards win for once."

"I wish I could meet him."

"I'd bring you along, but I can't invite a guest to someone else's party."

"I understand. Maybe another time. Tell him hello for me, though, and that I'm a big fan."

"I'll do that. Maybe I'll get an autograph for you, too."

"Gee, that would be swell."

"I'll see what I can do," he said, looking at me. "Tell you what, let's meet back up here on the sun deck again after dinner, as we approach Southampton, say about five thirty."

"Okay, I'd like that, though I can't promise my aunt won't be with me. She's hard to shake."

Simon laughed. "That's fine, I enjoy her company, too. Anyway, I better get going, I'm sure the champagne is already chilling. But I'll see you back here, same place, around half past five."

"Deal," I said. I watched him turn and walk away, then went back down the stairs to my cabin to pack what little was left, along with my toiletries and such, my tie and underwear I'd worn from last night, and the special souvenir I had acquired. When I finished, I went next door to help Verbina.

"I think I have everything in order, Heath. My dress from last night is put away, and I've got my other items all packed." She looked about and sighed. "It's been a lovely voyage. I hope you've enjoyed it."

"Oh gosh, I've enjoyed it ever so much, even more than I thought I would. Thank you again."

"I'm glad, and you're welcome." She looked at the clock on the nightstand. "It's ten minutes of four. We should go down for our last tea."

"That sounds so final," I said.

She touched my arm. "Remember what I said before—an end to one thing is also a beginning to something else."

"I suppose, though I think I prefer beginnings to endings."

"Some endings can be good even if they don't seem so at the time." She glanced about once more. "We have to be out of our cabins at six, and they're serving sandwiches and bullion directly after tea in the lounge, so I suppose we should just bring our bags with us."

"Oh, all right. I'll get mine, then, and I can help you with yours."

"Thank you, dear."

I returned to my cabin, gathered up my train case and bag, and then helped Verbina with her things.

"All set?" I asked, my one suitcase in my left, hers in my right, and my train case tucked under my arm.

She looked one final time around the cabin, then picked up her own train case and hatbox and nodded. "All set." The two of us found a table for two in the lounge, setting our luggage on the floor next to us.

The gathering for tea was lighter than normal, with many of the passengers having disembarked in Cherbourg, so we sat quietly, nibbling our sandwiches and sipping our tea. I did my best not to slurp or clink my spoon, and I think Verbina was pleased with my progress as we sat and listened to the harpist. In the past days she had sounded beautiful, but today she sounded mournful and sad, like a siren. Many of the other passengers had brought their carry-on luggage with them as well, piled about their tables, and it gave the moment an air of temporariness.

"Did you say they're also serving sandwiches here after this?" I said at last.

"Sandwiches and bullion, yes, here in the lounge, up until six p.m. I'm not all that hungry, but we should eat something. We won't get to the hotel until late."

"Yes, I suppose so. I feel like I've done enough eating on this crossing to last me a month, though."

"I know what you mean. Try as I might, I always manage to gain a pound or two on these ships. You could stand to put on a little weight, but not me."

"Oh go on, Auntie, you look swell, truly. Beautiful, even."

"Aww, that's sweet of you dear, thank you. But it's a constant battle. I think I'll pass on the bullion and just have one cucumber sandwich and another cup of tea."

"All right. I guess I could manage one cheese sandwich and one cucumber, and a cup of bullion with crackers."

"You might as well," she said. We ate quickly, me watching the time as it ticked slowly toward five thirty.

"What happens now?" I asked after we'd finished and a waiter had cleared our plates.

"The officials will come by soon enough. There will be declaration forms to fill out, a customs inspector, all the usual. It's the most tedious part of the crossing, but it doesn't usually take too long."

"Oh, I see." I glanced at my pocket watch again and smiled to myself. "It's just five thirty now. Do you think I have time to go up to the sun deck for a bit?"

"I suppose, but whatever for?"

"I'd like to get some fresh air."

"I could come with you, but we'd have to take our bags," she said.

"Yes, that would be a bother. Why don't you sit and relax and I'll just run up quick?"

"All right, Heath, but don't be long. Be back by six at the latest."

"Yes, ma'am."

I dashed off quickly before she could change her mind about tagging along, and then climbed up to the sun deck in search of Simon. Fortunately it didn't take long as he was right where I'd left him, as he'd said.

"Hey there," I said, trying to sound casual as I came up alongside him.

He turned and smiled at me. "Hello. You managed to shake your aunt?"

"Yes, I left her guarding the bags in the lounge. I have to be back by six, though."

"Yes, the customs fellows, inspectors and all that. They generally board via a tender at six o'clock, along with the pilot. I shall have to go too, of course."

"Great, we can go together. Where are your carry-on bags?"

"My room steward is watching over them for me. He'll bring them to the lounge when I'm ready."

"Oh, nice. How was Mr. Haines and his friend?"

"Pleasant. We had a good visit. I invited them to the house for the weekend, too, but they're otherwise occupied in London."

"That's too bad," I said, but I didn't really mean it. As thrilling as it would have been to meet William Haines and his friend, I wanted this weekend to be just about me and Simon. And Verbina by default.

"They'll visit another time, perhaps the week after. They're in London for two months."

"Gosh, that's a long time."

"Business interspersed with pleasure. Oh, I have something for you." Simon reached into his coat pocket and withdrew a rolled-up photograph he handed to me. It was a five-by-seven glossy head shot of William "Billy" Haines, signed *to Heath B, with affection, Billy*. I took it in both hands and stared at it, suddenly feeling a tad guilty for not wanting them to visit that weekend.

"Gosh, thanks, Simon! That's terrific."

Simon smiled. "Glad you like it. Billy keeps a few head shots around yet from his MGM days. Once in a while people still want one."

"Well, I sure do. I'll treasure it always."

"Good. I told him what a big fan you are." He looked briefly at his watch. "We should be docked by seven thirty or so."

"Will you be taking the train with us to London?" I said, rolling up the photo and putting it in the inside pocket of my suit coat for safekeeping.

"No, I have a car and driver waiting for me at the dock. My home isn't that far."

"Oh, that's nice for you, then."

"But I'll see you and your aunt soon enough, on Friday afternoon."

"Yes! Yes, indeed. I'm looking forward to it."

"Good, me too."

"Maybe that's the beginning Verbina mentioned earlier," I said.

"Maybe. But it too shall end, remember that."

My heart sank. "Why does it have to end?"

He sighed, looked out to sea, and then back at me. "Because it does, Heath. Everything begins, everything ends, one way or another. But don't think about endings now, focus on beginnings. Your first time in London, remember?"

"Oh, sure."

"Enjoy your time there," he said.

"Thanks, I will."

"I'm glad to hear it. London is a wonderful city."

"Yes, I suppose so," I said, rather unenthusiastically.

"You'll have a grand time, I'm sure of it." He glanced about to make sure no one was nearby. "By the way, I seem to have misplaced a pair of my undershorts. The pair of boxers I was wearing last night."

My face reddened. "Oh?"

"You didn't by chance see them anywhere, did you?"

"Well, uh, maybe perhaps I picked them up by mistake."

Simon looked stern. "By mistake, of course. I thought perhaps that's what happened."

I looked down at the deck, then at him, embarrassed at having been caught. "Do you mind terribly?"

He looked stern a moment longer and then broke into a grin, his eyes sparkling in the twilight. "Mind? I'm terribly flattered."

"I'd like to keep them, if I may."

"Consider it a gift. Another souvenir for you."

"Gosh, thanks ever so."

"You're welcome, though I do wish you would have just asked. I spent the better part of half an hour looking for them this morning, under the bed, under the chair, in the bed, behind the sofa—"

"I'm so sorry."

"Maybe you can make it up to me by giving me something of yours."

"Oh, sure! Of course, anything. What would you like?"

"Hmm. Let me think about that. But for now, we'd better get down to the lounge. It's almost six."

I looked at him again, so handsome, so distinguished, so mature. "Yes, I suppose so. Verbina will be waiting."

"You go on ahead, Heath. I have to check with my steward."

"Okay, see you in the lounge." I walked away, looking back once, but he was already striding off in the opposite direction, so I went inside and down to the lounge, back to Verbina.

The customs forms and paperwork didn't take long as we had nothing to declare, and we were soon cleared to A deck and the reception room, where we waited once more, Simon nowhere in sight. It was seven thirty when we docked in Southampton at the Cunard pier, the old, battered tugs nudging the ship into an open slot just behind the RMS *Scythia*, preparing to depart the next day. Soon the reception room doors on the starboard side opened, and we disembarked down the ramp and onto the pier, our carry-on bags in hand.

"Now what?" I said.

"Now we claim the rest of our luggage at customs and send it on to the train. Then we do the same," she said. "This way, dear. Don't dilly-dally."

"But where's Simon?" I said, looking at the many faces going by. "I didn't see him in the lounge or on A deck. Do you think he got off before us?"

"Disembarked before us, Heath, not 'got off,' and he did. I saw him. He probably claimed his luggage already and is on his way to Heatherwick. I believe he said he had a car and driver waiting for him."

"Yes, he did say that, but still, he said he'd see us in the lounge. I thought he'd wait to say goodbye."

"Whatever for? Didn't you say goodbye to him earlier? Besides, we'll see him in just a few days. Come on now, let's go. It's late and the train will be leaving soon."

I glanced about the crowded, bustling pier once more. "All right, I'm coming."

We claimed the rest of our luggage and had it sent on to the boat train, which seemed to have more cars carrying luggage than passengers. That done, we boarded at nine and found our first-class compartment in the second car, small but cozy and private. I stowed our carry-on bags in the overhead racks and had a seat opposite Verbina, who looked exhausted. Soon we were off, chugging slowly out of the station and on our way to London.

The train ride was pleasant, if uneventful. Auntie napped, and I read the *London Times* from that morning, which had been provided for us by the porter, along with more tea and finger sandwiches. I was anxious to catch up on the events of the world, as I had felt out of touch the past few days, but I was dismayed to find the paper full of distressing news and headlines. Japanese forces had captured Datong, the Chinese government had made a formal appeal to the League of Nations to take action against Japan, and Hitler had declared the failure of Franco's nationalists would "upset the balance of power in Europe." On top of that, I read that Ellis Parker Butler had died. He was one of my favorite authors.

Finally I gave up on the news and focused on my Oscar Wilde book, giving that up too just before the conductor announced our arrival. We pulled into Victoria Station at eleven on the dot, and with the assistance of several porters, managed to procure two cabs to the Grosvenor Hotel, which thankfully had two splendid rooms on reserve for us. It was nearly midnight before we checked in and got upstairs, Verbina declaring that unpacking could wait until morning, and I heartily agreed, as we were both exhausted.

CHAPTER TWELVE

Friday, September 17, 1937
London and on to Brockenhurst

We spent all day Wednesday and Thursday seeing many of the sights of the city. It was all thrilling and exciting, but what I was looking forward to most was Friday and seeing Simon again. The day came at last, and after breakfast the hotel doorman hailed us a cab to take us to Waterloo Station for the noon train to Brockenhurst. This time we only needed one cab, as we were traveling with just minimal luggage, having taken Simon's advice to leave most of our things in our hotel rooms. After all, we *were* getting the weekly rate.

The trip to the village of Brockenhurst was short, and I enjoyed sitting by the window, watching the little English villages and farmlands roll by as we rocked and swayed from side to side. Finally, the conductor announced our stop and the train ground slowly to a halt, letting off billows of steam.

"This is it!" I said excitedly, almost bouncing up and down in my seat.

"Yes," Verbina said, glancing out. "Looks pleasant enough. Too bad it's so overcast."

"It's all right. We're not here for the weather."

"I suppose. I hope Simon's on time picking us up and hasn't forgotten about us coming. Perhaps we should have sent a telegram reminding him."

"He'll be here," I said. "I bet he's been looking forward to seeing us again, too."

At least, I added to myself, *I hope he has.*

We gathered up our bags and disembarked on the platform of the tiny Brockenhurst station, noting the air was decidedly cooler and cleaner than it had been in London. Verbina adjusted her hat and pulled her coat about her, and I put my hat on and turned up the collar on my jacket. Both of us scanned the faces of the few people on or about the platform, but none of them were Simon. Verbina checked her watch, and I did the same.

"Well, the train was five minutes early," I said, setting our cases down.

"Yes," Verbina said, looking up and across the station area. "I suppose that's true."

"You two waiting for someone?" We both gazed at the little man who had come upon us. He was dressed in a dusty blue railroad uniform, his cap pushed back on his head, revealing a shock of white hair. "I'm the assistant station manager, Seamus Babcock. There's a telephone inside if you need it." One of his front teeth was gold and shiny, but the rest were gray and dull.

"Thank you, but he should be here presently," I said.

"Americans, eh?"

"Yes, sir, that's right. We're from Milwaukee, Wisconsin," I said.

He frowned. "Never heard of it."

"It's in the middle of the United States, on Lake Michigan," Verbina said. "One of the Great Lakes."

"If you say so, ma'am. Who's supposed to be meeting you here?"

"We're waiting on Lord Quimby, the Baron of Heatherwick," I said.

The little man's frown turned into a scowl. "Lord Quimby. You mean Simon Quimby. His father was the true Lord Quimby. I heard ol' Simon was back again. He comes and goes quite frequently these days."

"Yes, well, we all arrived together on the *Queen Mary* this past

Tuesday. He went on ahead while we stayed in London until today. We're visiting him for the weekend," Verbina said.

Mr. Babcock scratched the back of his leathery neck. "Know him well, do you?"

"No, not really. We just met on board a few days ago," I said. "Do you?"

He looked at me. "Well enough, I guess. Since he was knee-high to a grasshopper, anyway. He don't show his face in the village much anymore, since what he did to his own father, his flesh and blood, and after what happened to Miss Charlotte."

"What do you think he did to his father?" I said, somewhat annoyed.

"Heath, leave it alone," Verbina said, looking at me and placing a hand on my arm.

"Don't matter much what I think he did, sir, but some say he killed him. Some folks think he even killed his sister, Lady Charlotte, and made it look like an accident both times."

"That was never proven," I said. "None of it. He was cleared of any involvement in either death by the local authorities."

"Oh, so you know about all that, do you?"

"It's apparently not a secret," Verbina said.

"He'd like it to be. I'll wager it wasn't him who told you. There wasn't even a trial. Not enough evidence, they said. They never even found the murder weapon. There was just an enquiry, both times. Ha. *I* say ask Mrs. Devlin, the housekeeper at Heatherwick, about the bloody handkerchief she found of Sir Simon's on the floor of the murder room. If that isn't evidence, I don't know what is, but the inspector constable at the time, Alcott Wimbly, is a friend of Sir Simon's—make of that what you will. The official verdict was that it was a burglar killed Lord Lionel Quimby, and that Lady Charlotte Quimby died of accidental poisoning. Not bloody likely, in my opinion."

"Yes, well, thank you for your opinion, Mr. Babcock," Verbina said.

"Oughta be yours, ma'am. Poor Miss Charlotte. Awful what he did to her."

"We're aware of the rumors and innuendos, but it's just that, Mr. Babcock. Rumors and innuendos, vicious gossip," Verbina said.

"There's often truth to rumors and gossip, madam. Of course, some people think Lady Charlotte's death may have been suicide," the man said.

"I was wondering that myself," I said.

He stared at me, his brown eyes narrow. "I personally don't think so, but if she did kill herself, I bet Sir Simon drove her to it. I can't imagine her losing her father like that. They were close, you know, and Sir Simon was jealous. She had to live in that old house with a murderer, her beloved father gone. Can't blame her for offing herself under those circumstances."

"That's charitable of you, Mr. Babcock. However, if I'm not mistaken, I see Lord Quimby now, so we must be going," Verbina said.

"I'd watch your back if I were you, madam," Mr. Babcock said. "And you too, my good fellow."

I followed Verbina's gaze to the parking lot, where a distinguished, handsome, familiar gentleman was getting out of a boxy, yet sporty, four-door pale yellow car with whitewall tires. Simon appeared different, more like he had when we first met on deck—solemn, serious, and a little lost. Perhaps it was the sight of Seamus Babcock talking to us that did it. To spare him any embarrassment, I gave him a quick wave, picked up our cases, and started walking briskly to him, calling out over my shoulder, "Nice to have met you, Mr. Babcock," though I really could have done without it. I was pleased Verbina was following me, train case and hatbox in her hands, and we quickly reached the parking lot before Simon had gotten much farther than a few feet toward the station.

"Hello," he called out, though he wasn't smiling. He was staring past us, and a quick look back confirmed he was looking at Seamus Babcock, who was watching us from the platform, his hands thrust deeply into his pockets. Simon strode toward us and took one of the bags from me and Verbina's hatbox from her. "How was your trip? How was London?"

"Hello, Simon, thank you. Nice of you to meet us at the station,"

Verbina said. "The train ride was a bit dusty but no problems. London was charming, as always."

"Good, good. I hope you weren't waiting long. I got delayed by some bloody flock of sheep blocking the road."

"Not long at all, just a few minutes," I said.

"Glad to hear it." He put the bag and the hatbox into the trunk of his car, and I did the same with the ones I was still carrying. He closed the lid of the trunk and extended his hand for me to shake. "It's nice to see you." I shook his hand, but wished I could have embraced and hugged him instead.

"Likewise, Simon."

"How did you find London, Heath? Was it everything you'd hoped it would be?"

"Oh, sure. It's been a grand couple of days, though over-shadowed by all this talk of war and Hitler. One can't sit at a café or read a newspaper without being hit over the head with it."

"It's a grave situation," Simon said. "I admit I'm worried."

"Surely it will all blow over," Verbina said.

"Somehow, I don't think so. But let's not talk of it right now. What all did you see and do with your time?"

"Gosh, so much. We saw the Tower of London, Big Ben, Westminster Abbey, Tower Bridge, St. Paul's Cathedral, and more," I said. "I had no idea there would be so much to do."

Simon raised his eyebrows. "Indeed. You two covered a lot of ground in two days. Sounds busy."

"Sounds exhausting," Verbina said, "And it was."

"But fun," I said. "I'm looking forward to seeing more of it. We still want to see Windsor Castle, Hampton Court Palace, the zoo, Kew Gardens, and of course Royal Albert Hall, the theater, and the nightclubs."

"Well, I hope you won't regret your decision to spend a couple days here in the country. It's not nearly so exciting," Simon said.

"Oh no, I've been looking forward to this, too, very much."

"So have I," Verbina added. "Even more so after the last two days. My feet can use the rest, and so can the rest of me."

"You'll both have plenty of time to relax here. Heatherwick is nothing if not quiet and peaceful. And I've been looking forward to seeing you both again, also," he said, and for the first time since we saw him that day, there was a glint of a smile on his face, though he still looked back at the station.

"That's kind of you," Verbina said. "And thank you again for having us."

"Truly my pleasure. Anyway, this is my car, ready and willing to whisk you both away."

"It's quite an interesting automobile," Verbina said, looking it over. "I've not seen one like it before."

Simon patted the hood gently. "Thanks. She's a 1936 Ford Phaeton 68. I've got my eye on a Jaguar SS 100 3.5 liter roadster, though. Sporty little two-seater with a rag top."

"Jeepers, that sounds terrific," I said.

Simon grinned like a little kid. "With red wire rims and black leather seats. Of course, I'll keep this one for times like these, when I have more than one passenger."

"I've never ridden in a Jaguar before," I said. "Wouldn't that be something?"

"They're amazing vehicles, but unfortunately the finances don't allow for it right now. Soon, hopefully. Shall we?" He held open the back door and helped Verbina in, while I happily climbed in the front, then he went round and got behind the wheel, started the engine, and pulled away, glancing back once or twice in his rearview mirror. I suspected Mr. Babcock was still watching us, but I didn't want to look.

"What did Seamus Babcock want?" Simon said as he shifted gears.

"The station manager?" I said.

"Assistant station manager," Simon said. "I've known him my whole life, like I've known most people in the village, yet now I'm treated like an outcast by practically everyone."

"Oh, he just offered us the use of the telephone is all," Verbina said diplomatically.

"I'm sure. Did he know you were waiting for me?"

"We may have mentioned it," I said.

"It's all right. I know what he thinks, what he says, what they *all* say," Simon said, focusing on the road ahead of us. He seemed a good driver, attentive but not overly cautious.

"It's not fair," I said. "They don't know the truth."

Simon glanced over at me. "Do you know the truth?"

"Maybe not all of it, but I think I know *you*."

"That's charitable of you, Heath, but you *don't* know me, not really. I think we've been over this once or twice already."

"I'd like to get to know you, then," I said. "If you'll let me."

"I think we'll both get to know you better this weekend," Verbina said as we pulled onto the main street. "It seems so odd to be driving on the wrong side of the road. It takes me back to the time my first husband and I drove down here from London. Rather terrifying. I closed my eyes every time we met an oncoming vehicle, and the roads are so narrow."

"We don't drive on the wrong side, we drive on the left, which is the correct side," Simon said.

"We drive on the right back home, and our steering wheels are on the left," I said.

"Funny Americans," he said, with a genuine smile that time.

"I suppose neither is right or wrong, just different. Differently normal," I said.

"Differently normal, indeed. Welcome to Brockenhurst, by the way. This is Lymington Road, but we'll be turning left on Brookley Road soon, then another left on Burley. The house is just off Burley."

"The village is charming, Simon, so quaint," Verbina said, gazing out the window.

"I suppose it is that. It's the largest village by population within the New Forest in Hampshire, and it's not far from Southampton, where the ship docked. It's just about twenty-one kilometers from here."

"How much is that in miles?" I said.

"Roughly thirteen."

"Gosh, that's not far at all."

"No, it's convenient for when I want to go abroad. Have you had lunch?"

"Not yet, but we had a hearty breakfast," Verbina said from the back seat.

"A hearty breakfast is a must in my opinion. We should be to the house by twelve thirty or so. I'll have Mrs. Thorpe prepare a light meal. Dinner's not until eight, but we'll have tea at four."

"Sounds good," I said. I turned my attentions to the passing scenery out the window. We bounced along, turning slightly here and there, up a hill, and down a hill, until at last we reached a set of tall iron gates in the middle of a high stone wall that ran along the right side of the road. The gates were open, and Simon swung his car around and through it onto the pebble drive and past a small stone gatehouse.

"This is Heatherwick," he said, slowing down only slightly.

"Where?" I said, looking about at the towering trees on either side of the drive.

"This is the estate, the grounds. The house is over that slight hill up ahead and around the bend."

"You mean all this is yours? All these trees?" I said.

Simon laughed again. "Yes, every last one of them. And the pond and the stream, at least the part that runs through the property."

"Gosh," I said. We soon came upon a meadow that looked like it went on for miles, and then we climbed that small hill and rounded the bend. The house came suddenly into view, rising up from the ground proudly and stately, as if it had grown there over many, many years. It was the largest private house I'd ever seen in person.

"How big is Heatherwick?" I said. "The house, I mean."

"How big? Oh, I don't know exactly. There's the entrance hall, the main hall, a library, the study, a billiard room that was added about forty years ago or so, the dining room, breakfast room, a drawing room, and a conservatory on the ground floor, and seven bedrooms or so above. The attic holds a few more guest bedrooms as well as the female servant rooms, the trunk room, storage rooms, and the old playroom. The male staff are housed in the basement, near the kitchen and servant's hall. Off to the side and down the hill, near the kitchen yard and servant entrance, is the old stable and garage. Heatherwick's not all that large compared to other houses, I suppose."

"My folks live in a two-bedroom, one-bathroom, single-story house," I said, "with white clapboards and a little shed out back my dad parks his Buick in, and a garden next to that. My mom grows vegetables."

"Sounds perfectly sensible and charming," Simon said. "This place is too big for me by myself. I'm afraid these old estates are quickly growing impractical and out of fashion."

I didn't reply, but I looked in awe again at the large structure looming before us. The house was asymmetrical, the entrance set in the base of a square tower off to the right. A gabled wing on the far left projected forward slightly with another wing beyond that. To the right of the tower was more of the house, with a single, one-story addition to the right of that. The place was two stories high, with attic dormers above built of brick and stone in various shades of red, brown, tan, and beige, placed together like a puzzle. The English ivy covering the walls had grown over the years to almost become a part of the place, it seemed. The roof was of gray slate, and the windows were narrow and multipaned, some with slight arches, like eyebrows.

Simon brought his car to a stop in front of the house and switched off the engine, just behind a late-model black Packard.

"What's *he* doing here?" Simon muttered.

"Who?" I said.

Simon glanced sideways at me. "My cousin. Unless I miss my guess, that's his automobile."

"Oh," I said. I could tell by his tone that this was not happy news for Simon.

"Anyway, welcome to my home," he said, a little more cheerfully. He got out and opened the doors for Verbina and me, and the three of us stared up at the place. "It was built in 1796, just over a hundred and forty years ago, by my great-great-great-grandfather, Sirus Quimby, but it's been added on to here and there over the years."

"And it's all yours now?" I said.

"Yes, but it's really still ol' Sirus's house. I'm just the caretaker, as was my father, his father before him, and so on."

"It's lovely, Simon, simply lovely," Verbina said, looking up and side to side. "Just as I remembered it, perhaps even better. It may seem too big for you now, but when you're married and have children—"

"Yes, perhaps, Mrs. Partridge. But one can't foretell the future."

"But surely you wish to have an heir, to continue the bloodline, to keep Heatherwick in the family. Certainly Ruth St. James and yourself—"

"Should we get the bags?" I said, interrupting Verbina.

"No, let's go in," Simon said, looking at me. "It's gotten rather chilly, and I'm a bit knackered, as I'm sure you both are. I'll have Wigglesworth bring in your luggage and put the automobile away."

Verbina took my arm and we followed Simon up the ancient stone steps to the massive front door, set within a large arch in the base of the square tower. As we approached, the door was opened by a tall, thin man in black livery.

"Welcome home, sir," the man said. He appeared to be in his late sixties, possibly even older, clean-shaven, with silver-gray hair parted down the middle. His jawline was firm, with oversized ears on either side of his narrow head and a long, thin nose that gave him a severe, cold look.

"Thank you, Wigglesworth. You've assembled the staff, such as it is?"

"Yes, my lord. They're waiting for you in the great hall," Wigglesworth said, his voice flat, deep, and gravelly.

"Good."

"And your cousin, Mr. Wittenham, is here to see you, my lord. He's in the library. I've brought him tea and biscuits. He seems comfortable for the moment."

"I noticed his automobile."

"Yes, my lord. He insisted on waiting for you. Estate business."

"Very well, let's go in."

Wigglesworth ushered us into a long corridor, about eight feet wide by twenty-four feet deep, with a broad staircase at the far end of it. Simon and I removed our hats as Wigglesworth closed the front door behind us and led us a short distance down the corridor to a large doorway on the left that led to the main hall. It was a large room, about thirty by twenty-five feet, not counting a massive bay window toward the rear that overlooked a terrace.

An older woman, probably also in her sixties, in a long, dull gray dress, black lace shoes, and white apron, was standing just inside the hall, silver-white hair pinned neatly atop her head. Her face was deeply lined and her dark eyes set on either side of an aquiline nose. Next to her was a slightly shorter woman wearing a black dress and white apron and cap, with flame-red hair and laughing blue eyes. She appeared to be in her fifties and was pleasantly plump. Beyond her was a younger woman, attractive enough, and next to her an even younger girl, about seventeen or so. Last in line was an older man, probably in his seventies if not eighties. He was thin, wiry and weathered, his face craggy and creased, and he held his cap in his gnarled hands. Wigglesworth went into the hall and took his position at the front of the line, next to the first woman, all of them standing at attention, like good little soldiers in a row.

"This is Wigglesworth, Mrs. Jane Devlin, Mrs. Edna Thorpe, Agatha, Bonnie, and Bigsby," Simon said to us from within the arched doorway. Verbina and I stood next to him, all of us looking at the little group before us. "Henry Wigglesworth is the butler here, primarily in charge of the dining room, pantry, and wine cellar. You've been here, what? Forty years?"

"Forty-six, my lord," the severe-looking man said.

"Right. Mrs. Devlin there is the housekeeper, responsible for the house and the rest of the staff. She's been at Heatherwick forty-two years, I believe, is that right?"

"Yes, sir. Forty-two years this past May."

"Mrs. Thorpe has worked here twenty years. I remember that because I turned ten shortly after her arrival, and she made me the most marvelous birthday cake. She's the cook, and quite a good one, and in charge of the kitchen, of course."

Mrs. Thorpe looked quite pleased.

"Next to Mrs. Thorpe is Agatha. She's the kitchen maid and reports to Mrs. Thorpe, and Bonnie there is the chambermaid. They're both new here, having been hired just over two years ago. For some reason, we've always had trouble keeping the undermaids for very long. The young ones don't have the work ethic, you know, but hopefully that will change with Agatha and Bonnie. And finally there's our groundskeeper, Bigsby, an institution at Heatherwick. He was hired by my grandfather over fifty years ago. They'll all take fine care of you. Everyone, this is Mr. Barrington and his aunt, Mrs. Partridge. They'll be my guests until Sunday."

Each of them in turn bowed their heads slightly as they were introduced. I wasn't exactly sure what I was supposed to do, so I just kept my mouth shut, nodded, and fidgeted with my hat.

"Just the six servants, Simon?" Aunt Verbina said, surprised. "I seem to recall you having more when we were here last. There were two footmen, an underbutler, and I remember you had a chauffeur."

Simon shrugged. "One must cut corners where one can. I drive myself mostly, and Wigglesworth steps in when necessary. He's good with motorcars. Besides, Heatherwick is not a large house. It's just me now, and I'm not home all that much. When I am here, though, we generally get a couple of extra girls from the village, and sometimes a boy to serve if we're expecting a large number of guests." He looked at Mrs. Devlin. "I'm assuming you've arranged for additional help for the weekend?"

The old woman nodded. "Yes, my lord. Bess will be here later this evening to help in the kitchen for dinner, and another girl, I've forgotten her name, will be in tomorrow to help with the laundry and making up the rooms."

"Good, good. No boy this time, then?"

"No sir, with just two guests I can handle the serving," Wigglesworth said.

Simon looked at him. "All right, that will work. Bring the bags in from the car and take them up to the guest rooms, then, Wigglesworth. The tan one with the blue stripe and the small train case are Mr. Barrington's, the others belong to Mrs. Partridge."

"Yes, my lord," Wigglesworth said.

"When you've finished, you can put my auto away, I shan't be needing it anymore today, and besides it looks as though it may rain."

"Very good, my lord."

Simon turned back to the housekeeper. "And Mrs. Devlin, show Mr. Barrington and Mrs. Partridge to their rooms so they can get settled and freshen up."

"Yes, my lord."

Lastly he addressed the cook. "I know it's past noon, but we'd like a light lunch, nothing too heavy. You can take care of that, can't you, Mrs. Thorpe?"

"Yes, sir, of course. I've prepared a soup, which is still hot, and I can make some creamed carrots and bread and butter pudding."

"Good, good, that will suffice, see to it." He looked at his wristwatch. "It's twenty of one now, let's say lunch at one thirty." He looked at me and Verbina. "Once you two have settled in, unpacked, and freshened up, please join me in the dining room. It's the door just down this corridor, last one on the right across from the stairs."

"That sounds fine," Verbina said for both of us.

"Splendid," Simon said.

"I beg your pardon, my lord, but will Mr. Wittenham be staying for lunch?" Wigglesworth said.

Simon frowned. "You'd better set a place, though I'm not sure." He glanced toward the opposite side of the hall, where two doors stood on either side of a large tapestry. "I suppose I shall have to attend to him now."

"Yes, my lord," Wigglesworth said.

"Right." Simon turned once more to the rest of the staff. "You're all dismissed," he said, and then he strode past them across the massive hall, where he went into the door on the right side of the tapestry. It led to a smaller passage, and I saw he turned right, closing that door behind him.

Wigglesworth and Mrs. Thorpe also left to attend to their respective duties, followed by Agatha, Bonnie, and Bigsby. Mrs. Devlin looked at Verbina and me. "Your rooms are upstairs, if you'll follow me, please." She came into the corridor, turned left, and walked to the end, where she ascended the staircase to the second landing, turned, and then climbed up the remaining way, Verbina and I following behind. The stairs ended in an oddly shaped hall, with several doors opening off it. Just ahead on the right were two steps that led up to another longer, narrower hall that ran nearly the width of the house. Mrs. Devlin turned left, stopping at a door recessed into the wall.

"Your room is here, Mrs. Partridge. You have a lovely view of the back garden, as you can see." She opened the door and stepped aside as Verbina and I entered. It was spacious, with windows to the rear. The room was done in soft pinks and yellows, with green accents here and there, somewhat faded and worn but in good condition.

"Oh my, yes, it's charming. The room is quite pretty," Verbina said. "and looks very comfortable."

"I'm pleased you approve, madam. You have a private bath through that far door and a small dressing room, just here by the door to the hall. A fresh fire has been laid in the grate, should you need it, and there's a match safe on the mantel. It can get rather chilly here at night this time of year. If you need assistance with the fire, just let me or Wigglesworth know. Your call bell is here by the door."

"Thank you, Mrs. Devlin."

"Yes, madam. Will you require assistance unpacking?"

"No, I can do it. I left most of my clothes and hats in the hotel in London."

"Very good. If anything needs pressing, just let me know. I noticed you didn't bring your maid, madam. I will be happy to assist you with dressing or bathing if so required."

"Thank you, but I should be able to manage."

"Yes, madam." She turned to me. "Mr. Barrington, you're in the front of the house, on this side, with a view of the lawn. Just this way, sir," she said, stepping back out into the oddly shaped hall.

"I'll see you for lunch, Auntie," I said over my shoulder, following Mrs. Devlin out.

"All right, Heath. Don't be late," she said as I closed the door behind me. We walked across the corridor and toward the front of the house as I saw Wigglesworth over the rail struggling up the stairs with our bags. I felt a bit sorry for him.

"Where is Lord Quimby's room?" I said as we reached the long traverse hall once more.

Mrs. Devlin stopped. "Up those two steps and down the hall, there, sir, second from the last door on the left. Beyond that, the last door on the left, is Lady Charlotte's old room. It's empty now, except for the furniture. Such lovely things she had, such beautiful clothes. Sir Simon had all her possessions boxed up and taken to the attic, after...well, after she died, sir."

"Everything?"

"Yes, her books and letters, her journals, her drawings, her toiletries, and all of her clothes. Even her hairbrush, silver comb, and letter opener. She liked monograms, you know. Pretty much everything she owned was monogrammed, so no one else could use them, you see, after she died."

"Books, journals, and drawings. She sounds like someone I would have liked. Where do those other doors down there go?"

"The door at the far end of the hall is Lady Quimby's room, Simon and Charlotte's mother. It connects with Sir Lionel's, which is across from Lady Charlotte's room. Sir Lionel's is the largest bedroom in the house, with a lovely view of the back garden. It's empty now, too, though."

"I'm surprised Simon hasn't moved in there, then," I said.

Mrs. Devlin looked horrified. "Oh no, sir. That's where Sir Lionel was murdered, you know. Right awful. No one uses that room anymore, the same with Lady Charlotte's and even Lady Quimby's."

"Oh. Understandable, I suppose."

"Yes, Mr. Barrington. But your room is a good one also, a corner room, and it has a private bath. Just this way, sir," she said, continuing forward to a solid-looking door.

Mrs. Devlin opened the door to my room, which opened onto a small vestibule that led to the main room. I must say I was pleased at the accommodations, though secretly disappointed it didn't connect to Simon's room, and it wasn't even on the same side of the house. I looked about the spacious chamber, decorated in shades and layers of blue, but as in Verbina's room, the drapes, bedspread, pillows, and rugs were a bit past their prime.

"A fire has been laid in the grate for you, too, sir. And there's a cupboard to hang up your things besides the chest of drawers there. Is there anything else you require?"

"No, thank you, Mrs. Devlin. I should be fine."

"All right, sir. I hope you enjoy your stay. Please ring if we may be of assistance." She gave a small curtsy once more and left, closing the door behind her, but it wasn't more than a minute before Wigglesworth knocked. He brought my suitcase and train case in and set them down.

"Shall I unpack for you, sir?" he said, slightly out of breath.

"It's kind of you to offer, but no, thank you, Wigglesworth."

I noted a brief look of surprise crossed his face, but just as quickly vanished. "Very well, Mr. Barrington. Will you be needing assistance dressing?"

"Thanks so much, but I can manage on my own."

"As you wish, sir. Should you need anything at all, just ring."

"I will. I suppose people call you Wiggles," I said with a smile, trying to be friendly.

"No, sir, they don't." His tone was formal and dry, as always, his expression blank. I wondered if he ever smiled or laughed.

"You mean with a name like Wigglesworth, no one's ever called you Wiggles?"

"Well, there was a gentleman once, sir, who called me that. *Once*, sir."

"Oh, I see."

"Yes, sir. Good day, sir." He left, and I felt bad if I had offended him, but hoped he would forgive me. I unpacked quickly, then used the bathroom and freshened up. That done, I went out into the corridor, where I ran into Verbina, just coming out of her room.

"All settled in?" I said. She had removed her hat, gloves, and her stole, and looked somewhat refreshed.

"I think so." She lowered her voice and came closer to me. "I do hope we're not imposing too much by being here, though."

I looked at her in surprise. "What do you mean? This was all your idea in the first place."

"I know, I know. But did you hear what Simon said about the servants? Cutting corners, and all that? And what he said about not being able to afford the Jaguar right now, and then there's the worn draperies and furnishings. The family fortunes have dwindled. Simon would be wise to marry that Ruth St. James. Her family is extremely wealthy, and it's good, solid, old money."

"So?"

"So, as I've told you before, marriage is a business, a partnership, a sizing up of what each can bring to the table. Simon can offer Ruth a title, and Ruth can increase the Quimby coffers."

"You are not in the least bit romantic, are you, Auntie?"

"I'm pragmatic and a realist. Happily-ever-after has to be created and bartered for. It doesn't just happen. Now, let's go down to the dining room, it's one thirty."

CHAPTER THIRTEEN

Friday Afternoon, September 17, 1937
Heatherwick

She took my arm and we walked side by side down the broad stairs and into the dining room. Simon and a fetching young fellow I gathered was his cousin were already there. The dining room was well-lit and spacious, though as in the rooms upstairs, the décor was somewhat out of date, slightly faded, and worn.

Simon greeted us at the door. "Are your rooms satisfactory?"

"Oh yes, very much so, quite comfortable, thank you," I said for us.

"Good, I'm glad," he said, though he didn't look happy at all. "Well then, Mrs. Partridge, Mr. Barrington, I'd like you both to meet my cousin, Mr. Walter Wittenham of Munstead Wood in Long Wittenham, just north of here a ways. He'll be joining us for lunch. He's my mother's brother's son, so not a Quimby."

"As you delight in pointing out," Mr. Wittenham said, coming along beside him. "Although with the family curse, I guess I should be glad I'm not."

"How do you do?" Verbina and I said, and then Verbina added, "How nice to meet one of Simon's relatives, a Quimby or not. I'm so glad you could join us for lunch."

"How do you do? Simon insisted on my staying, didn't you, old boy?" Mr. Wittenham said.

"I wouldn't put it that way," Simon said. He moved to the head of the table and stood behind his chair. "Shall we be seated? Mrs. Partridge, please, to my left, Mr. Barrington on my right and, Walter, you can sit next to Mrs. Partridge."

"Delighted," Mr. Wittenham said. He held Verbina's chair for her and then sat down beside her, a broad smile on his face. He was clearly younger than Simon, but not by much, and handsome, with striking features, coal-black hair, and deep brown velvety eyes. His frame was thin and wiry, and I could tell he was in shape and strong. Still, I thought, he wasn't as attractive as Simon.

"Such a lovely room," Verbina said, placing her napkin in her lap and glancing about.

"Thank you. The dining room's a bit large, though. This table can seat at least eighteen comfortably."

"It's exactly as I remember it. Nothing has changed," she said.

"I'm afraid the whole house hasn't changed much since Mother died over twenty years ago. Father didn't like change, never saw the need, and I'm afraid I'm not here enough to give it much thought."

"I think my favorite part is the ceiling mural. It's so colorful, so classic," Auntie said.

Simon glanced up briefly. "Copied from some place in Italy, I think. Perhaps from a church or cathedral, I'm not really sure. My father was fond of it, but personally I think it's a bit much."

"Oh, no, the light from the chandelier really sets it off, in my opinion," she said.

"Well, I'll trust your judgment, Mrs. Partridge. Clearly you have excellent taste. What about the rest of the house?"

"I'd be delighted to give you some ideas if you wish, Simon, but really, it doesn't need a lot."

"No, I suppose not. But still, a freshening might be a good idea. Of course, I'll be getting some expert opinions when Mr. Haines and his friend visit. They've confirmed they're coming the first of next month."

"William Haines?" Verbina said.

"Yes, Mrs. Partridge. He and his business partner were on the ship with us and are acquaintances of mine."

"I'd heard they were aboard, but I wasn't aware you knew them. How nice."

"He's that actor fellow, right? Isn't he a...you know, a, uh, pansy?" Mr. Wittenham said.

"I didn't ask him," Simon said, staring harshly at his cousin.

"Well, that's what I've heard, and I would think *you'd* know. Besides, can you afford to be redecorating right now, Simon?" Mr. Wittenham said.

"What's that all supposed to mean?"

"Well, as the estate steward appointed by your father, I know a thing or two about the finances of Heatherwick, and as your cousin, about you."

"So you've just mentioned. No need to discuss your ridiculous opinions on either topic in front of my guests," Simon said. He turned to Verbina and me. "Let's eat, shall we?" He rang a bell, and Wigglesworth soon entered from the butler's pantry carrying a large ceramic soup tureen, followed shortly by the creamed carrots and bread and butter pudding, which I had never had before but soon discovered was delicious, made of buttered bread, raisins, eggs, cream, and nutmeg. I hadn't realized how hungry I was until the smell of the food hit me.

"Is this all you're serving, Simon?" Mr. Wittenham said, glancing down at his plate. "Are things really that bad?"

"Don't be rude on top of insulting. It's just a light lunch today because it's rather late. Sorry, I know you Olympians do like to eat."

"An Olympian?" Verbina said, intrigued.

"Simon likes to joke, but yes, Mrs. Partridge, I was a pole vaulter, track and field, in the 1928 Summer Olympics in Amsterdam. I was just a lad of nineteen."

"How marvelous," she said. "Do you know Lord Burghley? He medaled in '28 and '32, I believe. Did you medal?"

"Of course I know Lord Burghley, nice chap. And yes, he took the gold in '28 and the silver in '32. As for me—"

"No, Walter did not medal," Simon said.

Mr. Wittenham shot Simon a look. "True enough, cousin, but

at least I was on the Olympic team, which is more than you can say, and I still train, still keep physically fit. Track and field is my sport, though I'm good at almost anything physical."

"Yes, you can climb trees like a monkey," Simon said. "And you rather resemble one."

"I could pin you in a wrestling match. And I could have been in last year's Olympics in Berlin, except Violet didn't want me to go, what with the Nazis and Hitler and all."

"Violet is your wife?" Verbina said.

"That's right, a lovely woman, but a worrier. She begged me not to go to Berlin. Unfortunately, it might have been my last chance to medal. I'm not getting any younger, you know."

"That's so impressive that you were in any Olympics, Mr. Wittenham," Verbina said.

"I suppose so," I said. I didn't like Mr. Wittenham much, if for no other reason than Simon didn't seem to care for him.

"I highly doubt Violet begged you not to go to Berlin, Walter," Simon said. "Not from the way she behaves when I've seen you two together. I rather think she'd be glad to be rid of you for a spell."

"You're just jealous she chose me over you."

"She didn't. Father pawned her off on you to get her away from me. He felt she didn't have a large enough dowry to be a Quimby, and he thought I could do better. But she was clearly in love with me, and she always resented the old man for pushing her on to you. Can't say I blame her."

"Now you're being rude," Mr. Wittenham said. "You never cared for Violet, not in *that* way, but you didn't like her marrying me."

"I'd feel sorry for any woman marrying you," Simon said.

"Do you have children, Mr. Wittenham?" Verbina said, clearly in an effort to change the subject, and I cringed. For once, I wished she'd just shut up.

Mr. Wittenham turned to her, his fingers gripping the table edge. "Yes, we have a son, Cedric. He's nearly four now, growing like a weed. Takes after his old man, if I do say so myself. My wife and I are expecting our second any day now."

"How nice, congratulations."

"Thank you. You see, we will soon have two children, whereas Simon isn't even married yet."

"Uh, do you get to visit Heatherwick much?" Verbina said.

Mr. Wittenham scowled at Simon, who was scowling back at him. "Not much. My home is about an hour and half drive north from here. I had business this morning in Brockenhurst and thought I'd stop by while I was in the neighborhood and go over a few things with Simon since I'd heard he was back."

"If you'd telephoned first, I would have told you I had guests and not to come."

"And next week there would be a different excuse, but there are things we needed to review. In the old days, when Simon's father was alive, we were invited fairly regularly, often overnight. Now I only come when necessary to discuss family business. I'm the estate steward, as I believe I mentioned."

"Yes, you did mention that. Twice now," I said.

"As a matter of fact, the last time we were all here together was the night of Uncle Lionel's death two years ago."

"Oh really?" Verbina said.

"Yes, Mrs. Partridge. I remember that night well. So peculiar," Mr. Wittenham said.

"Must you bring that up again? Can't you let sleeping dogs lie?"

"No. Because it rattles my brain over and over. There are so many odd things about that evening I still can't figure out. A random burglar coming on the grounds, which seems a strange thing to do since the house is so far from the main road..."

"They say he may have been a vagabond, staying in the garden shed, unbeknownst to anyone," Simon said.

"Yes, I'm aware of what they said. Of what *you* said. Convenient, I say. And then this vagabond supposedly climbs that old tree outside Uncle's window, enters, stabs him, steals his wallet and watch, and flees back out the window and down the tree."

"That was the official report, yes," Simon said, irritation in his voice.

"And your friend the inspector constable found Uncle's empty wallet and his broken watch at the base of the tree. So strange."

"What's so strange about it?" Simon said.

"Well, for one thing, why was your father in bed, fully dressed including his shoes at that time of night, when we were all expecting him to return to the drawing room? After all, he'd said he was just going up to get a bromide."

"Yes, he was having trouble with his indigestion again. I remember Wigglesworth bringing him a peppermint tea just after Mrs. Devlin served dessert. Perhaps the bromide didn't help, and he decided to lie down for a bit. I guess we'll never know for sure."

"I guess we never will. Just like we'll never know how that bloody handkerchief of yours ended up on the floor of his room," Mr. Wittenham said, a wry smile on his face that for some reason made me want to slap him. "Funny how, even though you had motive and opportunity, and evidence was even found, the official result was that Uncle Lionel was killed by a random burglar."

"You know, Walter, I never said anything to the authorities, but you had motive and opportunity to kill my father that night, also."

"You must be joking," Walter said, suddenly looking indignant.

"Not a laughing matter. It's well known Father and I quarreled before dinner that night."

"As you two often did."

"*Occasionally* did. And Father jokingly told everyone at dinner he had cut me out of his will and was going to leave everything to you because you had produced a wife and heir, whereas I had not."

"And still haven't," Walter said.

"What more motive would you need than that?" Simon said, ignoring Walter's last comment. "Thinking you were to inherit Heatherwick and all that goes with her? Why not kill my father before he got the chance to change his mind."

"Don't be absurd. I knew Uncle was joking, we all did. Or maybe you're the only one who didn't. Maybe you killed him because you thought he was serious and you were angry."

"I never wanted Heatherwick all that much, so I certainly wouldn't have killed him over it."

"But surely you were angry and embarrassed that night about your father bringing up your lack of interest in women to all of us. I recall you telling him at dinner in this very room that you had no interest in finding a princess and didn't believe in fairy tales anymore, and he said something like, 'maybe you just believe in fairies and would rather find one of those.' Hmm, I wonder what he meant by that."

"He was just trying to annoy me."

"And he did a good job of it, I'd say. You must admit you're over thirty now and *still* haven't married. In fact, when is the last time you were even with a woman?"

"Vulgar. I think I'm through here," Simon said, standing up abruptly and dropping his napkin on his plate.

"Likewise," Walter said, getting to his feet as well. "On that we can agree. The food here is terrible. I'll see myself out."

Simon rang for service. "No, I'll have Wigglesworth show you to the door. Can't risk you pilfering the silver as you leave."

"That's fine," Walter said. "You couldn't afford to replace it. When your father died there was a fair amount of money in reserve, but you've blown through it in two years like a duck drinking water. All that travel and—"

"None of which is your concern," Simon said, his voice rising.

Wigglesworth entered from the pantry as Simon and Walter stared daggers at each other and Verbina and I sat in stunned silence.

"Show Mr. Wittenham to the door and get his hat, Wigglesworth."

"Yes, my lord."

Mr. Wittenham looked at Auntie and me, and then at Simon. "Good day to you, Mrs. Partridge, Mr. Barrington. Simon, give my best to your friend Mr. Haines. I'm *sure* you'll have a marvelous time together." He strode briskly out, an angry smirk on his face, with Wigglesworth following behind.

When they had gone, Simon looked at each of us in turn. "I apologize for that. Family matters should not be shared, nor quarrels done in public. I'm sorry."

"It's quite all right, Simon. We understand, don't we, Heath?"

"Yes, of course. I thought you handled yourself brilliantly. And I bet you could take him in a wrestling match," I said.

Simon smiled unexpectedly. "Thanks for that. I need to speak with Wigglesworth. Please, finish your lunch. I'll be right back." He strode out into the hall, closing the door behind him.

"Well, that was certainly something," Verbina said, pushing her plate away. "I think I've lost my appetite."

"Me too," I said. "I can't say I care for that Mr. Wittenham. He's a drip and a crumb."

"Meaning boring and uncouth," Verbina said.

"Yes! That's a humdinger, Auntie."

"Meaning remarkable or outstanding. You see, I can speak your college slang, but I must continue to remind you, my dear, that you are a gentleman, and a gentleman does not talk like a sophomore in school."

"I'm sorry, you're absolutely right. But he is boring and uncouth, I think. I don't like him."

"Nor I. There's something fishy about him. I wonder…"

"What do you wonder?" I said.

"Well, I'm no detective, but it seems to me that if Mr. Wittenham *did* believe Sir Lionel had changed his will in his favor, that would be a good motive indeed. Besides, he's an Olympian. Simon said Mr. Wittenham could climb a tree like a monkey. Who better to get in a second-story open window and kill Sir Lionel?"

"A vagabond, that's who," I said, but I had to admit hers was an interesting theory.

"Perhaps," she said. "But regardless, it's none of our concern, remember that."

Simon returned momentarily, and though I could see he was still visibly agitated, he put on his best face. "Anyone up for a game of whist?" he said.

"Oh, I do love card games, but I'm afraid I'm a bit tired. Would you mind terribly if I just went up to my room and rested for a while?" Verbina said, standing as I did the same.

"Not at all, please make yourself at home. It's just past two thirty now. Shall I have Mrs. Devlin rouse you for tea?"

"Yes, please, thank you," Verbina said. "I'm sure I'll be much better after a brief nap."

"I'll have her call you at half past three," Simon said as Verbina crossed to the door. I could tell her feet were killing her, but she'd never admit it in front of Simon.

"Have a good rest, Auntie," I said.

"Thank you, dear." She went out to the hall, closing the door behind us.

"Well, how about you, Heath? Two-handed whist?"

"I don't know how to play, I'm sorry."

"Oh bugger, but that's all right. I'd say we could go for a walk in the gardens, but it's started to rain," he said, looking out at the rain-spattered windows. "Chess?"

I shook my head. "I'm afraid I don't know that, either."

"Cribbage?"

My face brightened. "Yes, I know that one. I'll warn you I'm not that good, though."

"Excellent, then we shall play for money."

"What?"

"Just having a laugh, Heath. I don't get many of those, and I certainly need one after that unfortunate incident. Come on, let's go to the study."

"All right, lead the way," I said. We walked into the corridor and crossed to the main hall.

"Come on, the study is just through that door to the left of the tapestry."

"Where does the one on the right go?"

Simon paused. "To a small hall with a door on the right that leads to the library, a door on the left that also goes into the study, and one straight ahead that leads to the billiard room and a lavatory, which was carved out of the old gun room."

"Gun room?"

"Yes, when the billiard room was added on, they also included a vestibule, an outside entrance, and a small gun room. That way the men of the house could go out to shoot game without traipsing through the great hall. Father wasn't much for hunting, so he had the gun room converted to a toilet chamber. It's the only lavatory on this floor, old house you know. Rather inconvenient from the dining room and drawing room, but there was no place else for it."

"I suppose so," I said. "Still, at least it's indoors."

He laughed at that, and I was glad. "Yes, not so much when the house was built." He started moving forward again, toward the left door, and I followed behind, into the study. It was a decidedly masculine room, with dark paneling below solid green wallpaper, a beamed ceiling, and heavy gray and gold drapes that framed the three small windows. On the far wall was a massive marble fireplace with a painting of a distinguished gentleman above it.

"I hate English weather," Simon said, staring out one of the windows at the rain. "Bloody hate it, but at least Wigglesworth has laid a fire. Light it for me, will you, while I get the cards and the cribbage board? There's a match safe on the mantel."

"Sure," I said, walking over to it and doing as instructed. I was never a Boy Scout, but the fire lit on the first try, thanks most likely to Wigglesworth's skills, not mine. I stood and held out my hands to the growing warmth.

"Ah, much better," Simon said, coming up beside me as we both gazed at the flames taking hold of the tinder and the logs. "Sherry?"

"No, I'm fine for now, but please go ahead if you like."

"I do like," he said. "I'd offer you a martini, but I'd have to ask Mrs. Devlin for a pickle."

It was my turn to laugh now. "That's okay, I'm fine, it's a bit early for me."

"Suit yourself." He walked over to the sideboard and poured himself a small glass of sherry as the fire and the warmth grew.

"What's this?" I said, pointing to an inscription carved into the granite fireplace surround.

He walked back over and looked where I directed. "Hmm? Oh, you mean *Quem legari ad id tuam patres tui, Si tibi earn denuo possideres eam*," Simon said.

"Yes, what does it mean?"

"'That which thy fathers have bequeathed to thee, earn it anew if thou wouldst possess it.' It's a quote by Goethe. My father used to recite that fairly regularly to me."

"His way of saying you have to earn your keep?"

"Sort of, I think. He used to explain it by saying I would inherit this place, as he had, but I had to take care of it, make it mine, and earn the right to call it home. He told me his father used to say the same thing to him, and on and on, all the way back to old Sirus, I imagine, right after he had it inscribed."

"Is that Sirus Quimby in the painting?" I said, pointing above the fireplace.

"Him? No, that old boy's my grandfather, Lord Clarence Quimby. Always watching."

"Oh. He's handsome but stern looking."

"Yes, he was rather a severe chap, I'm told. He died before I was born."

"And passed everything on to your father, who in turn passed it to you."

"Yes. I don't know about my ancestors, but for me, earning my keep has been a daunting task. Sure you don't want a sherry?"

"Thanks but no, not right now."

"If you change your mind just say so. Shall we play?"

"Let's."

He brought his glass over to a small game table near one of the windows, not far from the fireplace, where he had set up the board and cards, and turned on a couple of lamps since it had grown rather dark inside. I followed him over and we sat across from each other at the table.

"Cut to see who deals?" Simon said.

"Fair enough," I said. He won the deal, and we began the first game. We played easily, conversing about the weather, politics, and automobiles but avoiding the subject of his cousin, his father, finances, and the ill-fated lunch. Simon ended up winning both of the two games we played. "What do I owe you?"

"I was just having a laugh about playing for money, Heath. You don't owe me anything. Want to play something else? Gin rummy, maybe? Surely you know how to play that."

"I do, but I think I'm played out for now. Besides," I said, glancing at the clock on the mantel below the painting, "it's nearly four, teatime."

"Blimey, you're right, and I've forgotten to ask Mrs. Devlin to rouse your aunt." He stood and rang the bell, which was answered shortly by Wigglesworth.

"Yes, my lord?" he said.

"Tell Mrs. Devlin to wake Mrs. Partridge for tea. We'll have it in the hall. Better light the fire in there, too. This bloody weather..."

"Yes, sir," he said, as he exited and closed the door behind him. Simon put his sherry glass away, and we went out into the hall over to a round table set in the bay window, surrounded by four chairs, opposite a massive fireplace. The windows in the bay looked out onto a flagstone terrace, with the lawns and gardens beyond that.

"Your groundskeeper Bigsby has his work cut out for him," I said, staring through the rain-spattered glass. "The lawns, the gardens, the drive and all must keep him quite busy."

"Yes, but we get a couple of young blokes from the village to do most of the heavy work. They report to Bigsby. It saves his pride, you know. Sometimes that's all we have in life."

"That's kind of you."

"I would hope people can show each other a little kindness and charity now and then, though lately it seems in short supply around here. Anyway, have a seat, won't you?"

"Thanks," I said, choosing a chair so I could both look out the window and at the hall. "This is such a large room."

"The hall? Yes, I suppose it is. It connects the east and west wings of the house, and the ceiling is slightly higher than the rest of the rooms on this floor. I remember some grand Christmas parties here when I was just a small lad. There was always a large tree almost touching the ceiling, four and a half meters high, beautifully decorated. And there were lots of flowers, all kinds. There was dancing, too, with music from a small orchestra, and beautiful women in lovely gowns, handsome men in tuxedos with white tie and tails..."

I closed my eyes briefly, imagining it all. I could almost hear the music. "It must have been grand," I said.

Simon looked thoughtful. "Yes, it was, once. But that was all a long time ago. This is the largest room in the house, but the furniture groupings help break it up. I like it because you have windows to the back here in the bay and windows to the front, on either side of the fireplace."

"So I see. It's spacious, yet intimate and well-lit."

"Exactly. Yet I'm sure Mr. Haines will have some ideas on how to make it even more so."

"I'm sure," I said. I was envious the two of them would be here alone with Simon, and I wished I could stay on. "Have you known them a long time?"

"Not really. We're more acquaintances than friends. We met in New York at the Saint Regis, in the bar, naturally. They seem like solid chaps, though. Ah, here's your aunt now."

I stood and saw Verbina coming in quickly, followed by Wigglesworth. She looked a bit harried.

"I'm so sorry I'm late, Simon, but I was fast asleep when Mrs. Devlin knocked."

"My fault entirely, Mrs. Partridge. I forgot to ask her to wake you until it was nearly four. I do apologize."

"He was engrossed in beating me at cribbage," I said as Wigglesworth tended to starting a fire in the massive fireplace. "He won both games and skunked me once."

"Oh, I do love cribbage. Perhaps we can play three-handed," she said.

"That would be lovely," Simon said. "We can play in here after tea. Let's be seated, shall we?"

He rang the servant call button and then took a seat with us at the small round table in the bay window. Mrs. Devlin entered with a silver tea service and a small silver cake stand, and I watched entranced as she poured and served, never once spilling a drop. The tea was hot, and it was accompanied by all kinds of little cakes and cucumber sandwiches as delicious as those on the *Queen Mary*. I felt once more that I could get used to living like this.

CHAPTER FOURTEEN

Friday Evening, September 17, 1937
Heatherwick

After tea, Wigglesworth cleared the dishes and the tablecloth, then set up the cribbage board and cards for us before leaving once more, perhaps to enjoy his own tea along with the leftover cakes and cucumber sandwiches we didn't finish. This time, Verbina won once, I won twice, and Simon won once. The time flew by, and before we knew it Wigglesworth was back, letting us know that dinner would be served shortly.

"Goodness," Verbina said, glancing at her watch, "it's seven thirty already. How did it get to be so late?"

"Easy to lose track of time on a gloomy day like this, when the lights are on and the fire is so warm and bright, and we're having such a pleasant evening," Simon said. He looked happy and content for the first time since he'd gotten home.

"Quite true. Well, I should go up and freshen before dinner. I'll see you two gentlemen shortly."

"We shall await your return," Simon said with a warm smile.

"*You* shall await her return," I said. "You shall await both our returns, in fact, for I have to go and freshen up, also. But I won't be long."

"I'll hold you to that. Mrs. Thorpe doesn't tolerate people late to the dining room table," Simon said with a mock stern look on his face.

"Yes, sir. I'll fetch the book I've been reading, too. I've marked a passage I thought you might like to hear. Perhaps we can discuss it after dinner."

"I'm intrigued."

"It's by Oscar Wilde."

"Oh yes, you mentioned that book on the ship. Best get going, though, or you'll be late, and there will be no pudding for you."

"All right, I'm going!"

Verbina and I went upstairs together, and we were back in the dining room ten minutes early. Simon was already there, waiting for us. I set the book on the sideboard and we took what by now were our usual seats. The meal was as delicious as I had expected, served with ample wine and good conversation. Any discussion of Mr. Wittenham and other delicate subjects were once more avoided. When the last of the dessert had been polished off, along with hot tea and American coffee, Verbina sat back with a satisfied sigh.

"That was superb. Whoever said English cooking is bland has not eaten Mrs. Thorpe's food."

"I'll be sure and pass on your compliments," Simon said. "And I quite heartily agree. I think it's only due to my traveling so much that I haven't gained a great deal of weight."

"Well, I shall sleep well tonight. And on that note, I think I'll go up to bed, if you gentlemen don't mind. It's been a long day," Verbina said.

"Of course. Breakfast is buffet style in the morning room, just through that door to the right of the fireplace. It's served between eight and ten. Come down as you wish, or if you prefer, Agatha could bring a tray up to you."

"Breakfast in bed? Oh my, doesn't that sound decadent? Do you think she'd mind?" Verbina said.

"Of course not, it's her job," Simon said. "I'll let Mrs. Devlin know in the morning to have Agatha bring you a tray—some orange juice, toast, eggs and sausages, or something. Say about nine?"

"Yes, nine would be perfect. What a treat, thank you."

"My pleasure."

"Are you coming up, Heath?" she said.

"Not just yet, Auntie. Soon, though."

"All right, then. Good night, gentlemen." She stood and so did we, and then she exited through the large doorway into the corridor.

"Fancy a cigar?" Simon said, looking at me.

"Why not?" I replied, though I'd only smoked one once and had nearly choked.

"Capital. Let's retire to the study. I'll have Wigglesworth get the fire going again."

"Good idea, it's gotten a bit chilly. Oh, and I'll just take my book along," I said, picking it up and tucking it under my arm. "I still want to read you that passage."

Once more the two of us traversed the main hall and went into the study. Living in a house like this certainly would be good exercise. Wigglesworth started the fire in the study once more, and then stood.

"Will there be anything else, my lord?"

"I shouldn't think so. Have the guest rooms been addressed for the evening?"

"Yes, sir, of course. Mrs. Devlin attended to Mrs. Partridge's room herself, and I," he looked at me, "turned down your bed, Mr. Barrington, though I couldn't locate your nightclothes. I generally lay them out for the guests."

"Oh, well, I must have forgotten to pack them," I said, embarrassed.

"You could borrow some of mine, if you wish," Simon said.

I very much liked the thought of sleeping in his pajamas. "That would be splendid, if you don't mind."

"Not at all, I have several pair. See to it, Wigglesworth. The blue pair, I think. We're about the same size."

"Yes, my lord."

"Thank you, Wigglesworth," I said. "That was very nice of you to turn down my bed. And thank you for getting the extra pajamas. You certainly keep busy, lighting all the fires, serving dinner, and whatnot."

That faint look of surprise crossed his face once more. "Yes, sir."

"That will be all, Wigglesworth," Simon said.

"Yes, sir. Good night, then, my lord, Mr. Barrington."

"Good night," I said.

When he had gone, I turned to Simon. "That's the second time Wigglesworth has looked at me strangely."

"It's because you thanked him and made a fuss about him turning down your bed."

I cocked my head, puzzled. "What's wrong with that?"

"It embarrassed him. One doesn't thank the servants, Heath."

"I was just being polite."

"They're just doing their jobs. Does a banker thank his tellers every time they wait on a customer? Does a restaurant manager thank his waiters every time they take someone's order?"

"Well, no, of course not, but still—"

"They're thanked at Christmas with a bonus and a fat goose, that's enough. It's just how it's done."

"All right, if that's how it's done," I said. It seemed the more I learned, the more I had to learn.

"It is. Wigglesworth is a proud man, and he takes his job seriously. He's worked at Heatherwick longer than I've been alive. His young niece worked here for a short time, too, as a chambermaid, about three years ago."

"Oh?"

"Clara, her name was. A pretty girl, hard to believe she was old Wigglesworth's niece. Father hired her and then fired her just a few months later."

"Why?"

"Rumor has it she was in the family way. Wigglesworth would never, ever, speak of it, nor would my father, but there was unmistakable tension between them after she left. I think Wigglesworth actually began to change toward my father around the time of the Gypsy girl, but it became more apparent after Clara left."

"Tension?"

"Yes. I'm not sure Father ever noticed, but I did, even as a child. Wigglesworth is a hard person to get to know, quite proper, rigid, and formal, but since I've known him my entire life, I sense things about him, how he feels about people, about guests, other staff members, and how he felt about my father."

"Interesting. Did you ever ask him about it?"

"Ask Wigglesworth? Of course not. He's the butler. I would never intrude into his life like that, though I will say he didn't seem to mourn Father's passing much. Rumor has it, you know, that he's related to Smith Wigglesworth, a noted evangelist who has been influential in the early history of Pentecostalism."

"I'm not familiar with Smith Wigglesworth," I said.

"I don't know much about him either, but I do recall one of his quotes. 'Great faith is the product of great fights. Great testimonies are the outcome of great tests. Great triumphs can only come out of great trials.' Smith Wigglesworth said that."

"Gee, he sounds like quite a figure, all right. And Wigglesworth is related to him?"

"That's what he claims, anyway, and I've no cause to doubt him."

"Gee," I said again. After that, neither of us said anything for a while, and the house fell quiet and still, except for the crackling of the wood now burning brightly in the grate, and the ticking of the mantel clock. Simon handed me a cigar, which he lit for me along with one for himself. I inhaled and started coughing almost immediately.

Simon patted me on the back, which didn't help. "Don't inhale, Heath, just let it happen, naturally."

I coughed a few more times, then tried again, this time managing not to choke.

"You all right, then? You look a bit green."

"Yes, I'm fine, thanks. Sorry."

"Don't apologize. Here, have a brandy. It will help." He poured a drink from one of the crystal decanters on the sideboard and handed it to me before pouring himself one.

I drank, feeling it burn down my throat but almost instantly warm me up. "Thanks," I said, feeling suddenly toasty and comfy.

"You're welcome. Please, sit," he said, indicating one of two dark brown leather wing chairs in front of the fireplace.

"This is nice," I said, sitting and gazing into the flames as I let the heat embrace me.

"Yes. Normally I hate this time of day, right before bed, when the servants have been dismissed and I'm all alone."

"But you're not alone tonight," I said.

"No, I'm not, and I'm bloody glad of it. I'm glad you both came for the weekend, truly." He touched the back of my hand, ever so gently. I was hot before, but now actual perspiration burst out on my forehead. "This is a lonely house, Heath," he said, retracting his hand from mine suddenly as he took another drink from his glass, his cigar in his other hand.

"I suppose it would be," I said. "It is big and isolated for one person. It's a bit of a ways from the village."

"Yes on both counts," he said. "I don't even use most of the rooms when I'm here by myself."

"Seven bedrooms on the second floor alone," I said.

He smiled. "Seven bedrooms on the first floor, actually. This is the ground floor, and above us is the first floor, and then the attic."

"Oh, right. I forgot that's how you do it here in England."

"Differently normal," we both said at the same time, and then we laughed.

"What's up in the attic again?" I said.

"The female servants rooms are up there, along with a couple of guest rooms. The rest is mostly just storage and the old trunk room, but that hasn't been used since the fire."

"Fire?"

"Yes, it happened while I was away at boarding school, so they can't blame me for that. No one was hurt, thankfully, but it destroyed the trunk room."

"How did it start?"

He looked slightly ill at ease. "Faulty wiring, probably. Father never had it investigated, and he didn't report it to the insurance company because he didn't want the rates to go up. You know how those places work."

"I suppose."

"He did have an electrician in afterward, though, to check the rest of the wiring in the house. He didn't want another fire breaking out."

"Certainly not. A wise precaution."

"Yes. There's an old playroom in the attic, too. Charlotte and I used to love to be up there hidden away, just the two of us. In fact, she used to go up there even as an adult. It was her sanctuary, I think."

"Were you close to your sister?"

"Close? I don't know, honestly. I tried to be, at least later on. She was six years younger than me, you see. Our mother died shortly after giving birth to her, so it was just the two of us and the old man. Charlotte was a bit simple, and she struggled sometimes with numbers. She never could get the hang of cribbage or whist, try as we might, or most any game, really, yet she excelled at reading and writing, things that didn't involve other people. She was a pretty girl, with lovely dark auburn locks and curls, and she grew into a lovely young woman, kind, gentle, childlike, but she changed as she grew."

"In what way?" I said.

"She became angry, but I couldn't figure out why. She stopped taking care of herself, not always combing her hair or cutting it short with scissors on a whim. She stopped wearing makeup and powder at times, stopped caring much about her figure. Still, Father adored her, much to my annoyance I have to admit, and I hate myself for having felt that way. Charlotte was an innocent caught up in an awful world, and I should have been there for her. I should have been her protector, but I was too involved in my own self. And then, when she killed herself, I felt like my world had ended."

"I'm so sorry, Simon," I said, feeling like I had opened a floodgate to his emotions. He probably needed to talk about this, but hadn't anyone who'd listen before. "So it *was* suicide? I had heard the official report was that it was an accident."

He took another drink and another puff on his cigar, the smoke billowing about his head. "My friend Alcott, the former inspector constable, stated officially that it was an accident because he thought it would be better for the family. Suicide can be scandalous and goes against the Church, not that I give a damn about that, but she wouldn't have been able to be buried in the family crypt in the churchyard or even have a proper funeral mass. And then there would have been the gossip. I just couldn't subject her memory to all that."

"Kind of him to protect both of you."

"Yes, that's true. I found her, you know, on the night she died. She'd taken that dose of poison. No one knew, and no one knew where she was, no one had seen her. When she didn't come down to dinner, I thought to check the old playroom in the attic. She used to go there fairly often, as I said, sometimes just to sit alone in the dark. Sometimes she actually played with the toys, even when she was grown. I didn't understand it then, but I think I do now."

"Finding her like that must have been awful for you."

"Yes, it was. It still haunts me. She was alive, but just barely. Her last words to me were 'I left a letter for you in the house.'"

"What did the letter say?"

"I never found it. The fact that she told me she wrote that letter is what led me to believe it was suicide, and at first I tried to convince everyone she had killed herself because of it, but Alcott told me why I shouldn't. Maybe it was foolish in hindsight, I don't know. My vacillating from suicide to accident probably raised more questions than not."

"You did what you thought was best at the time, and on the advice of a friend."

"I'm not so sure. Maybe it was an accident. Maybe she was just telling me she'd written me a letter, but it had nothing to do with her death."

"But you don't really believe that."

He shook his head slowly. "No, not really. Suicide just fits with her state of mind at that time. If only I knew what she had written. I've searched everywhere, but this house is so large, a letter like that could be tucked almost anywhere. I still search for it occasionally, though not as rigorously anymore. I've been through every one of the books in the library and in here, page by page. I've looked through all of her belongings, and I've looked through every drawer in the place. I don't understand why she couldn't be more specific as to where in the house she left it, but that was Charlotte."

"I wish I could have known her," I said.

"She would have liked you, I think, and you would have liked her, once you got to know her. But she was a hard person to get to know. At times she was timid and shy, other times volatile and angry. Some people think I had something to do with her death, and that hurts me greatly, truth be told. I don't mind them thinking I had something to do with my father's death, I don't even mind that idiot Walter thinking it, but for any of them to think I would hurt Charlotte…"

"I know you didn't have anything to do with either one."

Simon looked at me, his eyes moist. "Thanks for that, truly. I feel her presence sometimes, you know. I talk to her."

"That must be comforting."

"I don't know. Perhaps. Sometimes it's maddening, because I can almost hear her voice, hear her answering me when I speak to her. Sometimes I can smell her perfume, or I think I catch a glimpse of her going up the stairs to the playroom."

"The playroom and the toys are all still up there?"

"Yes, old, dusty and worn out, like everything else in this place."

"I'd like to see it, the playroom, I mean."

"Why?"

"I'm just curious. Old houses like this fascinate me."

"There's nothing up there that would interest you, Heath. Just dust, ghosts, and memories. I don't want anyone poking around, I'm sorry."

"It's okay, I understand. Sometimes it's best to let the past be the past, I suppose."

"Yes, I'd like to be able to do that myself. Maybe if I could find Charlotte's letter, things would be different depending on what it said. Perhaps I could let her go, let it be, and perhaps she could let go at last. If I could know she didn't blame me, you see? But I haven't found the letter, at least not yet. It's the curse, I think."

"Why do you keep going on about this supposed curse? Even your cousin mentioned it. Can't you just forget about it?"

"Because it's real, it must be. I can't not think it, after all that's happened. Mother dying just after childbirth, Charlotte being simple-minded, my father being killed, the fire, my being the way I am, Charlotte taking her own life. How could it *not* be the curse?"

"It could be a lot of things," I said quietly. "Women have childbirth-related deaths fairly often, and some children are born different. It happens."

"The doctor said mother died of puerperal fever, an infection contracted during the birth. He said it could have affected Charlotte, too, but what does he know?"

"He's a doctor, Simon. I'd say he knows a lot. As for your father being killed, it was a burglar, a vagabond, and you couldn't help that. And if Charlotte committed suicide, her reasons had nothing to do with you."

"You don't know that."

"You're right, I don't. But I do know one thing. You said you think the curse has something to do with you being the way you are, but there's nothing wrong with the way you are," I said.

"Of course you'd say that."

"Because it's true."

"The curse is true. Would you like to see it?"

"See what?"

"The curse, or the words of it, anyway. An old Gypsy woman left it in a bottle on the doorstep of the house. Father kept it all these years. He enjoyed showing it to people, making fun of it." Simon walked over to the bookcase behind the desk and extracted a volume titled *Legends, Myths, and Warriors of the Eighteenth Century*, which he set on the desktop. "Father pressed it in the pages of this book a long time ago."

Intrigued, I moved closer, looking at the yellowed parchment paper Simon took out from between the pages and set upon the desk.

"It's written in blood," Simon said.

I stood next to him then, almost touching him, as I looked at it. "How do you know it's blood? It's not red."

"Blood doesn't dry red, it dries brownish."

"Oh. Well, still. It could be anything, and probably not human blood. What does it say? It's hard to read."

"I can recite it almost from memory," Simon said.

A curse upon the Quimby clan,
every woman, child, and man.
Misfortune and mayhem to them befell
while they live beneath this spell.
The curse will stand and not be broken
until the truest words are spoken
by one whose heart is pure and strong,
who proves his worth and rights the wrong.
Consigned by the Queen to victory
to solve the hidden mystery.

"Gee, I said. "It's poetic, but it's just words on paper, Simon. Meaningless."

"Not meaningless if you're a Quimby. Walter's lucky he's a Wittenham, like he said. You know, I used to think if the curse were ever broken, I'd somehow change. I'd be attracted to girls, to women. Sometimes I still think that."

"Is that what you want?"

"Why wouldn't I? To not have to hide my feelings, my desires? To not have to pretend? I grew up playing a part, as did you, I'm sure, a version of myself I knew others wanted to see, and I had to do it to avoid humiliation and ostracization, but it wasn't the real me, or at least, not the complete me. I just want to be normal."

"I think you *are* normal, Simon, and so am I. We're just differently normal than everyone else, remember?"

He laughed rather bitterly. "Sure, differently normal. But I want to be normal normal."

"You know, I think now would be a good time to read you that passage I marked in my book."

"All right, go ahead."

"It's from Oscar Wilde's *The Soul of Man under Socialism*." I picked up the book from where I had laid it previously and opened it to the marked page. "'The things people say of a man do not alter a man. He is what he is. Public opinion is of no value whatsoever. Even if people employ actual violence, they are not to be violent in turn. That would be to fall to the same low level. After all, even in prison, a man can be quite free. His soul can be free. His personality can be untroubled. He can be at peace. And, above all things, they are not to interfere with other people or judge them in any way. Personality is a very mysterious thing. A man cannot always be estimated by what he does. He may keep the law, and yet be worthless. He may break the law, and yet be fine. He may be bad, without ever doing anything bad. He may commit a sin against society, and yet realize through that sin his true perfection.'"

"You're saying my sin, our sin, is our perfection?"

"I'm just quoting Mr. Wilde, but I imagine he knew a thing or two about such matters. He was in a position such as yours, you know, with societal expectations and whatnot."

"Maybe so, but he didn't have to contend with the Quimby curse."

"You can't blame who and what you are on the curse, or any of what's happened."

"Perhaps not, but it seems logical to me. That's what being like this is, a curse. You should know."

"I do know. I used to think I was the only one in the world who felt this way, but I'm discovering day by day there are lots of us, men and women, and we're not alone."

"I'm alone."

"You've got me."

Simon looked at me, but I couldn't read his expression. "Do I? I've no relations left, really, except for my idiotic cousin."

"Mr. Wittenham, you mean."

"The one and only. We don't get on very well, as I'm sure you've noticed. He's always been jealous of me, jealous of Heatherwick, jealous of the title, of everything, but Father seemed to like him well enough. He even made him the estate manager, as Walter pointed out at lunch. Father *did* make a point of telling Walter he had rewritten his will leaving Heatherwick to him and cutting me out entirely, but it was just a cruel joke. Father was trying to get back at me because of an argument we'd had before dinner. When Father's will was read a short while later, Walter was shocked to find out he wasn't in it at all, except to list him as the estate manager ad infinitum. He did that just to vex me, I think."

"Do you believe your father would have really changed it to cut you out if he had lived?"

"Walter tried to press that point, even hiring a solicitor, but the will stood. So, for better or worse, this place is all mine."

"It's a pretty nice place."

"To visit, perhaps. But do you know what it's like to live here by myself, day after day, with just ghosts and memories to keep me company? Do you have any idea?"

I wasn't sure if I was supposed to answer or not, so I took another puff on my cigar, another drink of my brandy, and looked into his beautiful eyes, noting the fire dancing in them.

"When I am home alone, which is most of the time since Charlotte died, my days are pretty much the same. I take my morning constitutional, weather permitting, and then retire to the library where I meet with Wigglesworth and Mrs. Devlin to approve the menus, get updates on the estate, sign checks, and pay bills. Then I usually read the morning paper and look through the post Wigglesworth has brought, make a few telephone calls, and do some correspondence. After lunch I'll sometimes nap, read a book, or play solitaire until teatime. After dinner, I usually sit in the drawing room and listen to my radio programs. Before bed, I review the evening post, and then it's time for slumber, only to get up and do it all over again, day after day after day, all by myself."

"Gee, that sounds awfully lonely."

"It's hell, in a word. That's why I travel so much, spending my inheritance. Why I don't like being here. I can't even go into Brockenhurst for a pint for people talking and whispering behind my back."

"That's sad."

"Yes. Sometimes when I get too lonely, I drive down to Battramsley, where I'm not really known, and visit a pub called the Pig and Pint for a whiskey and a game of darts. I use a false name and wear old clothes and a cap. It's what I have to do, living at Heatherwick and being who I am."

"Why do you stay, then? Why not sell the house and move to London, get a swanky flat in the heart of it all?"

"It's crossed my mind more than once. But the curse will just follow me wherever I go, until it's broken. And it's my obligation to stay here, isn't it? To society, to the servants, to my heritage, to continue Heatherwick, to marry, raise a family, and pass it on as my ancestors did."

"You told me you don't want that. You want to live your life."

He sighed and turned away. "I know. I always struggle with what I want versus what I feel I need to do. It's hard to explain, and for you to understand, I imagine. But when one is born to a family like mine, when one is a Quimby, a lord, a baron, and is raised to act a certain way, to behave in a particular manner, to realize your life is not really your own, well, it's different."

"Your life *is* your own, Simon, if only you'd realize it. If you sell Heatherwick, the servants may stay on or move on or retire, but they are not your obligation. You said yourself, they're your employees. And Heatherwick will go on with another family who will take care of it."

"I can't imagine anyone but a Quimby living here. I certainly can't imagine Walter Wittenham and his brood. I'm the sixth-generation Quimby, you know. It's my obligation to take care of it, and to pass it on to the seventh." He gazed at the fireplace then. "*Quem legari ad id tuam patres tui, Si tibi earn denuo possideres eam.*"

"That which thy fathers have bequeathed to thee, earn it anew if thou wouldst possess it," I said.

"Well done."

"But you don't have to possess it, Simon. Just because your father bequeathed it to you doesn't mean you have to keep it."

"You don't understand."

I shook my head slowly. "I guess I don't understand, you're right."

"I'm sorry, Heath, truly. Maybe if I ever found that letter Charlotte wrote, perhaps I'd be able to move on, but how could I leave now? What if I sold the house and someone else found it and just discarded it?"

"How do you know she even really wrote a letter? Maybe she meant to but never did."

"I can feel it. She told me she did, and I believe her. Charlotte was never known to lie. I don't think she had it in her."

"I guess it's your life to live."

"For better or worse, Gypsy curse and all."

"Why did this Gypsy curse your family, anyway?"

"My father used to say it was because her daughter was interested in him romantically, and he rejected her. But the old woman told a different tale to anyone who'd listen. She said her daughter and my father were having an affair, and he promised her a piece of land and some money, but when Father found out my mother was expecting with Charlotte, he broke it off cold with the girl and went back on all his promises."

"So the Gypsy mother was angry," I said.

"Yes, and she put the curse on us, and it just keeps coming true. I thought it might end with the old man's death, since he's the one who brought all this on, but it didn't."

"You mean when the burglar killed him."

"That's right. He died in his bed, probably napping."

"How awful," I said. "And the burglar was never found?"

"No. Probably some transient passing through, a vagabond, like I said at lunch. The constable thinks he may have been sleeping in the garden shed."

"Why?"

Simon shrugged. "These are difficult times financially for many people. The Depression has affected everyone, some more than others. It's not too far-fetched to imagine a poor man trudging down the road, seeing the gates to Heatherwick. He slips in, goes up the road to the house unnoticed, and makes himself comfortable out of the weather, in the shed. Then one night, he sees the open window and climbs up the tree to investigate."

"Intending to steal, but he ends up murdering your father in cold blood," I said.

"Yes. Father probably woke up and confronted him. Not being able to escape, the burglar grabbed the letter opener and stabbed him before he could summon help, and then stole his watch and wallet, escaping out the window. They found the broken watch and empty wallet at the base of the tree, dropped in haste by the burglar, no doubt."

"Were there any signs of a struggle?"

"No. Why? What's gotten into your head?"

"Well, if your father confronted the burglar it seems there would have been a struggle. And if he was napping and hadn't woken up, why would the burglar stab him?"

"I guess we'll never know."

"Say, I just had a thought. Was an autopsy done on your father?"

"An autopsy? No, there was no need. Cause of death was a stab wound directly to the heart. The death certificate lists it quite clearly."

"I was just thinking about your father being in bed, fully dressed, and no signs of a struggle. It's a bit odd, don't you think? You said he was probably napping, but surely he wouldn't have fallen asleep so soundly that he wouldn't have heard a burglar enter through the window. He would have had time to react, to pull the bell cord for a servant, to fight off the intruder, or something. Unless..."

"Unless what?"

"I recall one of our conversations on the ship, the second time I went to your cabin, when you pretended to slip me a Mickey. Maybe someone slipped your father a sleeping potion. Perhaps the real murderer drugged him at dinner to incapacitate him. They knew he'd go to his room, probably because he wasn't feeling well. They waited a short while for the potion to take effect, then stabbed him and stole his wallet and watch to make it look like a burglary."

"Because if he had been given a sleeping draught he would have been tired, causing him to lie down and fall deeply asleep. But why not poison instead of a sleeping draught? Wouldn't that have been easier than drugging him and then sneaking in to stab him?"

"Yes, but I've read that most poisons have ill effects, like vomiting or convulsions, things a doctor examining the body would have noticed. But a sleeping potion not so much."

Simon shook his head. "You will indeed make a first-rate detective one of these days, Heath. Or a first-rate murderer."

"The former, I think."

"Good to know. It's an interesting theory, but that would mean someone at dinner that night was a murderer."

"Or attending at dinner."

"Mrs. Devlin?"

"Possibly. Or even Wigglesworth. You mentioned he had brought your father a peppermint tea right after dinner, just after Mrs. Devlin served dessert. A sleeping potion could have easily been put into either of those, the tea or his piece of the dessert. And neither of them seemed too fond of your father. Then there was the incident with Wigglesworth's niece, Clara. Your father tossed her out on the street after she became in the family way. That would certainly have been a motive for Wigglesworth."

"Preposterous. Wigglesworth and Mrs. Devlin have been with the family for years."

"It's been known to happen, Simon."

"I suppose it has, but not with either of them. I still say it was a random burglar."

"Wouldn't it be worth investigating more fully? Perhaps speak to the current constable?"

"And say what? That you have a new theory on what *might* have happened? It's been two years, Heath, too late for an autopsy now. My father is dead and buried, let him rest. Digging it all up again will serve no purpose."

"But there may be a murderer in the house."

"Well, there's no one left to murder but me, and if that happens, so be it."

I stared at him and realized he looked overwhelmingly melancholy again. "All right, have it your way, then." I rubbed my eyes. "I think I'll go up to bed. I'm tired and it's gotten late."

"Yes, good idea. Sleep well. I'll see you in the morning. I may stay up and do some reading for a while. Speaking of that, don't forget your book."

"Right," I said, picking it up. "Good night, then." I tossed my cigar butt in the fire, set my glass on the desk, and left.

CHAPTER FIFTEEN

Saturday Morning, September 18, 1937
Heatherwick

I awoke at eight, and as I yawned and stretched, contemplating getting up, I fingered the fabric of Simon's blue flannel pajamas and thought of him. Though I didn't like wearing pajamas as a rule, I liked wearing his. I liked being here with him, mysteries and curses notwithstanding, and I wished he were sharing this bed with me. With one last stretch and a yawn, I slipped out of the warm, soft bed and opened the drapes. The rain had stopped, but it was still gray, overcast, and gloomy outside. It was chilly inside, too, as the fire had gone out.

I thought briefly of ringing for Wigglesworth but then decided against it as I padded quickly to the bathroom. I washed my face and shaved, dressing in my brown wool slacks, wool socks, a white button-down shirt, red tie, and a cream-colored sweater, with my brown leather loafers. At just a few minutes past nine, I glanced at myself one more time in the mirror and then slipped out into the hall. Mrs. Devlin was just leaving my aunt's room, having brought up her breakfast tray, I imagined. I wondered what had happened to Agatha.

"Good morning, Mrs. Devlin," I said.

She turned suddenly, and I could tell I had startled her. "Oh, good morning, sir. I hope you slept well."

"Quite well, thank you."

"Breakfast is in the morning room, sir, just through the dining room. It's set up on the buffet."

"Yes, I recall. I could use some black coffee and porridge."

"Would you prefer I bring you up a tray, then, also?"

"Oh, no, no. I'll go down presently and help myself."

"Very good, sir. We'll be in to make up your room shortly and lay a fresh fire for you for this evening."

"Thank you."

"Yes, sir. Was there anything else?"

"No, not really."

Mrs. Devlin nodded politely. "I'll leave you to it then, Mr. Barrington." She started toward the door to the servant's stairs.

"Is Lord Quimby up yet?" I said as an afterthought.

"Yes, sir," she said, stopping in her tracks and looking back at me. "The Baron is an early riser. He took his breakfast at eight o'clock sharp and then went for his morning constitutional. He hasn't returned yet."

"Oh." I climbed up the two steps into the long corridor that traversed the great hall below. On the wall opposite the windows was a portrait gallery, with dark oil paintings in heavy, ornate frames, filling the spaces from floor to ceiling and end to end. "Is this the Quimby family?" I said over my shoulder. Mrs. Devlin stepped closer and glanced up at me. "Most of them, sir, yes. It goes rather chronological. This first one there is Lord Sirus Quimby, painted in 1802."

I looked into the dark, narrow eyes of old Sirus. "Severe-looking chap."

"Yes, sir. But then, most folks looked stern in those days. Sitting for a portrait must have been rather dull and tedious."

"I suppose so," I said.

I walked slowly down the long hall, gazing at the many portraits as I went, and I noticed Mrs. Devlin had come up the steps and was following along.

"Why is this hall two steps up from the rest of the floor?" I said.

"It and the two bedrooms here, a guest room and Sir Simon's, are above the great hall, which is taller than the rest of the ground floor, so this area is raised to accommodate that."

"Oh, that makes sense. Who's in this large painting here?" I said, stopping.

"That one is old Lord Clarence Quimby, Sir Lionel's father, and that lady in the pink gown next to him is Sir Lionel's mother, Lady Elsbeth."

"Oh yes. There's a painting of him above the fireplace in the study, too. Simon's grandfather. I can see the family resemblance." I moved a bit farther on and stopped in front of a portrait of a handsome young gentleman sporting a striped coat and white trousers, a dog gazing up at him. "Ah, and here is Simon, I bet. He hasn't changed all that much. Was that his dog?"

"Yes, Mr. Barrington. That was done for his eighteenth birthday. He loved that pup. Buttons, his name was. Mr. Simon was heartbroken when he died."

I looked carefully at the painting, the brown and white dog sitting faithfully at his feet, a red ball in his mouth. Simon looked so happy then, so carefree, just a boy and his dog. Never trust someone who doesn't like dogs, my father always says, and I think he's right. Next to Simon's portrait was a slightly larger one, of an attractive, rather pale, red-haired man with bright blue eyes, dressed in a dark suit. A small but lovely dark-haired woman in an organdy dress stood by his side.

"Is this Sir Lionel and his wife?"

"It is," Mrs. Devlin said. "Sir Lionel and Lady Anne, the Baroness. Lady Anne was the former Anne Arbuthnot, of *the* Arbuthnots, a most noble family, sir."

"How interesting," I said, though the surname was meaningless to me.

"That painting was done just after they were married. Lady Charlotte looks like her, don't you think, sir, like her mother, Lady Anne?" She pointed just a bit farther down to a large painting of a young girl in an ornate gilt frame. I was mesmerized by it, for the girl looked so melancholy, yet so strikingly beautiful. Her expression was strange, though, not a smile, but not a frown, either. "That's Lady Charlotte, sir. Simon's sister, God rest her soul."

I moved closer to it. "She was a pretty girl indeed." I looked back and forth between her portrait and the one of her parents. "She did take after her mother, yet she had her father's blue eyes, I think."

"Yes, she got the best of the both of them. Still, poor Lady Charlotte. She was troubled. She struggled, you know, mentally. She was a bit simple, if you understand, sir."

"Simon mentioned that. How sad."

"It wasn't enough to be put away, sir, but she was forever childlike in many ways. The late Lord Quimby, Simon's father, had that portrait of her painted for her twentieth birthday. Just two years or so before she died."

I stepped closer and realized part of Lady Charlotte's odd expression was caused by a cut in the canvas that ran across the lower part of her face. It had been repaired, but not expertly enough. "What happened here?"

Mrs. Devlin clucked her tongue and shook her head, looking at me. "Isn't that awful, sir? Someone slashed it with a knife not long after it was hung here. Lord Quimby, Simon's father, was quite upset, naturally. He tried to have it repaired, but obviously you can still see it."

"Yes, it gives her a rather peculiar look. Who did it? How did it happen?"

"We don't know for certain, but some say that Sir Simon had something to do with it. Things started happening when he came home from university. It was almost like putting the cat amongst the pigeons, you know."

"Did Charlotte and Simon get along generally?"

"Oh, I suppose so, sir, but he always seemed to be jealous of Miss Charlotte." Mrs. Devlin looked away from me and back at the painting. "My, she loved that dress she was wearing. Pale green silk with a pink ribbon around the waist. It was her favorite. Funny…"

"What?"

"It wasn't amongst her things after she died. I packed everything up myself, and it was all put up in the attic. It didn't even cross my mind at the time, I was so upset. But I was looking at this picture a few months later, and I remembered that dress was missing. She wore it the night her father died, and I don't recall her wearing it since. I can't imagine what's happened to it."

"Maybe you just overlooked it in your state of mind at the time."

"I thought that, too, at first, sir. But I went up to the attic and looked through all those boxes and trunks I'd packed, and sure enough, it was missing."

"Curious. Maybe it brought back those awful memories of the night her father was killed, so she discarded it before she died."

"Queer, it is. If she wanted to get rid of it, she would have given it to me to dispose of. I mentioned it to Sir Simon, but he said I must have been mistaken about it being missing."

"Possible, I suppose."

"Possible but not likely." Mrs. Devlin glanced up and down the hallway, and then lowered her voice, looking at me. "Her death was listed as an accident, but Sir Simon claims it was suicide, you know. At least he did at first."

"I'd heard, yes. How terribly awful."

"But she didn't leave a note, and Sir Simon supposedly found her still alive, but just barely. He claims she uttered something about hiding a letter somewhere here in the house, but it's never been found."

"What do you think really happened?"

"Me, sir? Oh, not my place, not my place to say, sir."

"Clearly you don't think it was an accident *or* suicide."

"Well...no, sir, I don't. I will say that. No more than I think Sir Lionel's death was from a random burglar who'd been living in the garden shed. Not likely."

"So who do *you* think was responsible for Sir Lionel's death?" I said, bristling a bit. "Perhaps Mr. Wittenham?"

She nodded, looking thoughtful. "Aye, it could have been him, I suppose. There are those who think so, I'll admit, and he was here with his wife that night, staying in the room you're in."

"Certainly it could have been him, if not a burglar. Mr. Wittenham had a motive."

"Again, not my place to say, sir, but he wasn't the only one with a motive. Sir Simon was in the house both times, but Mr. Wittenham was only here the night Sir Lionel died. Sir Simon and his father didn't get along, not at all. Frequent arguments, you know. They didn't think we could hear, but we hear most everything."

"That's good to know."

"Oh, not that we mean to, sir. But when the two of them got to fighting, their voices got quite loud."

"I see. So they quarreled regularly? What about?"

"All sorts of things, sir. They butted heads regularly, like an old goat fighting the young one. Lady Charlotte heard those arguments, too. They frightened her. She'd sometimes go up to the attic to the old playroom and hide. I think she knew what happened the night Sir Lionel died, but she was too afraid to say anything."

"The official verdict was that Sir Lionel was killed by a random burglar. Why do you think otherwise? Is it because of the bloody handkerchief?"

Her eyes got wide. "Oh dear, yes, that's another thing. You heard about that, did you?"

"The assistant station manager, Mr. Babcock, mentioned it."

"It's true, sir, about the handkerchief, I mean. I found it on the floor of Sir Lionel's room the next day, almost under the bed. I knew it was Sir Simon's because of his monogram. The handkerchief had Sir Lionel's blood on it, I'm sure. He was stabbed, you know, but the actual murder weapon was never found."

"Yes, I'm aware of that. How do you know it was Sir Lionel's blood?" I said.

"It was a lot of blood. Where else would it have come from?"

"What did you do with the handkerchief?"

"Oh dear, oh dear, oh dear. I didn't right know what to do. I wanted to be loyal to the family, sir, but I felt I should do the right thing by Sir Lionel, so finally I showed it to the inspector constable, I did, and he presented it at the inquiry. Sir Simon said he didn't know how his handkerchief ended up on the floor of his father's room, but he figured he must have dropped it earlier in the day and the burglar picked it up after killing his father, used it, and then dropped it again."

"Maybe he did," I said.

"Oh, not bloody likely, I should think. But still the inspector seemed to believe it. Of course, he and Sir Simon are friends, you know. Can you imagine, sir, Lady Charlotte living in this house with her brother, knowing he killed their father? I'm not saying he did, of course, not my place, but if he did, it must have been awful for her. And perhaps the two of them argued about it. He realized she knew the truth, and he felt he had no choice—"

"So, you're saying he killed his sister, too."

"Oh, it's too awful to think about, sir. And certainly not my place to say."

"Certainly not, and yet you do. If you really think Simon is a murderer, why do you stay here? Surely he's not keeping you against your will. Why don't you go somewhere else?" I said, most annoyed.

Mrs. Devlin looked horrified, perhaps realizing at last that she'd said too much. "Oh, no, sir. I've worked here over thirty-five years, I'm nearly sixty. I couldn't just start over somewhere else, where would I go? There's no jobs to be had anywhere nowadays, you know, what with the Depression and all. I like it here, and Sir Simon is like my own son, he is. I used to change his nappy, I used to give him his baths and put him to bed. I raised him from a baby on, me and Mrs. Strobel, the old nanny. I raised him and Lady Charlotte both. I didn't mean to imply Sir Simon killed them, I was just supposing, you see? Just saying that *if* that's what happened, but of course I don't really think so, oh no. Sir Simon is a good man, a good employer, and he pays better than most. He's not even home very often, he travels so much, and when he is here, he doesn't ask much of us."

"In other words, you're paid well to do little. I can see why you wouldn't want to leave."

"I'm an old woman, sir. Where would I go?"

"I can think of a few places," I said. "I understand Wigglesworth's niece used to work here."

"Yes, Mr. Barrington, she did. Clara her name was, a pretty girl."

"But she didn't stay long, only three or four months."

"That's right, thereabouts. I couldn't say why she was discharged, though there was a rumor…"

"That she was in the family way."

Mrs. Devlin looked embarrassed. "Yes, sir. Oh dear, in my day young ladies didn't let themselves get into situations like that."

"I can assure you, young ladies have been getting themselves into situations like that for thousands of years, Mrs. Devlin. And it takes two, you know."

"I suppose that's true. But still, she seemed to be a nice girl."

"I've no doubt. So, she left abruptly?"

"Without so much as a goodbye. The last time I saw her was just after Sir Lionel's death. She came back and was in the kitchen yard, talking to her uncle Henry, Mr. Wigglesworth. He gave her an envelope, and she left."

"What was in the envelope?"

"Oh, I don't know, for sure, sir. Mr. Wigglesworth never said. I don't think he even knows I saw them out there talking. But I suspect it was money to pay for a doctor for the, you know, the baby, though Lord knows where he would have gotten any spare pounds."

"Something he'd saved up, perhaps. Sir Simon mentioned tension between his father and Wigglesworth. Were you aware of that?"

"Oh, I don't know much about that, sir. I do know ol' Mr. Wigglesworth didn't care much for Sir Lionel, but he wouldn't talk about it, with me or anyone that I know of."

"Did he always feel that way about Sir Lionel?"

Mrs. Devlin looked thoughtful. "Well, no, I don't think so. It started when there was the problem with the Gypsy girl, you know, and it got worse after his niece was let go."

"Interesting. So, this playroom up in the attic you mentioned, Mrs. Devlin. Simon mentioned it, too."

"Yes, sir, that's right. The children used to use it. It was quite gay up there once upon a time. And as I said, Lady Charlotte used to hide up there even as a young lady. I think she felt safe."

"May I see it?"

"The playroom, sir?"

"Yes, and the rest of the attic. I find these big old country houses fascinating."

She looked doubtful. "Oh, I don't know if Lord Quimby would approve, sir. The female servant rooms are all up there, along with the storage and trunk rooms, a couple of guest rooms, and the playroom, as I said."

"I don't think Mr. Simon would mind my having a look," I said, neglecting to mention that I'd already asked him and had been told no. "And I really have no interest in the female servant rooms, just the playroom."

"But he's funny about certain parts of the house, sir. Ever since I questioned him about Lady Charlotte's missing dress, he's kept that storeroom locked, and only he has the key. The playroom isn't locked, but I don't think he'd like anyone nosing about."

"I'll be as quiet as a mouse, Mrs. Devlin. Show me the way, will you? Besides, Sir Simon is still out on his walk, as you said. He'll never know, and I'll keep your thoughts and opinions about what you think happened to his father and his sister to myself."

She fidgeted with the collar on her dress and said "Oh dear" again a time or two under her breath, but then she nodded. "Yes, sir, just this way, then. I suppose maybe he wouldn't mind, but we'll have to be quick." We went back down the hall, around the corner, and past the main staircase to a door that led to a narrow staircase going up. "This is the attic stairs, sir, used by the family and guests. There's a spiral staircase just back there for the servants that goes from the basement all the way to the top."

We climbed up to the attic, her in the lead, the stairs creaking and groaning under our weight. "Watch your head up here, sir."

"Right, thanks," I said, as we reached the top, arriving under the eaves.

"The playroom is just here, Mr. Barrington. The family guest rooms are toward the front."

"Where does that go?" I said, gesturing at a door farther down a narrow hall.

"To the trunk and storage rooms. Beyond that are the female staff quarters. The male servants are housed in the basement, near the kitchen."

"You said the playroom is here?"

"Yes, sir." She looked troubled and fidgeted with the collar of her dress once more, but finally she opened a door just to our left, cringing as it squeaked rather loudly. "This is it, Mr. Barrington. The playroom," she said, turning on an overhead light.

It was under the right rear gable of the house, above Aunt Verbina's room, I imagined. It was quite spacious, filled with toy trains, a puppet theater, chests of clothes and costumes, musical instruments, balls, hoops, and child-sized furniture. The walls had been painted with circus animals and tents, the wide plank wood floor covered in multicolored rag rugs. The three narrow, arched windows overlooking the back garden had faded red, green, and yellow curtains covering them. I walked around the room slowly, the floor creaking every once in a while beneath my feet, and kicking up dust from the rag rugs.

"I'm surprised they've kept all this," I said between sneezes.

"God bless you, sir. Sentimental, perhaps, but most likely just forgotten. Out of sight, out of mind, you know."

"I suppose."

"It's probably been twenty years since Sir Simon played up here, though as I said, Lady Charlotte still came here often up until the day she died a year ago."

"To do what?"

"Hide away from the world, maybe. She was a sad child, an unhappy young lady, as I said before."

"Why do you think that was?"

"I think she was born sad, sir. Goodness knows Sir Lionel doted on her, so it wasn't for lack of attention, but she always seemed wistful and afraid of life. Perhaps it's because she never knew her mother, or felt guilty because of her mother dying right after her birth."

"Perhaps. Well, I can see how revisiting a room like this, full of happy memories, would be a good place to escape to, then."

"Yes, I suppose so, Mr. Barrington."

I marveled at a little wooden pirate ship in the corner, battered and bruised, just big enough for two or three children to sit on the deck. Next to it, a boy's blue and yellow cap hung from the yellowed tusk of a massive dingy gray elephant, with one eye missing. I wondered if the cap belonged to Simon. There was a little playhouse, too, with a small door and curtained windows that opened and shut. It was probably five feet tall, and about five by eight feet, with window boxes filled with silk flowers, a porch light that turned off and on, and even a little mailbox beside the front door. The inside of the house was filled with child-sized furniture, rugs, and dishes.

"Isn't that something?" the housekeeper said. "The lights even work, and at one time it had running water from a hose, but it leaked, so Sir Lionel had it disconnected."

"It's certainly something any little girl would love," I said. On the far wall of the playroom stood a little wooden spindled baby crib, and a shelf behind it held four dolls, three female and one male, dressed in finery from at least twenty years ago. As I got closer, I noticed all three of the girl dolls had been disfigured. One was completely beheaded, another had her hair chopped off, and the third had her face burned beyond recognition.

I shuddered and turned to look at Mrs. Devlin. "This doesn't look like typical child's play. What happened?"

She clucked her tongue again and pursed her lips. "I think it was Sir Simon again, Mr. Barrington, if you don't mind my saying so. Notice the boy doll is untouched. Lady Charlotte loved those dolls, so he did it to torment her, would be my guess." I tried to picture

Simon playing up here as a little boy, wearing that blue and yellow cap, running around in knee britches and bare feet, tormenting his little sister.

"I don't have any siblings, but I understand older brothers often torment the younger ones. It's what children do," I said.

"That may be, sir, but like you said before, that is more than normal child's play. It's not right, what he did to those dolls." She picked up one of them and examined it, shaking her head before putting it back on the shelf. "Frightening, really."

Both of us heard the creaking and groaning of the stairs just then, and we jumped in unison.

Mrs. Devlin looked panicked. "That may be Lord Quimby back from his walk. He can't find you here, sir, hide. There, behind the puppet theater."

I felt foolish yet terrified at the same time, the sight of those disfigured dolls still fresh in my mind as I crouched down behind the puppet theater just as the door from the hall squeaked open.

"Mrs. Devlin," I heard Simon say.

"Oh, my lord! You gave me a fright."

"I heard footsteps up here, and I thought I heard voices. What are you doing? Why are you here?"

"I thought I heard a mouse."

"That must have been a noisy mouse. Who were you talking to?"

"I heard scratching and squeaking, you see, as I was coming up to go to my room. I came in here to investigate. I was just muttering to myself."

"I see." He didn't sound convinced. I heard his footsteps as he began walking about, stopping every now and again. "Any sign of it?"

"Any sign of what?" Daft old woman.

"The mouse, of course. Any droppings? Anything chewed?"

"Oh, no, no sir, not that I can see, but this is the time of year they find their way indoors, you know."

He sighed audibly. "Yes, that's true. Better check the guest rooms and the rest of the attic. Be discreet. I don't want word of mice getting out to our guests."

"I understand."

"I suppose we should get another cat or two just to be safe. It's been a couple of years since old Mittens died."

"Cats are good luck for a house, they say."

"Well, we could certainly use that. Ask about in the village and the local farms and see if there are any kittens, though it may be the wrong season. Have them let you know."

"I will do that, Baron."

"Good." He looked about, taking it all in. I could just see him through a crack in the fold of the theater walls, and he looked lost in thought. "It's been a long time since I've been up here. I mean, except for last year when I found Lady Charlotte, of course." His expression was suddenly morose.

"Yes, milord. That was an awful night. I'll never forget it."

"I remember some good times, though, too, when we were young, playing with Charlotte, or playing by myself or even old Walter, back when we were just children."

"Yes, sir, I remember that, too."

"Time goes by. Look, there's my old puppet theater, a little worse for wear. Remember the show Charlotte and I put on for father and the staff?"

"I do recall that. Your father got it for you and Lady Charlotte for Christmas and you two put on a show you wrote yourself."

"That's right. Oh, it was terrible." I heard him laugh softly as the footsteps grew closer to me. I held my breath.

"I remember that, my lord. I thought it was quite entertaining. You were a creative lad, and so artistic. Always playing dress-up."

"I suppose so. Long-ago times. It looks so small now, it all does. Charlotte and I both fit back there with room to spare, now I doubt I could fit by myself."

The footsteps grew closer still, and I could feel my heart pounding. I also felt another sneeze coming on, and I scrunched my face up tight.

The sound of something falling stopped him in his tracks, but I couldn't see what it was.

"Oh dear, one of the dolls fell off the shelf," Mrs. Devlin said. "I must not have put it back properly."

"What were you doing with it?"

"Oh, I was just uh, checking to see if a mouse had maybe climbed up there, you see."

"Well, pick it up and put it back properly."

"Yes, my lord. Oh, look at your old pirate ship, sir. Remember that time you rode it down the stairs and broke the mast?"

I heard Simon chuckle then as he turned to look at it. "Oh, I'd forgotten about that. Father was furious, but it was worth it." He was moving away now. "I couldn't sit down for a week after that."

"Perhaps you might think about donating all this to charity, sir. I know some children would be so happy to have these things."

The footsteps stopped again. "Donate? This was our childhood. The happy part of it, anyway. Somewhat happy. Sometimes happy. Memories."

"Might be good to get the toys dusted off, my lord, put to good use again."

His laugh this time wasn't cheerful but more of a snort. "Father always said these toys would belong to our children someday. Some of them were his when he was a boy. That top over there, for one, the hoops, that old ball, and those marbles."

"Memories, sir."

"Yes, memories of him. This little rocking horse belonged to my mother, I'll keep that. And the wooden cup and ball toss game was hers, too, so that can stay, though I never was very good at it. The rest box up and give away, then clean this room top to bottom. It's filthy."

"Yes, my lord, if you're sure."

"I guess it's time," Simon said. "If I ever have children of my own, they'll get new things without so many memories attached. As for those dolls, I'll put them in the storage room with Charlotte's other things."

"Very good, sir."

"By the way, did Agatha bring Mrs. Partridge her breakfast tray?"

"Oh, Agatha was a bit under the weather this morning, my lord, so I took it up myself, sir, just a bit ago."

"Fine. And Mr. Barrington? Has he been down to breakfast?"

"I don't believe so, my lord, not yet."

"It's nearly ten, he must be sleeping in. Oh well, good for him. Keep the breakfast things out until he's finished, no need to rush. I'll be in my room until lunch. I'm afraid I have a bit of a headache."

"I'm sorry to hear that, my lord. May I bring you something?"

"No, I'll be all right, Mrs. Devlin. Let me know if you see any signs of mice." I heard his footsteps, then the hall door squeaked open and closed, and I breathed a sigh of relief as I climbed out from my hiding place.

Mrs. Devlin held a finger to her mouth indicating silence until she was sure Simon had gone down. She spoke then, softly, almost in a whisper.

"That was a fright. My poor heart is pounding," she said.

"Mine, too. Lucky that doll fell off the shelf when it did, or he would have found me for sure."

"Oh, indeed, sir. Funny about that, though. I'm sure I set it back properly before. Perhaps it was the ghost of Miss Charlotte distracting Sir Simon from finding you. I feel her presence sometimes, you know."

"I don't put much stock in ghosts, Mrs. Devlin, but I'll thank her anyway. Now I need to get down for breakfast," I said with one last sneeze.

CHAPTER SIXTEEN

Later Saturday Morning, September 18, 1937
Heatherwick

I went down to the morning room and found a delicious assortment of sausages, eggs, bacon, toast, black pudding, tomatoes, mushrooms, hot American coffee, and tea. Verbina was there, seated at the table, white linen napkin in her lap and a cup of black coffee before her.

"Good morning, Heath," she said.

"Auntie, I'm surprised to see you here. I thought you had a breakfast tray sent up to your room."

"Oh I did, and it was lovely and decadent, but they brought me tea, and I just really wanted coffee. I didn't have the heart to say anything."

"Ah, I see. Well, let me get a plate and I'll join you. Frankly I'm glad for the company. I've had a morning already."

"Goodness, do tell. I'm intrigued."

I filled up a plate and a cup and took a seat, recounting for her the details of the upstairs portrait gallery and the slashed painting of Charlotte, my experience in the playroom, the disfigured dolls, and how the doll fell off the shelf and saved me from almost being discovered hiding behind the puppet theater. When I had finished, Verbina looked surprisingly cross.

"Honestly, Heath, what would have happened had you been caught nosing about in the attic? It would have been most embarrassing. And grilling the servants like that, good heavens. We're Simon's guests, and we must respect his wishes and his home. Your actions reflect on me, too, you know, for better or worse. I told you before none of this is our concern."

It wasn't exactly the reaction I was expecting from her, and I instantly knew she was right, but I was still glad I did it. "Of course you're spot on, Auntie, you always seem to be. I'm sorry, I guess curiosity got the best of me."

"You should be sorry. I'm surprised at you, dear. This is not our business."

"I know, it's just that there are so many questions."

"The only question I want answered is if there is any more coffee," she said, putting her empty cup back on its saucer.

I shook my head. "I'm afraid I took the last of it. I don't think they expected you to be down, so they probably only made enough for two cups. I'll ring for some more." I pressed the call button on the wall, then took my seat again next to her.

"Thank you. I find I need at least two cups in the morning to get me going, the stronger and blacker the better," she said.

"I'm the same way. It must run in the family. Dr. Feldmeyer drank coffee, as I recall, even at dinner."

"That psychiatrist from the ship? Well, he was an American, too, you know. We Americans are fond of our coffee."

"Yes, we certainly are. I was thinking of him earlier, about what he had said—"

Wigglesworth entered from the pantry, which also serviced the dining room, before I could finish my thought. "You rang, sir, madam?"

"We seem to be out of coffee," I said.

"My apologies, Mr. Barrington. I'll bring some back momentarily."

"Very good," I said, resisting my natural urge to say "thank you."

"Yes, sir." When he had gone, I looked at Verbina once more and sighed, my earlier thought forgotten. "I've thought it several times this trip, but I truly could get used to living like this, Auntie," I said, leaning back, having finished most of my breakfast.

"The finer things in life never take long to get used to, and I hope you'll have many opportunities to enjoy them. You and Simon were up rather late last night, yes?"

"I guess. We had a long talk about this supposed Quimby curse, his father's death, his cousin, his sister, even Wigglesworth."

"It's nice he feels comfortable enough with you to talk of such private matters."

"Yes, it took some doing, but he finally opened up. And by the way, you'll be happy to know I slept in pajamas last night. Simon loaned me a pair of his."

Verbina raised an eyebrow ever so slightly. "How interesting. Did you sleep in your own room?"

"Of course I did. Where else would I sleep?"

"How—"

She was interrupted by the return of Wigglesworth with a silver coffee pot, filled to the top. He poured a fresh cup for each of us, then set the pot on the sideboard. "Will there be anything else at the moment?" he said, looking at each of us in turn.

I looked at Verbina, but she shook her head. "No, that will be all," I said, and then, perhaps because I didn't want Verbina to continue with the topic of Simon's pajamas, I said, "You've worked for the Quimbys a long time, haven't you, Wigglesworth?"

"Yes, sir, since I was fifteen, Mr. Barrington. I started as a hall boy and worked my way up to footman, underbutler, and finally butler."

"But there are no hall boys, footmen, or underbutlers working here now," I said.

"That's correct, sir. I'm afraid the house isn't what it once was, but then, nothing is, I suppose. The family stopped employing hall boys and footmen several years ago. And Sir Lionel's father was the last to have a valet, though I have acted unofficially in that capacity along with my other duties for both him and Sir Simon. It was a different house when the Baroness was alive. She was a kind woman, lovely and charming. It was tragic when she died. Things changed. And then Sir Lionel's murder…"

"I understand you were the one that found Sir Lionel that night."

"Heath, I don't think—" Verbina started to say.

"I'm just curious, Wigglesworth. Simon said I should ask you about it," which was a lie. I wondered what had gotten into me lately.

"Did he, sir? How curious."

"I asked him about it, but I think the memories were too painful, so he suggested I ask you. Do you remember that evening?" I said, pressing.

He looked uncomfortable, but finally he said, "Yes, sir, if that's what Lord Quimby wishes. It's a night I shall never forget. It was July twelfth, a warm evening, a tad muggy even."

"And Mr. Walter Wittenham and his wife were spending the night, along with their baby, I believe?"

"Yes, sir. Sir Lionel was fond of Mr. Wittenham and was anxious to see the baby, Cedric, who was just a little over a year old at that time."

"And I understand Simon and his father had had a disagreement that night before dinner," I said.

"I really couldn't say, sir."

"You couldn't or you won't?"

"It is my job, Mr. Barrington, to be discreet when it comes to private matters, and to never say what I think unless asked directly by my employer, sir."

"All right, fair enough. But it is true that at dinner Sir Lionel told Mr. Wittenham and everyone else that he had changed his will that day to give everything to him instead of Sir Simon," I said.

"Simon mentioned that, but he said it was a joke."

"Mr. Wittenham seemed to believe it, sir."

"Possibly. So, what happened after dinner?"

"Dinner ended just after nine. I brought Sir Lionel a peppermint tea right after dessert, as he suffered from indigestion."

"Sir Lionel asked for the tea?"

Wigglesworth's expression changed ever so slightly. "Well, no, sir, but he had frequent digestive problems, so I just assumed he'd want some, and I was correct. A good butler must anticipate the needs of his master."

"I suppose so. What then?" I said.

"Mrs. Devlin came in to help with clearing the dessert. Lady Charlotte excused herself to go to her room and get some aspirin because she had a headache. Sir Lionel finished his tea and said he was going up to his room to get a bromide. Mr. Wittenham went outside for some air and a cigarette, and Mrs. Wittenham went up to the nursery to check on the child. Sir Simon, by his own account, went to his room to get a gramophone record he was anxious for everyone to hear, 'Goody, Goody,' by the Benny Goodman orchestra. A most unusual name for a musical selection, I must say."

I smiled. "It's a catchy tune."

"Indeed it must be, sir."

"What then?"

"Before Sir Lionel went up, he asked me to serve mulled wine in the drawing room, so I went downstairs to the kitchen to prepare it."

"How long did that take you?" I said.

"Actually, while I was down in the kitchen, a call came from Lady Charlotte's bedroom. Mrs. Devlin usually attends to her, but she'd just gone up to her room in the attic to get her kidney pills, so I answered the call. Surprisingly, Sir Simon was the one who opened her door. He told me Lady Charlotte was in the bathroom, and he had pressed the button by mistake. He didn't seem quite himself. He was out of breath and nervous, but it's not my place to question, sir."

"How interesting," I said.

"I also noticed, sir, that there was a roaring fire going in her fireplace, along with the smell of something odd burning."

"But you said it was a warm night," I said.

"Yes, sir. I found that and the odor peculiar, but again, not my place to question, sir."

"So, then what?"

"I went back downstairs. Strangely I ran into Mrs. Devlin in the upstairs hall."

"But you said she had gone to the attic for her pills. Why was it strange to run into her?"

"Because there was no need for her to be there, you see. The servant stairs go from the basement to the attic. She had no reason to stop on the family bedroom floor. Servants must, above all else, be unobtrusive, unnoticed, and never be where we shouldn't be, sir."

"Did you ask her about it?"

"I did, sir. She told me she was coming to check on Lady Charlotte as she was concerned about her having the headache, but I told her I'd just come from her room and that Sir Simon was with her. We both returned to the kitchen together."

"Curious."

"It did seem odd to me, but then Mrs. Devlin can be an odd woman."

"So, you brought up the mulled wine," I said.

"That's right. I was the first one to the drawing room. Mrs. Wittenham arrived just after me, looking a bit distressed. It seems young Cedric was not behaving for the nanny. Mr. Wittenham came in shortly after, complaining about the heat of the night and the humidity, and I noticed he was perspiring. Sir Simon and Lady Charlotte came in together. Sir Simon, still in his green jacket and trousers, had the gramophone record under his arm, and Lady Charlotte, in a yellow dress with daisies on it, took a seat in the chair by the window while Simon put the record on the gramophone player. Sir Simon seemed agitated, and Lady Charlotte looked tired. It was nine thirty by that point, and I asked Sir Simon if he would like me to serve the mulled wine or wait for his father."

"What did he say?"

"He told me to serve and then go check on Sir Lionel if he hadn't come in by the time I was finished."

"And he didn't come in."

"No, sir. I went upstairs to his room at about a quarter of ten to see what was delaying him and if I could be of assistance. I knocked on the door, but there was no answer, so I entered and saw him in bed, fully dressed, his shirt blood soaked, his cold eyes staring lifelessly at the ceiling. He was dead, I knew it instantly."

"He was fully dressed in his bed?"

"Yes. I can't explain it unless he was just having a lie-down, but that seems unusual for that time of evening. The others were still expecting him in the drawing room. He even had his shoes on, and I have never known Sir Lionel to lie down in his bed with his shoes on. His trousers were also undone, probably because of his indigestion. The windows were open, too, although it was a warm night, as I mentioned, so that in itself wasn't all that out of the ordinary."

"Extraordinary, the whole thing," I said. My mind was whirling.

"I should say so, sir. I immediately phoned for the inspector constable from Lord Quimby's telephone in his room, and then returned to the drawing room to break the news to the others."

"What did you tell them?"

"I asked to speak to Sir Simon privately, and when he stepped into the corridor with me, I told him something had happened to their father, that he was dead in his room."

"And what was his reaction?"

"He was shocked, sir. He asked if I was sure, and I assured him I was. I told him it appeared to be foul play and that I had telephoned for the police. He went back into the drawing room to inform the others, then he told me to follow him upstairs to his father's room. We stayed there together until the constable arrived."

"I can see why that's a night you won't forget," Verbina said.

"Indeed, madam."

"Well, thank you, Wigglesworth. Let's not talk of this with Lord Quimby, though. No need to upset him by bringing up unpleasant memories," I said. "I think that's why he wanted you to tell me." That was a believable lie, I thought.

"Mum's the word, sir, madam," he said, and went back into the pantry, the door closing behind him.

"Honestly, Heath. Simon never told you to ask Wigglesworth about that, did he?"

"No, Auntie, not exactly. But I wanted to know –"

"Didn't I just finish telling you that none of this is our business, and that we're Simon's guests? I'm not sure exactly what kind of friendship you and Simon have developed, and I'm not sure I want to know, but I do know he would not tolerate you snooping about, questioning the servants, and prying into his family's personal matters, no matter how close you two have grown."

"I know, you're right," I said, feeling a tad ashamed. "But what do you make of it all?"

"What I make of it is of no concern to anyone."

"But you seemed interested in Wigglesworth's account of the fatal night. *You* don't think Simon is a murderer, do you?"

She set her coffee cup down and looked at me with a disapproving gaze. "All right, since you won't let this go, I'll just say this. You think you know Simon, but you don't."

"So, you *do* think he's a murderer?"

She gave me an exasperated look. "Oh, for heaven's sake. If I were a betting woman, which I'm not, my money would still be on Walter Wittenham."

"Really? Why?"

"Because he thought at dinner that Sir Lionel had changed his will in a fit of anger at Simon. He probably believed Sir Lionel would regret that decision and change the will back the next day when calmer heads prevailed."

"But he didn't really change the will," I said.

"Yes, but Mr. Wittenham probably *believed* he had. Even Wigglesworth thought so. After dinner, Sir Lionel told everyone that he was going up to his room to take a bromide. Walter went outside for some air and a smoke. Perhaps he saw Sir Lionel's open window and the tree beside it. Remember, Mr. Wittenham is a former Olympic athlete. He may have scaled that tree, looked in, saw Sir Lionel, and seized the opportunity to stab him."

"But there was no sign of a struggle."

"Oh? Well, perhaps Sir Lionel was in the bathroom when Walter entered. Walter waited outside the door until he came out, then he stabbed him and dragged his body onto the bed. All he had to do then was climb back down and return to the drawing room. Remember, Wigglesworth said Mr. Wittenham was perspiring, which would be only natural after going through all that."

"Goodness, Auntie, for not wanting to pry into family matters, you've certainly given this some thought."

"You asked, I told you."

"You certainly did. It could have just as easily been Mrs. Wittenham, though, you know. She had as much to lose as Walter did. Or should I say as much to gain? And she may have been angry with Sir Lionel for pawning her off on Walter to get her away from Simon. I wonder if anyone corroborated her story about going to the nursery with the nanny?"

"Hmm," Auntie said.

"And what about Mrs. Devlin? Wigglesworth found her on the family bedroom floor that night, and he admitted her being there was strange."

"Yes, that's true. I suppose it could have been Mrs. Wittenham or Mrs. Devlin, but stabbing someone is a man's murder, in my opinion."

"Don't be discriminatory, Auntie."

"Me? Never, but I think a woman would choose a gun or poison."

"Tell that to Lizzie Borden," I said.

"She was acquitted. Still, it could have been anyone, I suppose, that killed Lionel Quimby. Even Wigglesworth, when it comes right down to it."

"I was thinking that, too."

"But the damning evidence is the bloody handkerchief with Simon's monogram on it."

"Yes, found in Sir Lionel's room. But if you're right about Mr. Wittenham, perhaps he pilfered the handkerchief before going outside with the idea of using it to frame Simon."

"That was my thought, also. Walter certainly dislikes Simon, perhaps enough to frame him for murder. And I'm sure Simon has a whole drawer full of monogrammed handkerchiefs. He has probably left them all over the house, so it would have been an easy thing for Mr. Wittenham to obtain."

"It makes sense," I said. "Actually any one of them could have pilfered one of his handkerchiefs."

"I suppose," Verbina said.

"And what are your thoughts on Lady Charlotte's death?" I said.

"Suicide—on that I have no doubt. She was distraught over her father's death and prone to depression. It's quite logical."

"Yes, quite logical indeed."

"But the official verdicts, Heath, were that Sir Lionel's killer was a burglar and Lady Charlotte died from an accidental poisoning, and I say we leave it at that and drop the whole thing. If you like Simon as much as you say you do, you don't want to make him angry with you."

"But nobody seems to believe the official verdicts. Everyone seems to think Simon killed his father and perhaps even his sister. So why would he be angry with me if I could prove to the world that he didn't?"

"And what if you actually end up proving to the world that he is a murderer?"

"He's not, I know it. He'll be overjoyed when I prove his innocence. Maybe he'll even ask me to stay on here, as his companion or something."

She seemed to be studying me. "His companion or something. If I didn't know better, Heath, I'd say you have a schoolboy crush on Simon."

I felt my cheeks grow red, and I spilled my coffee. I laughed falsely. "What? A crush? Don't be ridiculous."

She looked at me sideways. "Oh, I'm just being a silly old woman, don't mind me. It's just the way you look at him, little things I've noticed. Like a student who admires his teacher, like any young boy admiring someone older."

"He's only eight years older than me."

"True, true."

"And I'm not a schoolboy anymore, Auntie, as you keep reminding me."

"Also true. But you still have some growing up to do. Things like this are a passing fancy, a phase so many young men go through."

"I don't know what you're talking about. I'm not going through a phase. He's just a friend, and I admire him."

"Naturally. I would never say you're not right, not me. You just need to get out more. Date, flirt, expand your horizons with a few pretty young things."

"Are you implying my thoughts of Simon are anything but friendly? Do I have something to prove?"

"No, dear. Certainly not to me, anyway. I'm sure it's all harmless and my imagination."

"Of course it's your imagination."

"It's just that I've had some experience in these things, you know. And I don't want to see you hurt, by Simon or by the world. I can't speak for Simon, but the world can be vicious and cruel. You may end up proving something, all right, but it might not be what you want it to be."

"What kind of experience have you had in these things?"

"That's not important. What is important is that you tread carefully in matters of the heart, and that you always be discreet and cautious in all things. It's fine and dandy to want to play house with Simon, the way young men sometimes do, but another thing entirely to live it."

"I hardly think Simon and I have been playing house, Auntie. We're just good friends." How did she know? I felt myself starting to perspire.

"You've been playing at something, my dear, both of you, and you can't fool me, try as you might. And I understand more than you think I do. Remember what I said before—you can trust me with secrets."

"Perhaps, but we're not playing house," I said. "Hmm. Playing house, playing house…"

"What are you on about?" she said, a quizzical look on her face.

"Hmm, what? Oh, I just thought of something, that's all. I wonder…"

"You're getting too old for this nonsense, Heath. Simon's not one of your bohemian friends from school. It's time to grow up, once and for all."

"I'm sorry, Auntie, but I need to go, will you excuse me?"

"Where are you off to?"

"To play house." I got up and gave her a peck on the cheek, then left hurriedly, through the dining room, out into the hall, and up, up to the attic.

CHAPTER SEVENTEEN

Saturday Afternoon, September 18, 1937
Heatherwick

My mission successful, I searched next for Simon, expecting to find him in his room. When he wasn't there, I checked the rest of the house and finally found him in the study, sitting with a snifter of brandy before the fire. He was staring into the flames looking lost.

"I thought you were in your room," I said as I came up beside him and stood next to his chair. "Mrs. Devlin mentioned you had a headache."

He looked up at me, his eyes red. "I *was* in my room, and I still have a headache. A right bloody throbbing one. Aspirin didn't seem to help, so I came down here for something stronger. That hasn't done much good either, though."

"Early in the day for a brandy, isn't it?" I said. "It's not even noon."

He looked over to the mantel clock. "Five minutes of, close enough. Did you want something?"

"Yes, I wanted to talk to you."

"I wanted to talk to you, too. Remember when you asked about the playroom yesterday?"

"Yes?" I said cautiously. Did he suspect I'd been in there? Did he know?

"I went up there today, thought I heard footsteps. Turns out it was Mrs. Devlin looking for a mouse. God knows there are often plenty of them about this time of year."

"Oh, I suppose so." So much for him not wanting his guests to know about the mice.

"I hadn't been there since the night Charlotte died. It brought back so many memories going up there again. I can't stand it, Heath, I just can't. I told her to box everything up and get rid of it, once and for all."

"That may be wise. Speaking of that, Simon, I have something for you. But before I give it to you, I'd like to ask you something, and I'd like you to tell me the truth."

He looked at me in surprise, setting his glass down. "What's this about? You seem so serious."

I took a deep breath. "I am serious. I want you to tell me what really happened the night your father died, and who really killed him. And I want you to tell me the truth, the whole truth."

"I don't know what you're talking about." He picked up his glass again and took a drink.

"I think you do, and I think you'll be interested in what I have for you when you tell me."

"What do you have for me?"

"First, tell me who *really* killed your father."

He finished the drink, set the empty glass down, and slowly rose to his feet, holding on to the mantel to steady himself. I wondered how many brandies he'd had already. "What do you mean, Barrington? What are you getting at? It was a burglar. We've been over this."

"That's not what really happened, though, is it?"

"It's all in writing in the official report, if you care to read it. I'm sure it's in a file down at the police station, not that it's any of your business."

I looked at him straight on. "You told me yourself there was tension between your father and Wigglesworth going back several years, but that it got worse after he fired Clara, Wigglesworth's niece."

"Yes, what of it?"

"Why the tension? I asked myself. And why was it so hard to keep the undermaids? You told me yesterday Agatha and Bonnie have only been here a little over two years, hired just before your father died. But the other staff members have been here thirty plus years. Why?"

"Young girls come and go. They don't have the work ethic the older ones do."

"Or is it because your father drove them off? He wanted more from them than just dusting and cleaning. Sexual favors, if you will."

Simon scowled. "That is rude and presumptuous. You don't know what you're talking about."

"Don't I? Wigglesworth slipped a sleeping draught into your father's peppermint tea. It'd be easy enough to do. Sir Lionel hadn't asked for the tea but drank it anyway when Wigglesworth brought it to him. Your father then went upstairs to take a bromide. Only he quickly became drowsy and passed out on his bed. Enter Wigglesworth, on the excuse that he was checking on Sir Lionel after he served the mulled wine in the drawing room. Wigglesworth stabs him through the heart, then he takes the watch and wallet, empties it of cash, which he later gives to Clara in an envelope in the kitchen yard, and then drops the empty wallet and the watch out the window."

"Ridiculous, utter nonsense."

"Mrs. Devlin saw him give Clara an envelope a few days later. You know it's true."

"So what? She's his niece."

"Yes, but in that particular envelope was payment taken from your father's wallet for a doctor because she was in the family way, and your father was the man responsible. But let's get back to the night of the murder. After killing your father, Wigglesworth took out a handkerchief of yours that he'd stolen, wiped up some of the blood, maybe cleaned off the murder weapon, which he pocketed to discard later, and then intentionally dropped your handkerchief on the floor of Sir Lionel's bedroom. He went back downstairs and announced your father had been murdered. He may have been planning on killing him after answering Miss Charlotte's call button, but he ran into Mrs. Devlin in the hall, delaying him."

"So the butler did it? That's absurd, Heath. Stop playing amateur sleuth. Wigglesworth would never kill my father."

"He chose that night because the house was full of suspects. Maybe he thought they'd pin it on Mr. Wittenham, or you obviously, because of the handkerchief. It would have been easy for him to obtain one from your room."

"You're crazy. There's no proof."

"Maybe, maybe not. But if I present my theory to the new constable, they'll at least question Wigglesworth. Maybe he'll ask Clara what was in that envelope her uncle gave her and she'll have to explain. The local paper would run a story, open the investigation again—"

"That would destroy and humiliate him and Clara. You can't do that. Wigglesworth didn't kill my father, I swear to you."

"I know that," I said softly, watching him. "At least I do now."

"What? What do you mean? What are you on about?"

"The fact that you know Wigglesworth didn't kill your father means you know who did."

"So that was a ruse? A game?"

"Call it what you will. Wigglesworth was a plausible suspect, but your reaction tells me he's innocent."

"All right. We both like games, so I'll play. Who do you think really killed the old man?"

"Why don't you tell me?"

"Oh, no. This is your game. Please continue. I'm absolutely fascinated, but let me get another drink first." He picked up the empty glass and walked somewhat unsteadily toward the sideboard, returning shortly with it three-quarters full. "Now then, pray tell, who do you think did the deed that dark night? Extra points if you say Wittenham."

I shook my head slowly. "No, sorry. Not your cousin, though I almost wish it had been. I'm sorry to say it, Simon, but *you* took your father's wallet and watch and threw the wallet out the window after you'd emptied it so it would look like a burglary. A few days later, you gave the cash to Wigglesworth to give to his niece, though you most likely didn't tell him where it came from. It was probably only fifty or perhaps a hundred pounds, but it made up in some small part for how she was treated by your father, and helped with her doctor bills."

He laughed now, spilling some of his drink. "Are you saying *I* killed him? Damn you, read the report. It was a *burglar*."

"No, Simon, it wasn't," I said softly. "I'm sorry, but you know it wasn't. You concocted that story, and your friend the constable probably went along with it out of loyalty to you and the family. I really wish you had trusted me enough to confide in me fully."

He looked angry and confused. He clenched his fists and stepped closer to me. I could smell the alcohol on his breath. We stared at each other intently and I wondered if he was going to strike me. I reached out slowly, gently, and touched his cheek with the back of my hand. He flinched and then suddenly relaxed. His expression softened, his eyes became moist and even more red.

"You *can* trust me, Simon. Will you tell me the rest of what happened, please?" I said. "It's time to confess. Keeping it in is killing you."

He took a large gulp of brandy. "All right, bloody hell, all right! Fine, I did take his wallet and watch. And the money. You were close, it was sixty-three pounds and some odd change."

"And you gave it to Wigglesworth to give to Clara to pay her medical bills."

"Yes. My father never admitted it, but I knew he was responsible for Clara being with child and so did Wigglesworth. And when the bastard found out she was expecting, he fired her and threw her out in the street without even a letter of reference."

"Harsh."

"Yes, so I had no problem taking the watch and wallet off his cold, dead body. I tossed them both out the window hoping to make it look like a burglary. It wasn't well thought out, but I didn't have much time to think. It wasn't premeditated."

"No, it wasn't. You had only moments to figure out what to do."

"That's right, but I didn't kill my father, Heath."

"I know you didn't."

He looked surprised and shocked. "For God's sake, why are you doing this to me? I thought we were friends."

"We *are* friends, Simon. That's why I'm trying to help you. It was Charlotte. Your sister killed your father, didn't she? She was tormented. Her disfigured dolls, her slashed portrait. Everyone thought she killed herself because she was heartbroken over your father's death, but she wasn't, was she? He did things to her, awful things no father should ever do. People said she was daddy's little girl, the apple of his eye, but they didn't know the dark, awful truth, did they?"

Simon shook his head slowly, tears welling up in his eyes. "No, they didn't. I didn't either, for quite some time," he said, so quietly now I had to almost put my ear to his mouth in order to hear.

"I think I know what happened," I said. "He followed her up to her room on the pretense of getting the bromide. He went into her room, as he had done so many times before, but she refused him that night. He got angry and attacked her, tearing and ripping her favorite dress, the green silk one with the pink ribbon. She grabbed the letter opener off her desk and thrust it into him in self-defense. And that's where you came in, isn't it?"

"That's right, though how could you have known?" Tears were running down his cheeks now.

"You mentioned to me last night Sir Lionel was stabbed with a letter opener, but no murder weapon was ever found, so how could you have known that's what was used? Then I remembered Mrs. Devlin telling me how practically everything in Charlotte's room was monogrammed, including that letter opener. Certainly you couldn't let anyone find it, so you wiped it clean of blood and prints and put it back on her desk."

"Charlotte loved monograms," Simon said. "She gave me all those monogrammed handkerchiefs. I got a box of them for nearly every birthday."

"Tell me in your own words, please, what happened that night. The complete truth this time." He slumped back down into the wing chair as he wiped away his tears with one of his monogramed handkerchiefs. I sat on the floor at his feet, my hand on his knee. After a couple more swallows of his drink, he spoke, looking down at me tenderly. "I went to my room that night to get a phonograph record I thought everyone might enjoy hearing, only it wasn't where I left it. I searched around before recalling Charlotte had borrowed it earlier. Her room is next door to mine, so I went out in the hall and knocked. There was no answer, so I opened the door and went in.

"Father was standing there, and as he turned to me I could see blood pouring out of a wound in his chest. His eyes were crazed. He tried to speak but no words came out. I noticed his trousers were undone and sagging. He staggered to the servant call button and pressed it before I could stop him. 'Call the doctor, call the constable,' he finally managed to say, as he coughed up blood, looking at me imploringly. I glanced at Charlotte. She was trembling in fear and shock. Her dress was torn and bloodstained, her face frozen in terror. In her hand she clutched the bloody letter opener, snatched up from the nearby desk. I looked back at my father and realized what had happened. Suddenly it all made sense. Everything did. I punched him hard in the face and he collapsed and died."

"I would have done the same, Simon. What happened next?"

"I pried the letter opener from Charlotte's hand and wiped it clean with my handkerchief, which I stupidly thrust into my pocket. I put the opener back on the desk, grabbed a clean dress from her wardrobe, and gave it to her, instructing her to go in the bathroom and change quickly. While she was doing that, I lit a fire in the fireplace and got it to a fairly good blaze. When Charlotte had changed, I snatched up her bloody, torn dress and threw it into the flames. When Wigglesworth knocked on the door, I told Charlotte to go back into the bathroom and take a sedative. I told Wigglesworth I had pressed the call button by mistake and he wasn't needed. I wasn't very believable, but I was making it up as I went along.

"When he was gone and the coast was clear, I dragged Father's body across the hall to his own room, put him in bed, opened the windows, emptied his wallet, and threw out the wallet and his watch. Then I left, my heart pounding. My handkerchief must have fallen out of my pocket as I was dragging him into his bed. I went back to Charlotte's room, grabbed the record, and the two of us went down to the drawing room as casually as we could. The sedative Charlotte took had calmed her considerably and she was groggy, but we tried to behave normally. I knew no one must find out she killed him. They'd have locked her away in an asylum, you see? I couldn't have that. It would have killed her, and me."

"I'm sorry," I said.

"Thank you. But I ask you again, how did you know? The letter opener notwithstanding."

"I didn't, at first. I started putting the clues together, though. I saw her disfigured dolls in the playroom—"

"The playroom? I told you I didn't want you to go there."

"I know, I'm sorry. But it wasn't just the dolls. I also saw her portrait in the hall that had been slashed across the face. And then I remembered something a psychologist at our dinner table on the ship had said, a Dr. Feldmeyer. He said people who have been sexually abused often exhibit self-doubt, self-loathing, and anger, and often blame themselves for the abuse, sometimes to the point of hurting themselves, or in extreme cases even suicide. Charlotte blamed herself for her father's abuse. She hated herself, hated being pretty, hated attention. She disfigured her dolls, cut her own hair, stopped wearing makeup, and slashed her own portrait across her face, didn't she?"

He finished his brandy and set the glass down, slowly, deliberately, and then looked at me again, touching the top of my head with his hand, stroking my hair. "Yes, though I didn't understand why at the time. Everyone thought *I* had mutilated those dolls and slashed her painting."

"Understandable, I suppose. Then there was Charlotte's dress that night. Mrs. Devlin mentioned upon my seeing the portrait in the hall that the dress Charlotte wore in it was her favorite, a green silk with a pink ribbon about the waist, and she was wearing it the night her father was killed. But Wigglesworth said Charlotte was wearing a yellow dress with daisies when he saw you and Charlotte in the drawing room before discovering your father's body. Why would she change out of her favorite dress so close to bedtime? Because her favorite dress was ripped, torn, and bloodstained, that's why. Wigglesworth mentioned seeing a roaring fire in the fireplace when he went to her room that night, even though it was a warm evening, and he reported an odd burning odor. The only thing I could think of was that you wanted to destroy something, though I wasn't sure what until he mentioned Charlotte was wearing a different dress moments later, and I recalled Mrs. Devlin saying the green silk dress wasn't amongst her things when she packed them up for storage after Charlotte's death."

"I did burn it, and it did give off a foul odor. Charlotte didn't want me to destroy it, but there was nothing else to be done. It couldn't have been cleaned or repaired without arousing suspicion."

"I suppose not."

"I never dreamed they'd try to finger me, but Mrs. Devlin found my bloody handkerchief on the floor of father's room the next day. I never noticed it when I went back in with Wigglesworth to wait for the constable. So people think I killed him and Charlotte was covering for me. People think she was so heartbroken over the whole affair, she killed herself. Or worse, that I killed her because she knew. I've had to live with that. So many regrets. Mostly I regret not realizing sooner what my father was doing to Charlotte. After she killed him, I figured out at least some of the things she had been going through. I tried to protect her, to make up for lost time, but it was too little, too late. So, I guess in some ways people are right about that. I suppose I did kill her."

"You didn't, Simon."

"In some ways I did. I should have known. I should have done something. Charlotte told me it started when I was twenty-two and away at university. She was just sixteen."

"A long time ago."

"Yes, I suppose so. As I said, I wasn't home much then. I came back for summers and holidays, but I honestly had no idea what was going on. When I *was* home, I could see Charlotte was acting differently, that she'd changed, but I didn't know why. I was actually jealous of her relationship with the old man, how he doted on her, bought her pretty dresses and things, talked about her all the time. I felt neglected. But after she killed him, she told me everything. Apparently, he used to take her to the trunk room in the attic, but after the fire up there, which I believe she started, he began coming to her room late at night. She told me she'd lie awake in the dark, staring at that doorknob, waiting for it to slowly turn, and for him to come in, wearing only his robe. It sickens me that I could have been so blind to it, so naïve. She was only a child, and his daughter!"

"It doesn't matter to people like that, Simon. Your father also molested, or tried to, most of the undermaids, didn't he? It's why they never stayed long. Wigglesworth may never have known or wanted to believe the whole truth about Sir Lionel, but certainly after his niece Clara ended up with child and was discharged, at that point he began to suspect, and his attitude toward your father changed even more."

"He suspected more than I did. But I don't think Wigglesworth knew exactly what was going on with Charlotte. He wouldn't have stood for it. He adored her, we all did. I think he thought it was just the undermaids the bastard was molesting, which is bad enough, but at least they were adults."

"You can't blame yourself. You were young and away much of the time, as you said."

He laughed bitterly, withdrawing his hand from my head and getting to his feet. "Father wanted me away as much as possible. One summer he even sent me to Canada for a holiday, all expenses paid. I was grateful. Grateful! Once the old man was dead and I realized all that had transpired, I tried to make things right. I tried to help her, but it was too late. I couldn't reach her, I couldn't help her, I was as helpless as she was. And then she killed herself, a year later, which caused me to be racked with even more guilt, wondering if covering up her deed had been the right choice." He filled his glass once more and sat back down.

"After she was gone, why didn't you come clean, tell the truth about everything?"

"Who'd believe me? I had no proof. Besides, it would implicate me in the murder, covering up and destroying evidence. And I couldn't have Charlotte's name dragged through the mud, her memory sullied. It would have made things worse, not better."

"Charlotte had nothing to be ashamed of. She did nothing wrong. Nothing. But Charlotte is dead. Protecting her now is only hurting you. You had no way of knowing what your father was doing to her. You can't blame yourself."

"Oh, but I *can* blame myself, and I do a bloody good job of it nearly every day. I should have known. Charlotte became more and more withdrawn as time went by, but I couldn't figure out why. I blame myself for not being closer to her, for not being able to protect her from him. And I blame myself for not being able to help her after his death. Once more I didn't know how to help, and I've had to live with that every second of every day since. I feel like she blamed me for not knowing, not stopping him. I was her big brother…"

"Maybe this will help," I said. I reached into my suit coat pocket and extracted the envelope I'd found. I stood then, and held it out for him.

He stared at it over the top of his glass. "What is that?"

"I found Charlotte's letter, Simon, the one you've been searching for."

His eyes grew large. "What? Where? How? I don't believe it. I've searched and searched for it, tearing the house apart, going through drawers, books, albums. Where could you have found it?"

"She didn't hide it in Heatherwick per se, Simon, but in the little mailbox of the playhouse. It's been there all this time. That's the house she meant. The playhouse. Her refuge."

He looked at me in disbelief, and then reached out a trembling hand for the envelope, dropping his glass to the floor, where it shattered.

"I…I can't believe it."

"It's true. Read it," I said.

He opened the envelope and withdrew the letter.

Dear Simon,

Don't blame yourself, please, and know that I don't blame you, I never could, I never would. You didn't know what Father had done to me. I kept it from you, and so did he. I can't go on feeling as I do and having to keep that secret. I killed him because I couldn't stand him touching me anymore, doing those awful things to me, and I couldn't stand myself, which is why I'm taking this poison. Death, I fear, is the only escape for me. What comes before death? What is death's prelude? Is it life? Is it end of life? Is it despair? I don't know, my love, but I never was very good at figuring things like that out. I do know that what comes after death is peace, and that is something that has eluded me for a very long time. Don't hate me and please don't forget me.

Love,
Charlotte

He shuddered then, and began weeping openly, sobbing almost uncontrollably, gulping for air, his chest heaving in and out. I reached down and lifted him up, taking him into my arms, comforting him as best I could. I felt awful that I'd brought this on, but maybe I helped somehow. We stood like that for some time, his head on my shoulder, arms wrapped tightly about my waist.

After a while he spoke, softly. "She didn't blame me, then."

"No, Simon, she didn't. She loved you. She knew you were trying to help."

"But it was too late."

"It was, then, but it's not now. It's not too late to help yourself," I said. "It's time to forgive yourself, to vindicate yourself, and to believe you are worthy of happiness."

He lifted his head and looked at me, wiping away tears. "I'm not so sure."

"I am."

He unwrapped his arms from my waist, took out a handkerchief, and wiped his eyes and blew his nose.

"You've always been sure of me. You never doubted me, did you, Heath?"

"No, not really."

"Why? You're the only one."

"Call it instinct, maybe. I don't know. When you care about someone, you have to believe."

"Thanks for that, truly." He looked about, and then back at me. "So much has changed. You've changed."

"Me? Really?"

"You've grown up a lot since that first day I met you on the deck of the *Queen Mary*. You're more confident, self-assured. Strong, mature, and not naïve anymore."

"In some ways I feel the same as I always did, but in other ways I feel like I've aged a hundred years."

"Well, you're a pretty handsome hundred-year-old," he said with a soft smile in his eyes. "You know, perhaps I need to change, too. Maybe I *can* find it in my heart to forgive myself now."

"It's what she would have wanted. A good start would be to give Charlotte's letter to the new inspector constable. Explain what happened. You can leave out certain details if you want, to protect yourself. It's the proof you need."

"But Charlotte's memory, her reputation..."

"Charlotte was an innocent. She did nothing wrong, Simon. Your father was the real culprit, and the world needs to know that."

"Yes, yes, I suppose you're right, the world needs to know, so that perhaps others will speak out against their attackers as well."

"Exactly. To know they've nothing to be ashamed of. Make the call to the constable, Simon, then you can move on with your life."

"My life, yes. I suppose I should get on with it, I'm over thirty, you know."

"And quite a catch, I must say. Do you mean to marry that woman?"

"Ruth? Maybe. I don't know yet. I know you don't understand, but it's not just producing an heir or living up to expectations."

"What else is there?"

"Money, if I may be frank. I don't think I can sustain Heatherwick without an influx of it, and Ruth St. James has it in abundance."

"You could sell. Maybe we could be confirmed bachelors together in a little flat in London."

He looked at me, just the hint of a smile on his lips, his eyes still red and puffy. "That would be nice. Nice for me, not so nice for you."

"Why not?"

"Because you don't belong in England, not long term. Trouble is coming, big trouble. It's brewing and bubbling like mad right now, and it's only a matter of time until it boils over. I'd like it if you were far away from it all and safe, back in Milwaukee, Wisconsin."

"Then why don't you come to America, too?"

He put his hand on my shoulder. "England is my home, Heatherwick is my home. I must stay and do what I can to defend her, to help her, to aid in any small way I can."

"Oh. So that's it, then."

"I'm afraid so, yes. That's how it must be."

"It wouldn't do any good to say I don't agree."

"No. Please try to understand."

I stared at him, fighting back tears of my own. "Okay."

"You can write to me. I'd be chuffed to bits, truly."

"I...I will, of course. And you write to me. And come visit."

"Perhaps. You know, you'll make a good policeman, and I have no doubt you'll make inspector someday."

"Detective."

"Oh, right. You'll make a jolly good detective one day, Heath Barrington. And you may end up meeting somebody closer to home."

"Not likely, Simon. Not anyone like you."

"No, not like me, at least I hope not! But a nice chap, someone you can be a confirmed bachelor with. As for me, well, time will tell. Who knows? I can't think of these things now."

"Promise me you'll at least forget about that bloody curse now," I said.

He laughed for the first time in what seemed a long time. "I just realized something. There is no more curse, you broke it. Don't you see? It's bloody amazing!"

"I broke it? How? What do you mean?" I looked at him, puzzled.

He strode purposefully to the book behind the desk and extracted the old parchment paper, reading aloud from it.

A curse upon the Quimby clan,
every woman, child, and man
Misfortune and mayhem to them befell
while they live beneath this spell.
The curse will stand and not be broken
until the truest words are spoken
by one whose heart is pure and strong,
who proves his worth and rights the wrong.
Consigned by the Queen to victory
to solve the hidden mystery.

"Yes, yes, I remember what it said, but what does it have to do with me?" I said, walking over to him.

"Don't you see? You spoke the truest words, and your heart is pure and strong. You believed in me, you told me you loved me. And you solved the hidden mystery."

"Well, gee, I don't know about all that. I mean, I figured a few things out—"

"You did more than that. And you were sent by the Queen, the RMS *Queen Mary*, just like the curse said."

"Now, that's a bit of a stretch, don't you think?" I said.

"I don't," he said firmly. "You were consigned by the Queen to victory, and you proved your worth and then some. I think you were brought here for a purpose, and you've been my salvation in more ways than one. I can't thank you enough, Heath Barrington. You changed my life. You saved my life."

"Well, gee, you changed my life, too, you know, forever and always. I…I do love you, I really do."

He came close to me once more and touched my cheek with the back of his hand. "You're sweet, but this isn't *Wuthering Heights*. No pining away for me, no tragedy, all right? I'm just your first love. There will be at least one other, I predict. It's the way of the world. For me, too, perhaps."

"All right. But first loves are important, and ones you never forget, at least I hope not."

"Never," he said. "You, Heathcliff, are unforgettable."

CHAPTER EIGHTEEN

Sunday Morning, September 18, 1937
Heatherwick

Charlotte's letter was in the hands of the new inspector constable, along with my written statement, and no doubt the revised and complete story would soon be reported in the local paper as well as the *London Times*. At least as complete as it needed to be. Some details would remain just between Simon and me.

"Well," Simon said as the three of us finished our breakfast in the morning room, "this has been quite an interesting weekend, to say the least." He looked tired but content.

"I'm afraid I'm still in the dark about most of it," Verbina said.

"I'll fill you in once we're back in London, Auntie. We have lots of time."

She looked at her watch. "Yes, but not lots of time to catch our train. We'd better get upstairs and finish packing."

"I'm nearly done," I said.

"Of course you are. Men."

I smiled. "Can't help it. You go on up, I'll be along shortly."

"I'll send Wigglesworth up in a few moments to get your bags, Mrs. Partridge, and yours when you're ready."

"Okay," I said. "I won't be long."

Verbina looked at each of us. "Well, thank you again for everything, Simon," Auntie said. "I hope we meet again soon."

"I hope so, too." The three of us got to our feet and Verbina exited.

"I hate goodbyes," Simon said to me when she'd gone.

"Me, too. Let's not, then."

"All right. What should we say instead?"

"Nothing. Just nothing. No words are needed, I don't think. And I won't forget you."

He smiled then. "I should hope not. You have my underwear to remember me by."

I laughed. "That's right, I do. I shall treasure it always. Say, I just realized I never gave you anything in return."

"But you have. You've given me more than I ever dreamed possible. You've given me my freedom, my self-worth, and my reputation back."

"Aw, I just figured out where the letter was and what had really happened, that's all."

"Both priceless gifts. But if you mistakenly leave a pair of *your* underwear in your room so I have something tangible to remember you by in case we never meet again, well…"

I grinned. "Now, that's a fair trade. But I predict we will meet again, Simon, you'll see. It's destiny."

"Well, destiny is not to be trifled with. What was it Charlotte said in her letter? 'What is death's prelude? Is it life?' To that I say a resounding yes. Yes, Charlotte, life is death's prelude, it must be. We must live our lives, each of us, to their fullest. And to help others do the same, to realize we are all more alike than different, and that it's okay to be…"

"Differently normal," we said together.

MYSTERY HISTORY

The *Queen Mary*'s maiden voyage was in May of 1936. She is permanently docked now in Long Beach, California, operating as a luxury hotel.

The *Queen Mary*, on average, took just over four days to cross from New York to Southampton. Her top speed record was three days, twenty-two hours, and forty-two minutes. She held the Blue Riband for speed in 1938 and maintained it until 1952, when she lost it to the S.S. *United States*.

The RMS *Scythia* was the longest-serving liner in the Cunard line until the *QE2*. Her maiden voyage was in 1921, and she sailed until 1958.

The New York Cunard Pier, number 90, was indeed located at number 90, 711 Twelfth Avenue.

The Stock Market Crash of 1929 plunged the country and the world into the Great Depression, resulting in breadlines and soup kitchens, and high unemployment that lasted until the United States entered World War II in 1941.

William "Billy" Haines was a huge movie star with MGM in the 1920s and early 1930s. When he refused to marry to hide his homosexuality, MGM fired him, and he started a successful interior design business with Jimmie Shields, his life partner.

Buster Crabbe was an American swimmer and film actor. He won the 1932 Olympic gold medal, which launched his movie career. He was often featured shirtless to show off his physique.

Upton Sinclair was an American author who wrote nearly one hundred books. He won the Pulitzer Prize for fiction in 1943.

Ellis Parker Butler, another of the authors mentioned in this book, was an American writer who died on September 13, 1937. He is most famous for his short story "Pigs Is Pigs."

Jean Harlow was an American film actress and sex symbol up until her untimely death at age twenty-six in 1937.

Wiltons of London was established in 1742, famous for oysters, wild fish and game, and traditional, old-fashioned hospitality. Wiltons gained a Royal Warrant for supplying oysters to the royal household in 1836.

The Woodlawn Woman's Club of Chicago was active between 1895 and 1954.

Lord Burghley did indeed win the gold medal in the 400 meter hurdles at the 1928 Summer Olympics, and in April of 1936 he did run one lap (400 yards) in evening dress around the promenade deck of the *Queen Mary* in under sixty seconds.

Smith Wigglesworth was an actual evangelist in England, who lived from 1859 to 1947. He dedicated his life to preaching and ministering, employing methods that were often controversial.

Heatherwick is a fictional estate created by the author, but the villages of Brockenhurst, Long Wittenham, and Battramsley are real.

Europe entered World War II on September 1, 1939. The United States got involved after the bombing of Pearl Harbor on December 7, 1941.

The working title of this book, believe it or not, was *The Curse of the Swamp People*. It was later changed to *The Quimby Curse* and finally to *Death's Prelude*, as suggested by Sandy Lowe of Bold Strokes Books. A much better choice!

About the Author

David S. Pederson was born in Leadville, Colorado, where his father was a miner. Soon after, the family relocated to Wisconsin, where David grew up, attending high school and university, majoring in business and creative writing. Landing a job in retail, he found himself relocating to New York, Massachusetts, and eventually back to Wisconsin. He and his husband now reside in the sunny Southwest.

His third book, *Death Checks In*, was a finalist for the 2019 Lambda Literary Awards. His fourth book, *Death Takes a Bow*, was a finalist for the 2020 Lambda Literary Awards.

He has written many short stories and poetry and is passionate about mysteries, old movies, and crime novels. When not reading, writing, or working in the furniture business, David also enjoys working out and studying classic ocean liners, floor plans, and historic homes.

David can be contacted at davidspederson@gmail.com or via his website, www.davidspederson.com.

Books Available From Bold Strokes Books

Death's Prelude by David S. Pederson. In this prequel to the Detective Heath Barrington Mystery series, Heath discovers that first love changes you forever and drives you to become the person you're destined to be. (978-1-63555-786-2)

His Brother's Viscount by Stephanie Lake. Hector Somerville wants to rekindle his illicit love affair with Viscount Wentworth, but he must overcome one problem: Wentworth still loves Hector's brother. (978-1-63555-805-0)

The Dubious Gift of Dragon Blood by J. Marshall Freeman. One day Crispin is a lonely high school student—the next he is fighting a war in a land ruled by dragons, his otherworldly boyfriend at his side. (978-1-63555-725-1)

Quake City by St John Karp. Can Andre find his best friend Amy before the night devolves into a nightmare of broken hearts, malevolent drag queens, and spontaneous human combustion? Or has it always happened this way, every night, at Aunty Bob's Quake City Club? (978-1-63555-723-7)

Death Overdue by David S. Pederson. Did Heath turn to murder in an alcohol-induced haze to solve the problem of his blackmailer, or was it someone else who brought about a death overdue? (978-1-63555-711-4)

Every Summer Day by Lee Patton. Meant to celebrate every summer day, Luke's journal instead chronicles a love affair as fast-moving and possibly as fatal as his brother's brain tumor. (978-1-63555-706-0)

Everyday People by Louis Barr. When film star Diana Danning hires private eye Clint Steele to find her son, Clint turns to his former West Point barracks mate, and ex-buddy with benefits, Mars Hauser to lend his cyber espionage and digital black ops skills to the case.(978-1-63555-698-8)

Cirque des Freaks and Other Tales of Horror by Julian Lopez. Explore the pleasure of horror in this compilation that delivers like the horror classics...good ole tales of terror. (978-1-63555-689-6)

Royal Street Reveillon by Greg Herren. In this Scotty Bradley mystery, someone is killing the stars of a reality show, and it's up to Scotty Bradley and the boys to find out who. (978-1-63555-545-5)

Death Takes a Bow by David S. Pederson. Alan Keys takes part in a local stage production, but when the leading man is murdered, his partner Detective Heath Barrington is thrust into the limelight to find the killer. (978-1-63555-472-4)

Accidental Prophet by Bud Gundy. Days after his grandmother dies, Drew Morten learns his true identity and finds himself racing against time to save civilization from the apocalypse. (978-1-63555-452-6)

In Case You Forgot by Fredrick Smith and Chaz Lamar. Zaire and Kenny, two newly single, Black, queer, and socially aware men, start again—in love, career, and life—in the West Hollywood neighborhood of LA. (978-1-63555-493-9)

Counting for Thunder by Phillip Irwin Cooper. A struggling actor returns to the Deep South to manage a family crisis but finds love and ultimately his own voice as his mother is regaining hers for possibly the last time. (978-1-63555-450-2)

Survivor's Guilt and Other Stories by Greg Herren. Award-winning author Greg Herren's short stories are finally pulled together into a single collection, including the Macavity Award–nominated title story and the first-ever Chanse MacLeod short story. (978-1-63555-413-7)

Exit Plans for Teenage Freaks by 'Nathan Burgoine. Cole always has a plan—especially for escaping his small-town reputation as "that kid who was kidnapped when he was four"—but when he teleports to a museum, it's time to face facts: it's possible he's a total freak after all. (978-1-163555-098-6)

Death Checks In by David S. Pederson. Despite Heath's promises to Alan to not get involved, Heath can't resist investigating a shopkeeper's murder in Chicago, which dashes their plans for a romantic weekend getaway. (978-1-163555-329-1)

Of Echoes Born by 'Nathan Burgoine. A collection of queer fantasy short stories set in Canada from Lambda Literary Award finalist 'Nathan Burgoine. (978-1-63555-096-2)